MW00626233

Forgive Me For I Have Sinned

A DARK COLLEGE ROMANCE

THE PREY SERIES
BOOK FOUR

CARMEN ROSALES

WWW.CARMENROSALES.COM

To my husband and my children,
Thank you for understanding me.

"The love we give away is the only love we keep."

ELBERT HUBBARD.

Also by Carmen Rosales

Like A Moth To A Flame

Love or Honor Coming Soon

For Give Me For I Have Sinned

What if everything they thought about you was a lie?
After Victoria's best friend dies, everything around her ceases to exist.
The man she loved all her life didn't want her anymore.
Her world crumbled.
Depression took her under.
All she has left is the will not to let others suffer under the Order's rules, but she has to play the part under the hands of the dangerous and depraved to save them.
It's the end of her senior year, and time has run out. Victoria has to marry under the Order's rules by the time she graduates from Kenyan, and her father has chosen her husband—Her ex-boyfriend's rival.
Alaric is the eldest of the sons of Kenyan, but he is darker. More sinister.
He doesn't play by anyone's rules—Except his own.
Alaric hates what Victoria's become after his cousin's death. He's heard the rumors around campus after he graduated. How dirty and twisted she is.

When he discovers whom she is marrying, revenge has never tasted so sweet.
Alaric has plans for her—Plans she never saw coming.
But what if he was wrong for letting her go, and now it's too late?

Carmen Rosales
Copyright © 2023 by Carmen Rosales
Cover Design © 2023 by Jay Aheer

All rights reserved.

No part of this book may be reproduced in any form or by any electronic or mechanical means, including information storage and retrieval systems, without written permission from the author, except for the use of brief quotations in a book review.

This book is a work of fiction. All character are fictional. Names, characters, places, and indigents are of the author's imagination. Any resemblance to any of the elements of events, locales, persons, living or dead, is coincidental.

Erotic Quill Publishing, LLC
3020 NE 41st Terrace STE 9 #243
Homestead, Fl. 33033

www.carmenrosales.com

Editing, Proofreading, by
Rebecca-Fairest Reviews Editing Services
ISBN 978-1-959888-29-1

Manufactured in the United States of America
First Edition April 2023

Dark Romance Reader

Dear Reader,

Please note, this is part of my dark room and is a Dark as F *ck Romance and is book four from the Prey Series.

This book may contain themes that can cause triggers for some. Please note there is list of triggers. If you don't have triggers, please move forward and read going in blind.

Please note: This is a series and will involve main characters in multiple POV's.

Please also note: This book is a work of fiction. It has dark elements. There are twists you may not see coming. I do not wish to offend anyone or make this other than what it is...a fictional story.

Trigger Warning

Dear Reader,

The triggers include depression, death, thoughts of suicide, acts of violence, and mental health. All sex is for the enjoyment of all characters involved. This series touches themes that might be triggering for some readers.

If you or know anyone you know that is suffering from mental health and needs help. Please call National Suicide Prevention Lifeline.

THE PREY SERIES

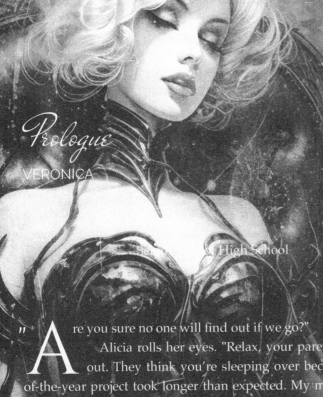

Senior of High School

"Are you sure no one will find out if we go?"

Alicia rolls her eyes. "Relax, your parents won't find out. They think you're sleeping over because our end-of-the-year project took longer than expected. My mother assured me it was alright with your mom. You want to see him, don't you?"

"Of course, I do. But I don't want to look desperate or stupid, showing up there uninvited."

Alicia snorts. "If my brother Reid gets to go, I get to go. And that means you can go too. Fuck what anyone else thinks."

I smirk, looking at her through the floor-length mirror in her bedroom. I turn to the side, knowing the black skirt is shorter than what my parents would allow me to wear and the thigh-high socks that stop an inch from the hem are way above mid-thigh, before I turn to face her completely.

"Stop lying," I tease. "You want to go because he'll be there."

Alicia has a major crush on Chase, but Chase is a scholarship student in his junior year at Kenyan and is considered Prey. It wasn't supposed to be serious between them; she isn't supposed to get attached when she has to marry within the Order, but to Alicia, it is, and that is what I'm afraid of, but if he makes her happy, then I'm not going to fill her head with what ifs. Since we both barely turned eighteen, me in August, and Alicia at the end of September, we've waited to go out and hang around college boys because we were both minors and still in high school.

This is technically our first college party and the first party of the year at Ohio University. Only the rich and, of course, the sons of Kenyan are invited. Even Draven, the evil Bedford twin, will probably be there, so they can confuse the shit out of the girls they fuck, thinking there is only one of them when there are indeed two.

"They will both be there, and this is our chance to get them to notice us!" she says with excitement.

"I-I don't know, Alicia. Do you honestly think he'll notice me?"

Pfft. "With those eyes, gorgeous hair, and awesome personality, Alaric would be an idiot not to notice you."

I know she's just being nice and doesn't want me to back out because that would mean she would show up alone like a lamb to a slaughterhouse, but my self-doubt comes from the other times I have seen him at family functions, and he didn't even say hi or notice that I was in the same room. I always blamed it on the age difference and the fact that I was probably too young because I was still in high school, and he's a hot shit college student, powerful, smart, and gorgeous, and one of the sons of Kenyan.

I swear there's never a time when he doesn't have a gorgeous woman on his arm, and that only fills me with jealousy because I want to be the only one on his arm holding his attention, even though I know it's impossible. But I would be happy with just one night with him. One night. It's all I've prayed for every night since the first time Alicia showed me a picture of her amazing cousin on her phone. Alaric Riodrick-Riordan.

Everyone looks up to him like he's a god.

Even me.

"You're my cousin Alicia's best friend from school...Veronica, right?" A warm feeling slides across my skin, hearing my name on his lips. Especially the way he says it.

"Yeah," I say softly, glad he can hear me even with the music blaring from inside the house.

"My name is Alaric."

I smile, trying to hide the nerves causing my heart to beat too fast and the palms of my hands to sweat. Thankful for the light October breeze beginning to caress my skin, hoping he doesn't notice how nervous I am.

"I know."

"How's that? I don't think we've ever met."

I was right. He never noticed me either time we were in the same room or when people talked about Alicia's best friend with the rich father that was a member of the Order. I'm used to it, though—no one giving a shit about me or who I am, except Alicia. To everyone else, I am invisible. But right now, I'm not. At least not to him. And it's all I ever wanted.

Not wanting to sound naïve and boring, I reply, "Then how do know my name?"

He grins. "You are...kind of a smart ass," he says, taking a sip out of a cup in his hand. It's whiskey. I recognize the sweet smell from my father's study when he calls for me. I always hated that smell, but right now, the fact that Alaric smells like it every time he speaks to me changes my perspective.

I glance to the left to see a group of guys who are drinking, looking this way with smirks on their faces. Two girls with them are covering their mouths in a fit of giggles. I'm unsure if they're drunk, and that's the reason, or if they know I'm still in high school and don't belong at a college party. I try not to think that they're judging me because my eyes are too light and my hair is nearly colorless, but most say the color is white.

I used to get teased all the time and sometimes still do. Veronica looks like an old hag with white hair, or her eyes are too light, the color of evil. Soulless. I would complain to my parents when I came home from school, but my father assured me I was beautiful and that having the lightest shade of eyes and hair makes me pure. He would say that it keeps the demons out of my head and not to listen to the kids at school because they are just jealous of me and my last name.

I tear my eyes away from them and look down at my fingers, playing with the hem of my skirt, and ask, "Do you know them?"

He looks up, knowing exactly who *they* are. "Just some friends from school. Don't mind them. They're just being stupid. It's initiation night for all the jocks from both schools. It's one of the few nights we all get along before the rivalry begins when the season starts. Football, guys from the swim team, baseball and basketball players. They all come to this party."

Initiation? "What do you mean?" I ask with a frown creasing between my brows.

"Don't worry about it." He stands up and holds out his hand. "Come on. Let's go somewhere private."

I look at his outstretched hand, and my lips curve into a smile, admiring how the tattoos of bones are drawn over the tops of his hands in deep shades of black and gray, giving the impression that his skin has disappeared. The way the muscles of his lean arms move with effort and his biceps flex by simply holding the cup. My eyes slide to his fitted white t-shirt, unable to obscure the hard body underneath until I reach his sinful mouth and his eyes that are the color of gray clouds.

I recognize a storm in their depths. A storm that calls to me, and I can't stop myself from saying, "Okay." Sliding my hand in his, knowing what going somewhere private means.

He guides me up the stairs, and I avoid the looks aimed my way and the raised brows as we pass. I. Ignore. All. Of. It.

It's my senior year, and yes, I'm still a virgin. So is Alicia.

Her brother scares every guy who tries to show her attention; meanwhile, my parents are hellbent on following the Order's traditions, and their rules, which dictate you have to be betrothed by the conclusion of your senior year of college. Unfortunately, this also means my father forbids me to have a boyfriend of my own choosing for fear of me choosing wrong and the fact that I'm an only child doesn't help because, in my case, it is up to me to form an alliance that is worthy of the Devlin name as the only heir.

Alaric is technically the oldest Riordan, being older than Reid and Alicia, but I haven't heard of him being betrothed to anyone yet and for a girl like me, it gives me hope.

He stops and opens the door at the end of the hall, and my stomach clenches in anticipation. I'm suddenly aware that my skirt is too short and my panties are wet. I wonder if a man like Alaric could tell. Probably.

The room is dark, except for the moonlight coming through the slit in the curtains. The bed is a full size with red and blue sheets. There are football pictures and trophies on a shelf on top of a desk. I stand in the middle of the room, not knowing what to do next. I didn't think that far ahead.

"Have a seat on the bed. I don't bite, Veronica."

I chew on my bottom lip nervously, watching him close the door, and when I do as he asks and sit down, I notice his eyes are on my exposed thighs, making the throbbing between my legs worse.

I slide my hands between my thighs under his watchful gaze and squeeze them together, trying to calm the pulsing that won't stop. I'm obviously nervous, but I don't want to seem like a scared virgin and risk him leaving me here and walking out.

He smiles and hands me the red cup with the whiskey in it. "Here, have some. It looks like you could use it."

I take it because it's where his lips have been. I want nothing more than to drink from him—to be here with him. I take a small sip and feel the liquid burning me from the inside, giving me the courage to relax. I take another sip, and I'm surprised how smooth it is the second time it slides down my throat. Bumps on my skin rise all over my arms under my long-sleeve shirt from the alcohol coursing through my stomach.

I hand him the cup, and he places it on the dresser by the bed. "I'm not twenty-one," I blurt and close my eyes, wanting to kick myself.

"I know. You're obviously not twenty-one if you're still in high school. You're eighteen, and that is all that matters."

I avert my gaze. "Of course."

It's not like I haven't had alcohol before. Alicia and I have snuck some from her parents' liquor cabinet when they went out for dinner. A few sips of alcohol from him will not kill me or send me to hell. I drank from his cup, so I'm sure he didn't lace it with anything. A guy like Alaric Riordan doesn't have to stoop so low to get a girl.

The bed dips when he sits close, and all I can think about is the heat coming off his body and the whiff of his masculine cologne mixed with his scent. A scent I'll commit to memory because I know that whatever happens tonight with him in this room will never happen again, unless he wants it to.

"You know it's a shame."

"What is?" I ask, pinching my eyebrows together a little confused.

He turns slightly toward me, sliding his finger up the side of my thigh, causing the throbbing to worsen by the second between my legs. Shit. "That it is my last year at college, and by the time it will be your freshman year, I'll have graduated."

I let out a slow breath. "Why is that?"

He leans close, his hand sliding over my right thigh, stopping between my legs, and whispers, "Because I won't be around to always do this." He kisses my cheek and the area right under my ear, causing the tiny hairs to rise all over my skin. "Is this okay?"

I nod and let out a slow breath I didn't realize I was holding. Maybe I should tell him it's my first time, but then my mind screams at me that I shouldn't because I would never get a chance with him again if he stopped. This is not the place I planned to lose my V-card, but all I know is that I want it to be him and no one else, which means it's now or never with him.

"You don't have to do anything you don't want to," he says when his lips brush mine.

"I want to," I reply breathlessly.

He smiles, and it's my first time seeing his perfect white teeth. He takes my lips softly and then roughly. One minute he's kissing me, and the next, I have my shirt off and skirt bunched around my waist. The tiny white thong I purchased online without my parents knowing is pushed aside. My freshly waxed pussy glistens from how wet I am for him and drips down my thighs. He holds himself above me without his shirt, and I'm too busy looking at all his ink to care that he's seeing me practically naked.

"Damn, you're fucking hot. Do you know that? Those fucking socks are driving me insane. It's like you're innocent but sinful at the same time."

"Like you," I counter.

He chuckles, and his gray eyes meet my light ones. "We both know there is nothing innocent about me." He unzips his jeans and takes himself out. Fuck, he's huge. He fists himself and I'm mesmerized at seeing him like this. All I can think about is if he will be able to fit inside me and if I can handle what comes next.

I remember overhearing Lindsey and Rachel in the girls' locker room at school during fourth period after P.E. talking about doing It. Lindsay told Rachel that it hurts at first, like a giant sting that burns for a minute, then it feels so good and that it only hurts the first time. After that, it always would feel good, she amended, if the guy you were doing it with knew what he was doing. She said she did it four times with Tristan Minnis, the football team's star quarterback.

Feeling the first brush from the tip of Alaric's cock brings me back to the present. I hear the tear from the wrapper of the condom between his teeth, and his gray eyes flick to mine.

"Are you sure?"

I nod. "Yeah, I'm sure."

Not wanting him to have second thoughts, I slide my hands up the hard muscles on his chest and widen my legs for him while he expertly slides on the condom like he has done it hundreds of times before, and I know he has, but this time, it's with me.

He lowers his head and sucks the swell of my left breast, pulling the bra cup down to lick my nipple. He doesn't suck it like I'm expecting and then does the same to the right, trailing his tongue up between the valley of my breasts and stopping at my parted lips.

For one second, our eyes meet, and I'm lost. I have the man of my dreams looking at me like I'm something special, and he is about to make love to me. I know this means more to me than it does to him, but I don't care.

The head of his cock crowns my opening above my panties when he pushes against me, feeling how hot and wet I am. He closes the space between us, and his lips crash against mine. Our tongues meet, sucking and tasting.

After a few seconds, his lips pull away and his hands slide down my body, my hips lifting off the bed in anticipation. He slides my panties slowly down my legs, leaving me in only my thigh-high socks.

"Open your legs, and let me see your pink pussy," he demands. I open them as wide as my thighs allow and watch his eyes drink me in. "You are so wet, Veronica. Is this for me?"

"Yes," I hiss.

I want him so much. I get wet with just the way he looks at me— like I'm his.

His tongue peeks out and licks his lips while fisting his cock and pushes the tip inside. I close my eyes to brace myself for the sting I know is coming. I'm sure it will be good because Alaric isn't some boy in high school that has only had sex a couple of times; he's a man that knows what he's doing.

He thrusts into me hard, and I gasp from the pain, holding in the sob that wants to cross my lips. It hurts like hell, causing tears to escape my eyes, pooling on my lashes. He fucks me hard like an animal. Thrust after thrust like a man possessed. He isn't soft like I expected but rough.

"Fuck!" he roars. "Your pussy is so tight," he says with a groan, pumping into me savagely.

God, it burns. The sting's not getting any better like I thought it would. My legs shake from the pain, but it must be different for everyone. At least my first time is with Alaric, I keep telling myself.

He's sweating, his hair sticking to his forehead. His tattoos shine from the layer of sweat on his skin. His breaths come in hard and fast. I feel his hand sliding down, gripping my ass between me and the mattress, plunging deeper, causing a strangled groan to escape my lips from the pain. I feel myself stiffen, and something hot floods inside me. I think he came inside the condom. Even if it didn't feel good for me, I blame it on it being my first time, but I was glad I could pleasure him.

When he pushes himself up on the bed, I'm glad it's dark in the room with only our shadows and the moonlight, so he doesn't see the wetness on my lashes or see me wince when he pulls out.

I hear his phone ding with an incoming message. I watch him walk over and fish his phone out of his jeans from the floor and then pull them on after disposing of the condom, admiring the muscles on his back and his trim waist. I push off the bed with my hands and gather my clothes, so I don't look like an idiot lying on the bed with my legs wide open. I didn't have an orgasm, but I don't think I could with how much it hurt.

As I pull my shirt over my head, the bedroom door flies open, and the group of guys that were downstairs are standing at the threshold, laughing and pointing at me. I hastily look around for my skirt and panties, covering myself from their gazes and trying to tune out the abysmal sound of laughter bouncing off the walls in the bedroom.

"I hope she was a good fuck, Riordan. I was wondering who was going to tap that," one of the guys with brown hair says.

I look over at Alaric and can see his lips turn into a frown from the glow of the screen of his phone. Right then the girls that were with the guys walk in and turn on the lights. The brunette points between my thighs with a hideous laugh. I look down between them in abject horror. There's blood. Lots of blood all over my thighs and in between my legs.

"Dude, she had her period!"

The blonde girl pushes the brunette to the side and covers her mouth. "Eww, gross!"

My head begins to spin, but Alaric is frozen, still looking at his phone. His eyes go dark like a storm raging, and it's about to destroy everything in its path. I hear the voices resonating around the room, saying different things about me.

"—Dude, you fucked her on her period—"

I think it was Dorian Black, from the sound of his voice. I remember him from the day we went to a gala, and my father said he went to Kenyan with the older Riordan. The others I don't know, but I can still hear their crude statements.

"—That is so disgusting—"

"—They could have used the shower. What a disgusting whore—"

"—she ruined the sheets on the bed—"

I don't have my period, but it's not like I'm going to scream and tell them I was a virgin. What good would that do? How could a night that was supposed to be unforgettable in a good way turn out to be so wrong in the worst way? Can it get any worse?

I spoke too soon because all of a sudden, they begin chanting, "Whore! Whore! Whore!"

I look up at Alaric and expect him to defend me or kick everyone out, but I'm met with an evil smirk.

"Alaric?" I croak with dread and panic bubbling inside me. He looks over at the group of people, not doing anything to stop them from forming a circle around me as I stand, taunting me as I try to wipe the blood away but fail miserably.

"Stop it!" I scream.

But they don't stop the incantation. The guys and girls by the door and in the hallway begin to chant in tandem. "Whore! Whore! Whore!

Alaric bends down with a malicious smile plastered on his face, picks up my white thong and skirt, and throws it in my face. I flinch when it hits my mouth, falling to the floor at my feet. I bend to pick it up slide them on and grab my shoes to run the fuck out of here. I straighten when the sounds of them chanting begin to subside, but then I hear Alaric when he says, "She was a lousy fuck. All she did was lie there on her back." His hard gaze lands on mine, but I can't clearly see his face because the tears won't stop falling. And his next words slice me deeper than anything ever could, scarring me forever. "It's safe to say that you are the worst fuck I have ever had. Now I have to clean myself by scrubbing my skin from your nasty period blood, you filthy whore." He pauses. "You're so disgusting."

Flailing my arm while holding my shoes with the other, I scramble to leave the bedroom, not caring if my legs are sticky and full of blood.

I run down the stairs, the sobs rising from my throat without restraint. My hair is plastered to my face from the wetness of my sweat and tears. The smell of sex lingers on my skin. I don't look for Alicia or anyone as I run outside, almost face-planting on the sidewalk, falling and scraping my knees and making a hole in my socks. I finally find my footing and run away from the chanting of the word, Whore, and the sound of disgust in Alaric's voice.

I make it home, ignoring every message from Alicia on the way. I took the public bus and sat in the back, ignoring the weird glances cast my way and the embarrassment of having blood smeared on my thighs. It was the first time I met Dorothy. The only person that helped me. She worked in a small restaurant on the edge of town and was on her way to work. She handed me a pack of tissues. I was relieved she didn't ask questions about the blood or the holes in my socks. All she told me was that she lived on the outskirts of Kenyan, and if I wanted a cup of coffee, I could visit her anytime during the night shift at the restaurant to talk. She hated taking the bus, but her license was suspended. My mother never talked to me. That is what I saw in Dorothy even for a moment, a mother figure.

I shut the front door when I make it home and turn, trying to make my way down the stairs to my room, but I pause when I hear my father's irritated voice. "I've been waiting for you, Veronica." I was wrong if I thought this was the worst night of my existence. It was going to get worse. A lot worse. "I got a call tonight," he says in a harsh tone. His hard eyes slide down my tattered clothes until he stops where there's dried blood stained on my skirt. I knew someone from the Order would call him eventually after what happened. There was no way anyone there wouldn't.

"I'm s—"

He backhands me across the face, whipping my head back. Pain radiates on the side of my skull, dulling the burning sensation between my legs.

For the rest of the night, I pray and pay for my sins. I didn't know what he meant when he said the word sin, but I quickly found out, and it's where my nightmares begin. What happened at the frat party was child's play compared to this. Tonight taught me a valuable lesson. I learned how quickly you could yearn for something or someone, only to loathe it and wish it never happened the next.

Which is why I promise myself never to fall in love again.

CHAPTER 1

Veronica

PRESENT DAY

"Why are you sitting out here alone?" I look up to see Jess standing by my boots.

Looking around at the headstones, I can see why sitting out here by myself on a grave would seem a little odd, but nothing about this place is normal.

My eyes finally rest on her concerned expression, not wanting to tell her why I'm here. "What are you doing walking alone in the cemetery without your future hubby? I thought you would be busy making babies," I tease. She shifts nervously on her feet and all that tells me is that she isn't alone. Reid is probably with her, and she convinced him to let her walk over here.

"I worry about you. I keep thinking about what you said that day in my dorm room."

I wipe crumbs of dirt and leaves off my wool plaid skirt when I move to get up. That was three weeks ago when the cat was out of the bag with Reid, and he finally revealed himself. I shouldn't have said anything. My problems are not anyone else's but my own. And besides, no one can do shit about it. My fate is sealed, stamped, and delivered to the highest bidder who my father deems suitable with the approval of the Order. A nightmare I have to live with for the rest of my life.

I give her a dry smile and do what I do best, lie. "I'll be fine, Jess. It's just an arranged marriage." I look at the gate, not wanting her to notice the headstone I am leaning against and give more of myself away. "You should go. He's overprotective of you, as he should be." She looks over, I follow her line of sight, and I see Reid waiting by the pillar, glaring at me. "He doesn't like me."

He never did.

She waves, and I notice his eyes soften for a fraction when they land on her. "He'll come around."

I laugh through my nose. "No, he won't."

He would rather see me die and be buried here, so he could piss on my grave and take a shit in each flower holder every time he walks through the cemetery to visit his sister. If he ever does. No one comes to visit her. It's too painful for him and his family. Everyone deals with loss and pain differently. Reid deals with it in his way, and I deal with it in mine. But I owe it to my best friend to visit her and let her know I'll keep my promise. Always.

I slide my hair over my shoulder, needing to head home or face my father's wrath. I slide my phone out of my pocket, acting like someone sent me a message. "I gotta go. See you around?"

She nods. "Yeah," she says softly, sliding her hair behind her ear and stepping back. "Do you want to hang out with me and Gia? Maybe go shopping or something."

I hate turning her down when she is trying to be a friend. Even though I don't deserve it for what I did to her, even if my inner motives came from a good place. But in everyone's eyes, I don't deserve anything. Not even a friend. With my best friend dead, I have to agree with them. Jess is better off staying away from me. I did what had to be done— what needed to be done.

I glance down at my shoes that belonged to Alicia, allowing a few seconds to pass so I can paste a fake grin on my face, so the lie that slips off my lips doesn't sit in my conscience like a heavy brick when I look up. "Yeah, let me know, and I'll meet up with you guys."

Making my way down the hallway to the room I call a torture chamber, I check the time on my phone. I have two hours before my late shift at the small restaurant on the edge of town begins. It's been two years, to be exact. I caved one night visiting Dorothy and asked if I could work the night shift during the week and she agreed.

I push the door open, hearing it groan on its old hinges. This house is one of the oldest besides Kenyan. It still has servants' quarters in the basement, keeping in tune with the ancient Victorian era my father refuses to change.

I look to my left and see the man I loathe with every fiber of my being. A man that is part of my living nightmare. "Good, you're here."

His voice feels like a snake's venom sliding through my veins, shutting my organs down one by one. The smell of his preferred whiskey reminds me of the past and present.

"I am," I quip.

I watch as he widens his legs in the chair he is sitting in with a predatory smile, hoping he can find something I did wrong in his eyes.

"You know I don't like to be kept waiting, Veronica. Tell me, how was your day?"

I close my eyes and tell him what he wants to hear. The sins I committed because he loves to make me pay.

"Will that be all?" I ask the couple seated at table fourteen with a smile, placing the plate on the table.

"Yes," the guy says first, as I notice his girlfriend looking straight at him. Probably to see if he's flirting. I hate that feeling. When you like someone so much and hope they are into you the same way you are into them, you're looking for signs because you feel insecure.

I smile at her and avoid looking at her boyfriend to ensure she doesn't feel threatened by me. "We have a new Oreo shake if you're interested. It goes great with the burgers." I smile, looking at her.

She sags in relief, and I make sure to avoid any and all eye contact with her boyfriend. A man that doesn't make sure he only has eyes for his girl sucks in my book.

I glance over at Dorothy as she walks my way and softly says, "Hey, love. Table twelve just sat down, and eleven will be ready to be seated."

I smile. "You got it, Dorothy."

Dorothy knows more about the gossip in Kenyan than I do. She knows most of the parents and the kids who go there. Especially the late Mrs. Bedford, Draven and Dravin's mother. They were fond of each other. I remember the day I found out how close they were when I came to visit Dorothy during her shift, needing a job.

It's funny how a place and its people remind you of certain events in your life that mean the most, but at the same time end in the worst. It didn't stop the night of the party. If anyone mentioned me around Alaric, he would tell people I was a lying whore behind my back and that I was looking to make an alliance because of my father's greed. Alicia told me everything she heard him say about me. Of course, that wasn't true. She was only one person that I confided in and told the truth, and now she's dead.

I pull the ticket off my next order by the kitchen and place the hot plate on the tray. "Is it true you used to be blonde?"

I look over at my friend and co-worker Adam and pinch my brows in confusion for a split second, but then I remember I'm at work, and the fake Veronica Devlin was left home in the dark mansion of hell. "In high school. Who told you that?"

It must have been Dorothy. She is the only one that has seen me with my colorless, platinum-blonde hair. Hair that was dyed because my father liked it the shade of platinum, but hair can only take so much damage, and my scalp could only take so much pain. Now I use pricey extensions and wigs. The only thing my father would pay for, sparing no expense in the way he wanted me to look.

"Dorothy. She said you are one of the few women she knows that can pull off extreme looks like that." He leans close and says softly, "I like your dark hair, honestly."

Adam is about to graduate high school and will be a freshman at Ohio University. It's a rival school, but he doesn't know I attend Kenyon. He also doesn't know who my father or mother is, and I'd like to keep it that way. He started working here his senior year of high school, needing the extra money for college. He secured a scholarship, but he has to pay for additional expenses.

"Thanks," I say, grabbing the tray and heading to the next table.

I place the plates and notice the Ohio State jackets on the two guys sitting across each other in the booth. *Shit.* I don't wear makeup, false lashes, or anything I wear to school so that no one recognizes me when I work here. It is also why I stuck to the night shift on weekdays only.

"Hey, don't I know you?"

I stiffen slightly and look up and meet moss-green eyes. "No."

He points at me when he picks up his fork, but I let my eyes focus on his jacket, so I don't give myself away. "Are you sure? You look familiar, but I can't remember where." I don't answer because I'm sure it's from one of the parties at Kenyon.

"Maybe because you only remember the back of their heads when you fuck them from behind, Matt." His friend sitting opposite him says with a smirk.

Matt shrugs, but I feel the way his eyes travel over my waitress uniform, undressing me with his eyes as I move to the next table. *Dick.* "I haven't fucked *her* because I would have remembered," he says between bites, and I look back with a glare. "There is no way you could forget a girl that looks like that." He pauses and takes a sip of his soda. "I would love to see her eyes when I take her."

Adam slams the plastic tub on the table, making the dirty plates and forks clank inside. "I think you two need to leave," he grits out.

My eyes widen in panic because that would mean I lose tips from a table, or worse, they leave, and I have to pay for their meals.

I walk back to their table and stop next to Matt, who's looking over at Adam. "It's alright, Adam. They must have me confused with someone else. Right, boys?" I purr on the last part.

Matt arches a brow, and Adam looks like I kicked him, but my eyes give him a pleading look.

"Right, gorgeous. How about you let me take you out, and you could be that girl."

I'd rather eat my own vomit.

"I can't; I have a boyfriend," I lie.

Matt looks around mockingly. "I don't see him anywhere, and besides, what kind of guy lets his girl work the night shift at a twenty-four-hour restaurant and not expect guys to hit on her. You're better off with someone like me."

Let me guess, I'll work the dayshift to soothe your ego. I want to say the words, but the fact is, I don't want to lose this job or let Dorothy down.

"Table is ready," Adam says behind me before storming off.

I know he thinks he is trying to be a man by defending me, but you can't change who people are or how they think. I deal with assholes like this all the time. These guys are elementary to what I'm used to dealing with at Kenyan.

"Now that your little boyfriend stormed off. How about it?"

I look down at Matt and his friend, my lips lifting in a sardonic smile. "Is that where I see how big you really are?" I bite my bottom lip and slide my hand down my skirt, watching Matt's eyes widen, my demeanor changing like a flip of a switch. I lean close. "On second thought, I think I'll pass. Taking a girl from behind can only mean one thing. You're a selfish prick that only cares about your own pleasure...which also means—" I pinch my fingers together, leaving a small space in between—"You have a small pathetic excuse of a cock and to be honest, I wouldn't want to look at your ugly mug of a face either while I fake it."

His friend chuckles. "Damn."

I straighten and give him my resting bitch face. "Total waste of my time." When Adam walks back, I place my work face back on, fixing the pin on my uniform and smile. "Will that be all for you boys?"

CHAPTER 2
Alaric

"An alliance between Riodrick and Riordan Holdings and Black Capital investments would benefit the Order, Alaric."

I lean back in the executive chair, looking at the amber liquid in my whiskey glass with three ice cubes, watching it melt, just like my patience as I try to hold myself back from reaching over and strangling Dorian Black. He has something up his sleeve. It is why I accepted this meeting in the first place. Dorian Black is a snake. A venomous one.

But if he's a snake, then I'm the wolf.

I place my elbow on the table and put my forefinger on my lips, acting like I'm considering investing in his piece of shit company that makes in profit what I pay in toilet paper for one of my buildings.

"Send me you're Profit and Loss statements. I need to look over them," I state, calling his bluff.

His right eye twitches, and I watch his jaw harden slightly. He won't send it because we both know what I'll find. Loss and little profit.

He needs capital to fund his spending habits, but I'm not the asshole that will support it. Riodrick legacy of hotels comes from my grandmother on my mother's side and the last name Riordan from my father. We use both as a surname interchangeably since my father merged both estates into one and named me and my cousins both Riodrick-Riordan out of respect for the alliance when my uncle and father married their wives. Alliances are everything to the Order and it is how we control the world. In Dorian Black's case, he wants power and money. That much is obvious. He will have to ask the Bedfords to form any business alliance, and good luck with the twins. They will hang him by his balls. Literally.

"What's to think about, Alaric. You don't need P and L's to make a decision. You were summa cum laude at Kenyon, for Christ's sake. We're friends. We go way back...since high school. Then four years at Kenyon." *Yeah, four years of me watching you be a prick.* "We had one fallout." He snaps his fingers, and my eyes harden, hearing the words slide off his lips. "Senior year at the initiation party."

I yawn, feigning boredom. "So," I drawl.

Motherfucker. He wants to throw the steak at the wolf to see if he is hungry so he can bare his teeth. But all I do is give him a grin. I could care less about that party and what happened. It's in the past, and yes, I slipped. Once.

"Get to the point, Dorian. I don't have time for a college reunion. I give three fucks about what happened at that party any more than you do."

"Oh, you don't–"

"No," I grit.

My jaw hardens every time I'm reminded about that night and that lying, manipulative cunt and one of the reasons my cousin Alicia is dead. I could care less about her.

The door to the boardroom opens, and my father and uncle stroll in along with Dorian's father. "Did you two boys wrap things up?" Mr. Black says with a smile.

I'm hardly a boy, but his wife and daughter know that personally. He glances at me when he sits like he won the deal of a lifetime. *In your dreams, asshole.* I will not ever go into business with the Black family in this generation or the next. My father knows that, but he does what I ask, and since my cousin Reid will take over his share of his hotels, he thinks I have a purpose. I do. Just not the way he thinks I do. Keep your moves private. Calculation is key, and timing is everything in business. Like when you want to strangle your opponent, and that someone right now is Dorian. *Not yet.*

"I'm finished," I reply, picking up my whiskey glass and downing the three fingers that are left before getting up.

"Wait!" I look up at Dorian and see the desperation crossing his features. "I-I can get you the reports."

"Riordan?" Mr. Black nudges his head toward me, speaking to my father like I'm not here. "Talk to Alaric." Like that's going to change the outcome of my decision. Desperate pig.

"I'm afraid it's up to Alaric. He makes all the business decisions, and if he disagrees, I'm afraid it stands, Black," my father replies.

"Alaric?" Dorian calls out.

"The answer is no, Dorian. I have no interest in merging with you because we both know the truth, and I hate wasting my time. You would have sent me the reports if you were serious and a two hundred and fifty million investment is steep, even for you. You and your father can see yourselves out," I say as I move to walk out of the boardroom, hearing his parting shot.

"You will regret it, Alaric. I promise you that!"

"That's enough, Dorian. He said no, and we don't beg," Mr. Black scolds.

That should be the least of his worries. I don't do well with threats.

I walk into my office and shut the door.

"Took you long enough." I turn my head and look at the woman I have chained to the wall, giving her about twenty feet to walk around. And I was being generous. Not because I give a shit but because it gives her the ability to use the toilet. I have no interest in sending someone in to clean up her mess.

"I had a business meeting."

She rolls her eyes. "Of course, you did. You always have meetings. You hold the majority share of both Riodrick-Riordan holdings. Billionaires are found at meetings."

"I'm a busy man," I reply, unbuckling my pants, and watch as she falls to her knees, hearing the chains rattle. She takes me in her mouth, and I hear her moan.

"Can you take it?" I push harder down her throat, making her gag, watching the tears pool in her eyes, just the way I like it. "No?" I grip her auburn-colored hair when she doesn't speak, fisting it in my fingers and looking at the color. Never a blonde or a brunette, unless it is for a reason, but never for pleasure. I pull, arching her neck, so she can take me deeper, watching her eyes roll back in her skull. In three seconds, her air constricts, and if she is as good as she says, she will know to relax her throat and breathe through her nose. If not, she will struggle to breathe. Not my problem. She should have known better than to want to fuck and suck my cock.

I hear her gag and watch the drool slide down her chin while I fuck her face, pulling her hair. I grip the side of her head and pick up speed, fucking her mouth and watching her struggle.

"Just a little more." She nods, but I can tell this is hard for her. She can't take it. Pathetic. All that talk that she can take me. She stops and whips her head back, gasping for air.

"I-I can't," she gasps.

Of course, you can't. You like to fuck rich men for money. That is why she took the job as secretary for Dorian Black. So she can spread her legs and hope to get lucky. I asked her to give me information on Dorian's company, and she thought I was a bigger fish she could catch for a payday, so she folded. The problem is, she didn't know I was an apex predator. I eat the fish and the one trying to catch them.

I pull out and put myself away and step back. "Then get up and get out."

Her eyes look between the door and me. "B-but," she stammers.

I unhook the cuff and chains around her wrist, throat, slide a stack of bills from my wallet, and let them fall at her feet. She looks down at the money with an angry expression. "I'm not a whore," she seethes.

I button my pants, folding my belt, itching to take shower to wash the smell of her off me. "Could've fooled me." I pull the chain and hook it back in place while she tries to cover herself, like she just wasn't prancing around naked in my office, waiting to fuck me like a good little whore.

"Fuck you."

I look up at the ceiling for a second and sigh. "Stop being pathetic. Take the money and get out. It's what you wanted, right? An expensive dinner. Some money to shop to buy a purse and shoes. Except the fucking is obviously off the menu because you couldn't keep up your end, and now, I'm bored." I meet her sour expression while she looks for her clothes. "I have more respect for a prostitute than a gold-digging bitch. At least a prostitute is honest and doesn't hide what she is after. I respect that more than a two-bit lying secretary that spreads her legs for a man in a fifteen-thousand-dollar suit and then gets mad when the guy is being generous in giving her what she wanted all along, even when she couldn't keep up her end.

"You're an asshole."

I walk up and grip her by her neck. "Watch your mouth, Elaine. Don't piss me off. Get up. Get your coin and get out."

She shakes her head in disbelief. Her angry tears run down her cheeks. Tears that do nothing for me.

"You used me."

I did, but I paid her for it. It wasn't like I forced her to do anything. I release her, getting annoyed. "It was nice doing business with you, Elaine."

I sit in my office chair, waiting for her to leave, so I can shower, but of course, she just keeps ranting.

"I didn't think the rumors were true. You are a sadistic fuck. There is no one you care about, is there? You treat all women like animals."

"You should see how I treat men. Count yourself lucky. Here's a tip. You should work on pleasuring a man if you're after his money. Your performance is lacking, and now I have to think of someone else to get off."

She stomps toward the door and says, "Fuck you," before the door slams shut.

I glance at the floor and smile. She took the money. Some people don't like hearing the truth. She's lucky I didn't kill her for her filthy mouth. I should have choked her with my dick, but then I'd have to clean up the mess, and it's bad enough that I need a shower. Besides, I might need her to give me more information on Dorian. I have a feeling he isn't going to let shit go. He likes to dig things up and use it against you. The mention of the initiation party years ago struck a nerve, making my dick twitch in my pants, but that was what he was after. A reaction. One I would never give when it comes to her. She was a one-off. A moment of weakness. And what do you do to a weakness? You destroy it.

CHAPTER 3
Veronica

"Are you sure my dad left for his trip this weekend?" I ask Marissa, zipping up an overnight bag. I promised Adam and his mother I would babysit his younger sister Melody, so she doesn't get any ideas about bringing boys to the house when no one is around. He has another sister named Madison who started at Ohio State last year, making her a sophomore, and she lives off-campus. This is Adam's freshman year at Ohio State and one of the reasons he feels he had to protect me against those assholes at my table the other day. He said they are on the football team, and off the field, they think girls will just sleep with them.

"Yes, Miss Devlin." I look up, hearing my last name. A name I hate being associated with because of my father.

"Please don't call me that. Veronica is fine."

"I'm sorry, Veronica. You deserve to be addressed with the utmost respect, you know."

In middle school, I used to think I was Cinderella, residing as a servant, and my real mother was the evil stepmother. Except my mother isn't evil. She is just a victim of her own mistakes, and one of them was marrying Charles Devlin. These days she can be found traveling or hopped up on sedatives in her bedroom. She's high most of the time and doesn't care about me as long as I keep Daddy happy. Glancing at the ceiling for a few seconds with the pseudo-redwood and peeling walls I have lived in since I was twelve, I'm reminded of just how messed up my life is.

"Did he say when he would be back?"

"Monday afternoon," she replies, looking down at the uneven floors.

I sag in relief and dread at the same time. He always makes sure he is back by Monday afternoon to ensure I'm home and my heart and mind can break again.

"I'll be back by then. I have to babysit for Adam and his parents. Adam is going to a college party with his older sister. Adam told me Melody is at it again with a boy, and his parents caught him in her room last weekend. His parents are going to visit family and Melody is hellbent on staying."

Marissa snickers. "That child is a wild one. You never snuck boys in your room."

I mockingly point both of my index fingers to the floor and walls. "Look around you, Marissa. A boy wouldn't sneak in a room without windows, and every boy I have encountered is afraid of me. Courtesy of Mr. Devlin."

Her eyes soften, and I hate the pity mirrored behind them. I don't want or need it because that is not how you survive. That is how they destroy you from the inside.

"Do you want popcorn?" I ask Melody, rummaging through the pantry of Adam's house. "We could watch a movie...*Insidious* is streaming."

After I find the packet of microwavable popcorn, I look up to see Melody grinning like she won something on her phone. The boy she snuck into her room last weekend probably sent her a message. When I was fourteen, Alicia showed me a picture of Reid, Alaric, the Bedford twins, and Valen at the lake house they visited that summer. One look at Alaric's perfect face, and I was a goner. Starstruck is what they call it. Alicia and the Riordan's invited me, but I couldn't go. One week without me in the house was a death sentence to Charles Devlin.

I sit down next to her with the bowl of freshly-made popcorn and the irresistible smell has her looking up. Amusement twitches my lips when she tilts the screen so I can't see the text messages on her phone.

"We can watch whatever you want," she finally says.

This means she will be on her phone during the entire movie. As long as she stays out of trouble, then all is good. I could care less what she does on her phone, if her parents allow her to have one. I promised Adam I would watch her, and he promised me fifty bucks for the trouble. I didn't agree because of the money. Well, not entirely. I like being around Adam and his family. I get to be myself and feel...normal.

I find *Insidious* and press play but then notice the grin wiping right off Melody's face and a stream of curse words flying from her mouth.

I raise my eyebrows. "Whoa, do your parents know you use such colorful language?"

"That piece of shit. He lied!" she yells, slamming her hand on the cushions of the couch.

I look at the hurtful expression in her eyes with her ash blonde wavy hair framing her face, hating that someone made her feel this way. Especially some guy that hurt her.

"They all do."

"How would you know?" she snaps. "Adam says he has never seen you even look at another guy since he's known you. I told him it's probably because you like girls."

I snort and almost choke on a piece of popcorn. "I have no issues with people who do, but I assure you, I don't like girls." I tilt my head to the side. "What did he lie about?"

Her eyes are glassy, meaning he either told her he wasn't seeing anyone and he is or that he's somewhere with someone he shouldn't be.

"I can't tell you because you'll tell my brother, and then he'll tell my parents."

I stuff a couple of popped kernels in my mouth and raise a brow. "Try me."

How bad could it be?

She slides a piece of her hair behind her ear, nervously looking between me and her phone. Another message dings on her screen, and she opens it. I watch the fury and hurt swirl in her expression like a tornado at whatever was just sent. The world is crumbling around her in her mind, and she cannot stop it from happening. It's the type of shit that scars you even though those who did it don't deserve you. I sit up, watching her lip tremble, and feel bad for her. The same way I do for all Prey on campus. The ones walking in blindly, only to be slaughtered emotionally by the privileged.

She finally holds up her phone with an audible sigh, and there is a picture of a guy and a girl. His hand is up her skirt, and her tongue is down his throat while she sits on his lap. "He said he was going to sleep early because he had practice in the morning. He's a senior and got a full ride playing football at OSU."

"But you're fourteen," I say. *I think.*

"Sixteen. I will be seventeen in the fall when he starts his freshman year. It's not too much of an age gap, but my parents and brother think he's too old for me."

Her parents and siblings don't trust her to be home alone and now I get why. Guys don't always have a girl's best interest at heart.

I should say she is too young, but then I would be a hypocrite. Alaric was a senior in college when I was a senior in high school, and it didn't stop me. But I was eighteen and a legal adult. I can't tell her that because she will shut down and not tell me. Instead, I go for the let him go. You could find someone better speech.

"You can do so much better."

More tears.

I look at her phone as more messages with pictures come in from social media, with his hand up the other girl's skirt, probably fingering her, and I notice it's somewhere familiar. The outdoor patio. The chairs and benches. A party at a frat house near the college in Ohio. The same one Adam and his sister are probably at right now. I overheard the party was tonight around campus at Kenyan on Friday before the next season starts.

"Does your brother know who he is?" She nods.

Shit.

She looks down, twisting her fingers in her lap as the movie plays. "He snuck in my room, and we...got caught–" she trails off.

"Fucking." I finish for her.

She waves her hand, rolling her eyes and says, "Yeah."

Little shit. I never had a sister. The only one I considered a sister was Alicia. I had no siblings to look up to or to take care of.

I hand her phone back, and she sniffles. "I gave him my V-card. It wasn't like I didn't wait. He said all the right things." It feels like déjà vu.

"That's what some of them do. They're good ones out there, but you need time to figure it out, if not, it can get messy sometimes. He told you that because he knows you wouldn't show up."

She glares. "I would, but you're here."

"So...what...you're just going to show up there and do what exactly? Rip her off of him. The damage is done. You can't take away what you saw on your phone...what everyone saw."

"You're right, but when my brother finds out he's there and what he's doing with whoever, he will kick his ass. He will prob-ably get kicked out of Ohio before he even gets to start football, and my sister will probably do the same to the girl my now ex-boyfriend is currently finger-fucking. It's what I would do."

She's probably right.

I slide my cell phone out and text Valen because I know he is probably there. It's initiation night.

Veronica: Where are you?

Valen: Why do you want to know? Are you all out of fresh victims already?

Veronica: No. I'm bored actually. I wanted to see what you jock losers are up to.

Valen: Ohio frat party. The jocks' initiation party.

Veronica: Why are you there?

Valen: You know why.

Valen wants no-strings sex to feed his addiction. A good-looking guy like Valen and one of the sons of Kenyan will have no issues getting pussy.

Veronica: Be careful. They get attached.

I love teasing him. He thinks it's some twisted scheme I'm up to, but if he only knew the real me, maybe he would think differently.

Valen: Are you coming to rescue me, Veronica? Do you need me to FEED your demons?

Since Reid and Jess happened, Valen has spiraled into a fuck frenzy.

Veronica: You know you couldn't satisfy me. I wonder if your balls ever dropped.

Valen: Come over and find out. Tell me how big they are.;)

He's drunk or almost there. He would have never offered, otherwise.

Veronica: Maybe I will.

Not for what he thinks, but I need to help my friends out before they screw up their lives over some asshole with a hard-on for naïve girls. At least I think they are *my* friends. I glance at Melody, watching her wipe the tears from her red-rimmed eyes. "Did your parents leave the keys to their second car? Can you drive?" I ask.

She nods. "Where are we going?"

"To make sure your brother and sister don't fuck up what they worked so hard for, but I need something to wear to a frat party."

She smiles, her eyes lighting up. "Yeah, I have the spare key to their car, and I have something you could wear, but how are you going to get in? You need to know someone."

"I do."

"Who?"

I don't *really* need to know anyone. My reputation proceeds me, but I can't tell Melody that. Or Adam. Or anyone. I just hope this doesn't blow up in my face. Reid and the Bedford twins don't hang out at parties since their wives are at home. Valen is obviously drunk or on some type of drug. I can use Melody as an excuse for showing up and confronting the little prick before Adam and his sister find out.

It's not like anyone will announce who I am to the entire room like a bunch of idiots. Adam thinks I live in a small house on the outskirts of Kenyan with only my mom. I always make an excuse when he sometimes gives me a ride home because it's raining, and I ask him to leave me at the corner, or my mother will freak out if she sees me alone with a guy. I hate lying, but lies are comfortable to tell because they are easy and hide the truth.

CHAPTER 4
Alaric

I'm home getting ready to call it quits from my computer. I've been digging into Dorian Black's finances. He's in the red but barely scraping by. He could turn it around, but he's too stupid to do the work. *Lazy prick.* The last thing you need is a lazy CEO running a business's hard-earned dollars into the ground. Expenditures are through the roof. He wouldn't have to decrease his spending habits if he put in more effort. It is probably why he wanted me to merge with him, so I could be the ducky to do all the work while he played.

I've worked my ass off so I was allowed a free pass on the marrying requirement at the end of my senior year in college. Cash is king in the Order's world. And I know how to make loads of it from a laptop.

My phone rings, and I look at the incoming call. Reid.

"What," I answer impatiently.

"I need you to do something for me."

"I have. I got Tara off your back. You got the girl. She accepted your crazy ass and married you. Now what?"

"I need you to go check on Valen. He's at a frat party. Initiation night."

"And? He's a big boy. He can handle himself. We both know why he's there. What's the problem?"

"He's drunk and high, Alaric. After the whole Jess thing—"

"What? He has a problem getting pussy. He'll fuck five more and get over it. He has to marry Melissa. Get to the point," I grit.

I'm annoyed. I'm not his savior. He needs to get his shit together. I lean back, hearing the leather in my chair groan like my patience.

"He's there alone, and I don't trust anyone else to get him out of trouble."

I let out a puff of air from my mouth, pinching my nose. "Fine. I'll go get him but make sure it's the last time, Reid. I don't have time for this shit."

"Not everyone is a killer like you, Alaric."

He means Valen doesn't have a strong mind to handle his own shit because he fell for a girl that wasn't his.

"You know what they say, killers are smart. Most of them are geniuses."

"Whatever, dick." And hangs up.

Now that my night is screwed. I have to get mentally prepared to go to the last place I ever thought I would end up at: an initiation party. Some people might recognize me; some might not. I am one of the sons of Kenyan because my uncle and father are brothers as well as founders of the Order. I just choose to be excluded from the whole Sons of Kenyan dynamic when they all hang out. I'm not in college anymore, but I still have a reputation.

I'm untouchable.

The dealmaker and dealbreaker.

The sinner.

Now I have to help one of our own from doing something stupid he will regret later at a frat party.

I check the time, and it's half past eleven at night. I'm getting dressed like I'm still in college because I can't show up dressed in a suit to a college party, looking like a fucking parent who is searching for his kid.

Heading out in my Ferrari SF90 Stradale, I take the highway, remembering the last time I was at a college party that wasn't in Kenyan, and all I can think about is *her*. Tears falling from her eyes, the color of the clearest blue sky like fat drops on a window pane, play on my mind like a loop and I hate the memory. I grip the steering wheel and shift the car, pressing the gas and hearing it roar down the road.

Follow the rules.

Fuck the rules and fuck her.

She deserved it.

I pull up on the same street, and nothing has changed since I graduated college. People milling about. Cars parked down the road. The faint thumping music. People with Solo cups in their hands, drunk and high, laughing without a care in the world, except for who they are going to fuck next. Or making sure they have the answers to the next test and work turned in for class, so they can stay and do it all over again the next weekend.

I shut the door of my car and arm the alarm. "Hey, nice car, man," one of the guys says from the porch. "You borrowed it from your dad?"

I almost choke on my spit and clear my throat. "Yeah, man, my parents are divorced 'n shit. My dad lets me borrow it when he's out of town."

"Not a bad way to get pussy."

I walk up the steps and smirk. "Yeah, the car gets the chicks every time."

I can tell the guy is high as a kite, practically falling over the wooden railing.

Fucking idiot.

I'm going to kill Reid. I hate these Ohio pricks. Most of them think they're hot shit and think every girl is a game because they play a sport.

"Go on in, man; there's plenty of liquor and pussy." He laughs. I blink. "Just pick one. This one hot chick came in with another one all pissed and shit. She has dark hair, but she has these eyes. All the guys are going crazy over her."

I raise my brows, pulling open the door. "I bet."

I need to find Valen and get the fuck out of here before I lose it and punch someone, or worse, make them disappear. I just hope I don't find him fucking in a room somewhere.

Making my way through the throng of bodies, I walk toward the back patio, where a group of people are forming a circle around a girl losing her shit and screaming at a guy with a girl in his lap.

"You fucking asshole!" she yells.

The girl sitting in the guy's lap tears her lips from his neck. "Get lost, bitch," she snarls.

The guy angles his head, wide-eyed, and lifts his hands in mock surrender like the girl fell on his lap and he doesn't know how she got there. "Melody, it's not what you think."

Laughter. "Damn, dude," one guy says. "That's fucked up. You got caught. Own that shit."

The girl with ash blonde hair turns around, and I notice that she's young. She has to be fifteen or sixteen tops. This asshole is fucking a sixteen-year-old?

Valen comes up behind me, and I roll my eyes because he keeps looking at a girl with the same ash-blonde hair arguing with a guy on the other side. The guy pushes her to the side when she steps in front of him, but I don't miss Valen's hands balling into fists or the hard set of his jaw. Interesting.

"Adam, stop!" she screams when he lunges toward the guy with the girl on his lap.

He doesn't. Adam walks up and punches the guy in the face, causing the girl to fall off his lap. "You think my little sister is some whore you can play with? Huh, bitch!"

The guy gets up and rushes Adam to the floor, and they go at it. Blow for blow. Fists flying. Flesh connecting with flesh.

"Stop it! Both of you!" I hear a loud voice that I recognize, causing me to whip my head in that direction.

"No fucking way! She came!" Valen points, and I follow, landing on eyes that haunt my dreams. "I dig the hair," he adds.

"Shut the fuck up." I growl.

I don't want her to notice me. Not yet. Why is she here? Veronica looks...different. She's not the same girl I first met and decided to fuck that night. I look around but don't see a guy then I remember what the dork out front said about the girl with the eyes. She came with a female. Putting two and two together. She showed up with the young girl. The question is, how does she know a girl that young, and why the change of hair?

I watch when another asshole from Ohio with a football jacket saunters up next to her. I try to relax when I catch myself grinding my teeth with how he eats her up with his eyes. But what I notice are his hands.

CHAPTER 5

Veronica

This is exactly why I came. To avoid this crap. I knew this would get out of hand.

"Adam, get off of him, I demand.

Adam looks up, his eyes full of anger, and I notice a cut on his bottom lip already swelling. He might hate me right now, but I'm helping him out. He can get kicked off the team or lose his spot, or worse, get expelled, losing his scholarship before setting foot on campus.

Matt from the restaurant the other day comes up behind me. "You changed your mind, princess?" I flinch at the word *princess*. I turn to face him and watch his eyes slide down my face landing on the swell of my breasts.

He thinks it's cute. To me, it's the same as calling me a worthless whore.

"Fuck off, Matt. She didn't come here for that," Adam tells him, wiping his hands on his jeans.

"I doubt that, Adam. You need to worry about Zack fucking around with your little sister. It's initiation night, and she's fair game. You come; you play."

I glance at Adam, but he looks away. He knew. He wanted me to watch Melody, so she wouldn't show up or find out.

My eyes narrow on Matt, but I plaster a fake smile, making it appear to him that I'm game. Melody steps back and stands behind her brother and her sister, Madison. I reminded Melody right before we walked in that whatever happened and whatever I did, not to interfere.

I lick my bottom lip, scraping my teeth along the skin and pulling it in my mouth, slowly, watching Matt's eyes follow the movement. "Oh yeah? How does that work?" I ask, playing dumb.

I know first-hand how it works, but he doesn't know that, and without my blonde hair and normal clothes, he probably wouldn't know that I'm not from here but from Kenyan. Initiation night at an Ohio frat party means they make men out of the freshman jocks coming in. Testing to see what they can handle and can't. With pussy. Or dick. Or both. It just depends. It also lets everyone know who's easy.

Matt grins and looks around as everyone goes silent, waiting for him to answer. "Depends on what you want and what you can take."

I get closer, letting him think he will get what he wants. "Is that why you invite girls to come here? Get them drunk. Maybe a little high to see how far their legs spread." I close the rest of the space between us, sliding my hand up the stuffed crotch of his jeans, watching the lust pool in his eyes.

When I look behind Matt, I meet gray eyes glaring at me.

Alaric.

My heart begins to beat hard inside my chest. Awareness that he's watching me, causing the nerves to rattle under my skin. Reid must have called him to rescue his friend from fucking everyone inside the frat house. Valen looks between me and Alaric, knowing a storm is brewing. You can feel the tension crackling like static electricity.

I almost laugh because my hand is still on Matt's pegged jeans. I was right. Matt's cock is small, but I'm surprised, he's about six-two. Poor guy. No wonder he treats girls like he does because he lacks in the dick department.

My eyes flick to Matt's, and he has a bitter smile. "Did you think I wouldn't figure out who you were? You're Veronica Devlin and a skank. Everyone in this frat house knows who you are." He lowers his voice. "But I don't think your friends here know that. Do they?"

I'm used to it hearing the rumors about me, but it doesn't matter because I have to marry someone. Even if they don't like what they hear about me, true or not. It buys me time. I stopped caring what they all thought anyway. The man standing behind Matt saw that my reputation here and on campus at Kenyan was tarnished. It doesn't stop the guys wanting to fuck me, though. I just use it to my advantage. Like right now. I don't want Adam and his sisters to know about my past or who I really am coming from these people.

"Tell you what? I'll leave quietly, and I won't tell everyone here how small your hard cock feels in my hand." I lean close and lick his earlobe, causing him to shudder then whisper, "It will be our little secret. Because we both know they will all believe it coming from me. The skaaank."

His eyes darken, and he leans in, placing his lips close to my cheek. "Kiss me. I will make this all go away...if you kiss me. Right now...we both get what we want."

He doesn't want me. He wants to show people he can get any girl he wants, including me. It's all a show. I don't want to kiss him. I want to rip his dick off because guys like him use girls and then talk about them like they mean nothing.

My eyes flick to Alaric briefly and then back to Matt. *Stop thinking about it too much, Veronica. Remember what he did to you every time you see him.* Then the words *whore* and *disgusting* fill my head like a mantra. I look at Matt's moss-green eyes, sliding my hands up his chest. He pulls me closer, and I want to cringe when I feel his small, hard cock on my belly.

He angles his head and takes my lips in a punishing kiss. He tastes like alcohol and pepperoni, and I want to gag, but anyone looking at us would never know it. It seems like I did come here because of him. His hands slide down to grip my ass under my skirt, and my eyes pop open, and I tear my lips from his, taking three steps back.

He bites his bottom lip. "Fuck."

I sink my teeth into the soft skin of my lower lip, tasting blood to mask the disgusting taste of his spit. His eyes are full of hunger and something I recognize. The predatory look that he would force himself on me if I wasn't standing in the middle of the back patio of a frat house full of people. Matt wouldn't ask. He would take.

"Adam, take Melody and Madison home," I say, without looking their way, but from the corner of my eye, I see him push Melody and Madison toward the exit, without looking at me and storming off.

Matt flicks his gaze to Zack. "You're off the team. Get your shit and get out."

"What the fuck, Matt! It's initiation night!"

"I know, and I'm the captain. You're a freshman, and you broke the rules. No girlfriends showing up on initiation night."

"What about her?" Zack points in my direction.

Matt smirks, and everyone snickers. "She's not my girlfriend. She came to play."

I walk down the sidewalk toward the bus stop. I remember where it is and know the route back to Kenyan. My babysitting duties are over, but I dread going home, so I decide to head to the dorms instead. I check the time, and a laugh almost bubbles up my throat. 1:30 a.m. This was nearly the same time I ran out of this same frat house the night with Alaric.

The night my whole world turned to shit and has been since then. My life keeps getting better, but not in a good way. Every time I think I've made friends, it all turns to shit because of my past. Because of Alaric. I tried texting Adam, but he ignored my texts and calls. I probably lost a friend, but if he knew who I really was, he probably would tell me to go to hell and fuck off anyway. *I did what was right,* I tell myself. It felt dirty, but it was worth it.

I hear a roaring engine from a car coming down the street

behind me, but I keep walking, ignoring the sound getting louder. I look straight ahead, counting the concrete slabs from the sidewalk in my head, walking past the frat houses on fraternity row.

I watch the sleek black car pull up ahead by the curb. The taillights glow red like evil eyes. I pause for a second but continue to walk and decide just to ignore it. The dark-tinted window slides down when I'm about to pass the car, and I recognize the tattoos on the hands gripping the steering wheel, which only causes me to walk faster.

"Where's your driver?" he calls out.

I keep walking. I've never spoken to Alaric since that night and don't plan to. Ever.

The car crawls forward, but I keep walking.

"Stop being stupid and get in. It isn't safe walking out here alone. I'll take you home."

He didn't care that night, and I made it to hell just fine. This night is no different, but my father isn't waiting to make me pay for my so-called sins this time.

I don't stop and he continues to follow me until I reach the bus stop. I sit and check the time, fifteen minutes until the last bus for the night. If I missed it, I would have to call a cab or an Uber. I like to avoid spending money if I don't have to, so I'll wait for the bus.

"Are you joking right now? The bus?"

Yeah, asshole. It's called public transportation, but a stuck-up dick like him probably has never been on a bus.

"So you're going to sit out here alone until a bus comes with who knows what on it." I roll my eyes and look away. "I'm going to call your father."

My head snaps in his direction as sheer terror flows through my veins. "Fuck off!" I yell angrily.

"She speaks. That got your attention, didn't it? You don't want to piss off Daddy, huh?"

A brief gust of rage flows through me, but I tamper it down. He's just patronizing me. Trying to get under my skin. *Refrain from showing him a reaction, Veronica.*

His gray eyes slide over my crossed legs, making me wish I had pants on. I don't want him looking at me. It confuses me. And the fact that I hated what he did to me doesn't help. I've paid for it with my body and my blood.

"I'm not going to lie and say I wasn't surprised to see you there, but then I saw you with the Ohio State QB, I figured you must have run out of cocks to fuck. I thought you would have toned it down by now, but I guess I was right the first time. You are a whore."

"So I've heard," I reply sarcastically. "Are you done? Because it seems like you love to keep tabs on me since you know how many cocks I take."

"Not at all. That is just what I overhear. I was being generous since I saw to it Valen made it home. I owe it to the Order and all."

"You mean you don't want people pointing fingers if something happens to me and you happened to drive by. Trust me, no one would care."

"That is not true. Your father would be devastated."

A maniacal laugh bubbles out of my throat, and I do what I do best, act like they expect me to, so I don't fall into a self-deprecating puddle of self-pity. I widen my legs so that my panty-covered pussy is exposed. I watch his eyes flick between my gaze and my panties. Maybe he'll leave. "Is this what you were hoping for?" I purr, pasting a fake salacious smile on my lips. "You know, ever since you fucked me like a rabid dog and told everyone what you thought about me, it's made them curious to see if it's true. All they want is to fuck me." I slouch on the bench, widening my legs, and watch him blink in confusion when I finally say, "Thank you for making me their filthy whore. It reminds me of how much I hate you." I snap my legs closed. "Now fuck off."

He shakes his head offended but grinning. "You're just pissed off that you were outed and couldn't trap me. Come to think of it, are you still desperate and fuck random guys on your period?"

I'm relieved the lights of the bus appear, and he will have no choice but to pull away from the curb. After all this time, he still thinks of me the same way. I was so stupid in thinking he was different from the rest. He was a mistake. Poor judgment because I was trying to find someone to feel something genuine with just once. But it's too late for me. The damage is done, because I chose wrong.

I get up when it gets closer and walk toward the curb, not answering him, waiting for the bus to open its doors so I can get on. I sit in the back, relieved there are only two other people on, and watch as Alaric pulls away from the curb, roaring down the street.

I close my eyes and remember the night I walked in on him with another girl. It was at a Kenyan party after a swim meet. I was surprised he showed up since he had graduated. Reid was acting his usual self. It was six months into our freshman year, and Alicia was already gone. They killed her for eloping with Prey. It was a message. Loud and clear, and my father was part of it because he voted like an executioner.

Nothing has mattered since Alicia's death. I hide the pain along with my little notes of self-pity. I have no one but my regrets to keep me company. I should have told Reid when she promised me not to tell anyone she was leaving with Chase, but I didn't. I promised her I wouldn't and that I would make sure Reid found his happily ever after.

After I found out that my father voted for them to kill her, I knew it had everything to do with me. No one knew, but I did. Charles Devlin voted yes because of *me*. If I wasn't her friend to begin with, maybe she would still be alive, which makes it all my fault. I should have known Charles Devlin would take the one pure thing I had: my best friend.

That night at the party in Kenyan, I walked up to the house looking for the bathroom. I didn't think anything of it when Reid looked at me, but I knew it wasn't really Reid. His eyes told me it wasn't. They were dark and malicious with intent. They told me I deserved what I would see and feel. I opened the door, and he was fucking Becca Hales from behind. She hated me. But I'll never forgot the look in his eyes when he saw me standing at the threshold or how he told her she was beautiful and felt good. The way he held her and placed soft kisses on her neck. The way he never was with me—the way no one has ever touched me.

Because girls like me didn't deserve pleasure. They deserved pain.

And I believed it.

I watch the streetlights glow through the big windows of the bus as we pass. My eyes feel heavy, so I decide to close them for five minutes until the bus arrive on campus.

I nod and wash myself, listening to the sounds of his heavy breathing. A cold chill slides down my arms, and a knot forms in my throat, trying not to let the sob escape from my lips as he pleasures himself.

"So beautiful. The devil was the most beautiful angel God had ever created. It is no wonder he would create something so exquisite. Spread your pussy for me, princess," he demands, while he beats his dick faster.

The sound makes me want to throw up. I keep my eyes shut because if I open them, I don't want to cry out and make it worse. I do as he asks and hate myself every time. Every time he makes me bathe in front of him. I just clean myself and imagine there is someone else in the room.

Someone I want.

Who I always wanted.

I say his name repeatedly in my head, trying to picture the only time he looked at me like I was something. I shouldn't because of what he did, but no one has ever looked at me any different.

I jerk, waking up when I hear someone's voice. "Ma'am."

My eyes try to adjust to the bright light. "Huh?"

"This is the last stop. Kenyan."

"Shit." I look around, relieved it's just the bus driver. He looks like Mortimer Snerd sitting behind the wheel.

I walk down the aisle, cursing myself for falling asleep. "Err, thank you."

"Be careful," he says as I run off the bus in front of Drury Hall.

CHAPTER 6

Veronica

I run inside Drury as I head to the showers located in the female dorms. I don't want to go home, but I desperately need a shower to scrub my body. If I go home right now, I know I'll fall asleep and I'm afraid I'll have the same dream. I feel numb. Seeing Alaric again and reminding me how he hurt me triggered this need to forget. I keep glancing at the skirt I borrowed from Melody to see if there is blood.

I enter the back door with the skeleton key I found one night in the library when the librarian was busy in the back room and walk down the dark corridor, bypassing the overnight security guard. By the time I enter the shower, I'm out of breath. My lungs burn with trying to stay hidden from security. I close my eyes and look down at my hands. They're trembling.

When I calm down, I turn on the shower, hearing the water hit the tile, and watch the steam from the scalding hot water rise to the ceiling. I remember overhearing Draven saying that his twin hated bathtubs because that is where they found his mother after she slit her wrists. I have to say I agree with him in hating them—especially being inside them. The Bedford twins have their reasons, and I have mine.

After getting undressed, I stand under the spray and look

down at the razor blade in my hand. I started cutting when I was twelve. Alicia helped me stop for a while, but after Alaric and then her death, I couldn't stop. Whenever I couldn't cope or hated myself for something I did, I'd cut. It reminds me that I'm still alive—that I'm still here and most importantly, it's pain I can control, making sure it's hidden. The most important part was keeping it hidden from my father by cutting the skin near my inner ankles, inner thighs, or places no one would ever look or notice.

I sit on the tile, push my hair to the side and find a spot near my ankle. I press the tip, closing my eyes, and feel the first sting like the rush of a million needles. I watch the drop of blood flow down my heel to the tile floor. My eyes sting a bit from the heat of the water as I watch the blood flow like a river to the center, gurgling down the drain.

I find another spot when the bleeding becomes too much, watching the blood pool and mix with the water. I slide my fingers down my thighs, seeing the faint bruises, and find a spot scraping the back of my neck with my blunt nails. Tears fall down my cheeks, hating myself like I do every day. I hate my existence, but I have learned to help others in a way. They don't see it, but I don't care.

"Is this how you deal with shit?" I freeze. I look at the blade between my fingers close to the skin on my thigh. "Look at me, Veronica."

I turn around slowly, not caring if I'm naked. *I stopped caring a long time ago.* My dark hair is plastered on the top of my head like a helmet, but I keep my eyes on the tile, watching the blood flow from the cut on my ankle, bleeding out like the tears on my cheeks.

"W-what do you want, Valen? Why are you here?"

"Look at me, Veronica."

I raise my head slowly and see him leaning on the tile far enough so he doesn't get wet, but I don't meet his eyes because that's the last thing I need. Pity.

"Give me the blade."

"No."

"You're stronger than this."

I laugh, baring my teeth, and tap my temple with my finger. "You don't know what I am." I pause. "I-I don't know what I am. The Bible says if you kill yourself, you go straight to hell, but God didn't specify what that hell was." I get up and angle my head, trying not to break down in front of him. The sound of the water gets louder as my heart beats erratically inside my chest.

He tries to move forward, but I step back under the spray, looking at him boldly. "Go home, Valen."

"I'm not. I'm not leaving you here." He rolls his eyes. "Fine," he mutters, removing his shirt, pants, and shoes.

"I'm not going to kill myself," I say with wide eyes, instantly turning around.

"Tell me what's wrong, Veronica. You can't go home like this. I can't leave you like this. Tell me what to do or what you need."

He stands behind me when I turn around and shut my eyes, hoping he gives up and goes away. I don't know why he followed me or how he knew I was here, but it doesn't matter right now. I feel dirty, ugly, and worthless.

"Do you think I'm a good person?" I ask, my voice breaking.

I know he doesn't. No one does, but I need to hear it. I need him to say it. Because one thing Valen is, he's honest. There is no bullshitting with him. He just has a sex addiction. A woman wouldn't know if he wants her for real or if he's just trying to feed his demons, but when he's done, he regrets it as soon as it's over. I've seen how he shuts down right after at Kenyan parties when he comes out of a bedroom after fucking some girl. It's like an off button. Everything shuts down, and the lust in his eyes dies like it never happened, except for Jess. He fell for her, but he saw how Jess looked at Reid and he looked at her. I think we all did.

"I think we all have good in us...you know." I nod. "But whatever you are going through right now, I just need you to trust me. I need you to give me the blade, sweetheart."

I nod again and hand it to him, watching him place it on the brown bench attached to the tiled wall beside his shirt and jeans.

"I'm not trying to kill myself. I need you to know that."

He nods. "You need to feel the pain."

Tears slide down my cheeks because he gets it. He gets me.

"All I've ever known is pain."

He looks confused under the water, causing his hair to stick to his forehead. Water slides down his chiseled chest. Valen is built like a swimmer with little to no body fat on his tall frame. He's good-looking but a heartbreaker.

"What do you mean?"

I cringe inwardly because I said too much. I place my finger over my lips. "Shh." The skin between his brows crinkles, so I slide my finger to my ear and tap slowly and whisper, "It's not what you know but what you see and hear."

"Da-fuq?"

I shake my head, frustrated that he doesn't understand. I look down at my feet, the blood slowing its descent on the tile and walk to the next stall and turn on the water and then the next one, so the sound of water echoes louder against the tiled walls. I walk back, not caring I'm leaving footprints stained with blood on the floor.

He wipes the water from his face and steps close. I place my finger over his lips, telling him to be quiet. I pull his head down, so our lips almost brush and whisper, "They can hear you if they are listening." He raises his brow like I'm fucking crazy, and to most people, I sound like I am. He stands numbly when I turn around and slide my naturally dark hair to the side, and I hear the audible intake of his breath.

My hands begin to tremble at what he sees—what I'm allowing him to see. I turn around to see his expression and widen my eyes while keeping my finger to my lips, so he will remain quiet, shaking my head. His eyes widen in disbelief.

"You can leave now. I need to get back home. You were great, by the way." His lips drop open. "This stays between us," I drone on. "You wouldn't want Melissa to know about us."

Crazy talk. All of it.
But he knows.
He gets it.
He gets me.
And he knows he can't utter a word.
To anyone.

CHAPTER 7
Alaric

I bang my fist on the steering wheel repeatedly. "Fuck! Fuck! Fuck!" I look down at my hands, smeared with blood from my split knuckles. I lost control. I always lose control when it comes to her. I don't even feel the sting from the skin that's torn.

"Do you regret it?" Reid asks through the Bluetooth in my car.

Do I regret it?

"No."

"Relax, you didn't kill him, so stop beating yourself up over it."

I slide my black hooded sweater off my head and wipe my hands on it. "Yeah, but I'm trying to *not* kill people."

He snorts. "I hate to break it to you, but that is part of what you do, Alaric."

I let out an audible breath. "Whatever."

"Did Valen get home safe?"

"I'm not an Uber, and he wasn't drunk. He left in his car before—"

"You went back."

"Yeah, and I sent someone to clean it up when I was done."

"Do you need anything from me besides therapy?"

I laugh, and then it fades a little. "I don't need therapy. I need you to handle your boy."

"This is not about him, Alaric. It's about her. It's always been about her for you. Ever since that night, it's like—"

"Like what?" I snap, pinching my nose, not caring if I get blood all over my face. I'm parked in front of my house. I need a shower and a drink.

"Like you feel guilt for once in your life and not the angry kind. Everything that has to do with her is hot and cold. But you don't have to worry for much longer. The next meeting. Her father is going to announce who she's going to marry. Her time has run out. No man or son of one wants to marry her."

Her words play in my head, haunting me. 'All they want is to fuck me.'

Good, I tell myself.

"Jess is worried about her for whatever reason. She keeps asking me if I know who she'll end up with."

"Why the fuck should she care? Whoever the prick picks to marry her crazy ass is doing everyone a favor."

"She won't tell me, but Jess is…delicate."

He told me what happened, and I facilitated the vote, and the Order didn't get involved. I'm on the Consortium, but I have the most influence out of all the members of the Order. I cleaned up the mess.

"It's not our problem. There is nothing we can do. It could be anyone that isn't betrothed."

"Who do you think it is?" he asks, and that funny dread creeps up, but I push it down, like a weakness I must eliminate.

"I don't know, and I don't care. Every time she is around, lives are ruined. No one can do anything about it anyway. Rules are rules." I think about Alicia, and a surge of anger for being unable to save my flesh and blood sparks fury like a gout of flames within me. "Fuck her. I gotta go."

Placing my hands on the tile in my shower, I let the hot water beat down on my back, releasing the tension. The glass shower door opens behind me. Cold hands slide around my waist.

"You need me?"

I don't respond.

I need release. The hard, unforgiving kind. The brutal kind that calms me. I push off the tile and turn, looking at Sasha, my secretary. Her small breasts don't do it for me, but she is nothing I like, which is what I want. To escape from what I like, to focus on what I need. I press the screen, and Disturbed's "Down with the Sickness" plays through the speakers.

I grip Sasha by the throat, guiding her so she can get on her knees. I pump my cock and push the head inside her mouth to the back of her throat, and she takes it.

She takes it all. I fuck her hard, constricting the air from her lungs. Tears are pooling in her eyes. Spit is running down her chin, foaming on the bottom, trying not to choke on my size. I fuck her mouth hard and fast, not caring. Not giving a fuck. I close my eyes and see clear blue, which pushes me over the edge. My fingers fist Sasha's hair, causing her to cry out. The music and water drown out her screams, and then she sputters when I come down her throat.

When I pull out, I hear a string of curses. "You motherfucker! I couldn't breathe."

I walk out after I wash her spit and cum off my cock. "You should've held your breath longer." I grab the towel off the hook and turn my head. "You can see yourself out."

"I don't know why I agree to this shit."

Because I'm a Riodrick-Riordan. I'm a billionaire who can give you what no man can. Money, protection, and a life you could only dream of, and the best part of all, I'm forbidden fruit. The kind you want the most because I'm unattainable. A challenge.

I scratch my left brow as I watch her small, curveless body and small tits bounce with too-large nipples as she scrambles to dry herself and get her clothes on. She knows what I want, and the last thing I need is her running her mouth. I'm not a nice man. I never said I was. I'm not romantic or want more than what I ask. She came here. I didn't force her, but that is the problem with some people who don't know how to take no for an answer when they want more. They expect more because they feel that they can meet your needs.

"Then don't."

She slides her shirt over her almost flat chest. "Don't what?"

"Don't agree to do it. I asked specifically for one thing, you came, and now it's over."

She looks defeated, but that doesn't stop her from sinking her self-esteem even lower. "I'm sorry I overreacted. I'm leaving. I just—"

I stare at the wall, not caring what she is trying to say. I try to keep things convenient with the whole boss and secretary thing because I don't feel like dating women who think I can give them more when I don't. It's not her; I feel like this about every woman. I just like my dick licked. I'm a man. Sue me.

"I will always want more from you, Alaric," she continues. I roll my eyes when I give her my back and wait…until I hear the door shut and watch the screen by my bed as she walks out the front door into her car from the surveillance camera.

Relief.

It's what I feel after she leaves. It's how I feel after every woman leaves when I'm done.

Except for one woman.

And all I can think about is destroying her.

CHAPTER 8
Veronica

"You should know... that I detest having to wait, Veronica."

My ears become assaulted by the clinking sounds of the buckle, which sound like nails being dragged over a chalkboard. "Get in the bath, Princess."

I take another step forward while observing the heated steam from the ancient tub. I can't help but pray that something will drag me under and drown me once I step inside.

As I undress, taking care not to get any water on the extensions of my platinum hair, my heart beats so hard in my chest, and my voice is screaming inside my head to turn around and run. But I can't. They would just kill me and make it look self-inflicted. Sometimes I wish I had the balls to do it myself.

Sometimes.

The steaming hot water causes me to wince from the discomfort it causes on my skin. I close my eyes as I take the bar of soap in both hands and work it into a lather. The smell of some weird leaves I hate slides over my skin like a ritual.

"You are such a good girl. I love to watch you purge yourself of the wrongs you've done, the sins you've committed, Veronica. You're a sinner because you were consummated by sin—born out of it. In the eyes *of God, you are an abomination that is on par with having a kid with a bastard, and I will be your savior, but you must pray for forgiveness."*

I look to the corner of the room and see a red dot of light flashing like a tiny beacon. Something was in front of it, but it was unmistakable, and I didn't imagine it. It looks like a recording device.

"What is that?" I ask, pointing to the corner where the light was flashing, making sure to never maintain eye contact. I hate to see the glint of mockery and spite every time I ask about something.

I hear the groaning of the chair but keep washing my skin over and over, acclimating to the heat of the water.

"It's nothing. There's nothing. Now show us how you let him put it in you. What did you say? Everyone knows you're very clever. Like a demon sucking cock to the root. So persuasive in doing what is needed and then expiated...sin is committed because it lives inside all of us. But we have to learn to live sinlessly in a world plagued by demons." I look up and see eyes that glitter hypnotically and a dry smile aimed at my body. "You sin with pleasure, Veronica, and here is where you will repent with pain." The leather belt slaps against my thighs as the sound of my voice gasping from the bite of the sting on my wet thighs fills the room. Rough fingers pull them apart, leaving white marks that then turn red with angry welts on my skin. "He wasn't yours to take!"

I push the wooden door to the confessional, knowing the priest is still here. I keep the hood from my coat in place and the rosary between my hands as if I'm praying.

"Welcome, my child. If we confess our sins, God is faithful, forgives, and cleanses us. But we must confess our sins."

I follow and motion the sign of the cross. "Forgive me, Father, for I have sinned. It's been two weeks since my last confession. I have tried to be good, but the voices inside my head won't stop. They don't help. I want to do good, but I have to repent for the sins I have already committed."

"What kind?"

"Sex. The kind out of wedlock, and I think of sex and what it does. How it destroys. I also keep thinking...what does God think of fatherless children? I mean, if they didn't have one."

"God says he is the father to the fatherless. There is a place for them with the Lord." I wonder where that place is because if he was a father, why do I feel so alone and unloved. Why do I feel so much pain? "Are you fatherless, my child?"

I shake my head. "No. I have a father."

I do, and I don't because he hates me.

"Then you have nothing to worry about."

"What if I feel like he isn't."

"Parents are to bring their child's discipline to the Lord. Now tell me about these voices and thoughts–"

After I've said my prayers, I walk up to the fourth floor inside the left wing on campus and into Dr. Wick's office for my scheduled appointment.

"I'm glad you could make it, Veronica."

"I'm ecstatic to be here," I respond, taking a seat after shutting the door.

She crosses her legs like a queen, but it's mostly because she is squeezed into a black pencil skirt, and there is no other option.

I open the inner pocket of my coat and light a Virginia Slims, taking a drag and exhaling with an audible sigh of relief, watching the smoke in the air like a dark cloud.

"Do you have to smoke in here?"

"I prefer weed. But if I have to be here and they are paying you to, then yes." I tap the middle of the cancer stick with my middle finger so the ash can fall to the floor, hoping I make a hole in the carpet. Maybe she would remember me by the burnt hole and not forget me as soon as she closes the file after telling my father everything I've said because this bitch doesn't know the meaning of patient confidentiality.

"How are the voices? The dreams?"

I take a drag, exhale, and tamp the cigarette on the plastic arm of the chair, and I smile inwardly because she's annoyed. But so am I because it's the same narrative.

"They're still there." I tap my temple and smile. "The voices in my head keep telling me to do stuff."

"Like?"

I watch her solemnly as she waits for my answer. "Like fucking, Mrs. Wick. They tell me to fuck, and then I have these dreams where they tell me that I have sinned. In those dreams, I'm nothing but a sinner."

She shifts in her seat uncomfortably and places her thumb on her bottom lip like she is thinking, but she isn't. She's listening.

"Is that the only time you have intercourse? When the voices tell you to?"

I laugh hysterically. "Well, of course. They tell me who to fuck and how hard I need to fuck them."

"How do you feel after?"

"How do you feel after you fuck, Dr. Wick?"

"We are not discussing me. We are discussing you."

"Of course!" I snap my fingers looking up at the ceiling. "It started when I was twelve, you know—the voices telling me to do it, but it didn't manifest until the sacrifice."

"The night they all ridiculed you at the party?" My head whips forward, and I snap my fingers, watching with glee as she jolts like she is zapped in her chair. "You're really on to something there, doc."

"What am I on?"

"Some good shit. You need to give me some."

"What do you want me to give you?"

"Something to sleep like happy pills. My mother is on them all the time. You should see her. She's perfect."

I need the pills to sleep because I'm tired, not from the night shifts with Dorothy at the restaurant, but from not being able to get actual sleep when I do come home. Nothing has helped. Not tea or reading. Nothing.

I watch her tear the paper off the prescription pad after she writes something on it, so I can give it to the front desk before I leave. She probably gave me tranquilizers, and I need them.

She hands me the script and asks, "Are you sleeping at all?"

"Sometimes. It's why I want the pills."

"I suggest relaxation and massages. A spa to relieve anxiety and thoughts that can cause you not to sleep. I will make a note and send a treatment plan. The sleeping pills will help, but I need you to try to curve your *actions* and avoid what triggers them."

"You want me to avoid being around men, so I don't fuck."

She gives me a pointed look, and I raise my arms and stretch like a cat waking up from a nap. "Alright, doc. I'll avoid all the triggers but can't make any promises." I sigh. "I have to get married soon you know."

"Do you know to who?"

I grin. "Are you asking if I know who will put their semen inside me? The one they call a sinner. Whore. The answer is no, Dr. Wick. I don't know who will make me bleed in sacrifice."

A glimmer of sadness crosses her features for a second, and then it's gone. Her mask is back in place, and I go for the kill because...why not. She doesn't care. She is getting paid to do a job.

"How's your daughter, Dr. Wick? I heard she was going through...a rough patch."

Her head lifts, her eyes flat. "Times up. I will have to see you more often since you're on sleeping medication. If it doesn't work, I recommend observation."

She is trying to deviate from what happened to her daughter. After Dravin fucked her ten ways from Sunday, the girl got attached. Poor thing needs therapy, from what I heard.

"Don't be so hard on her, Dr. Wick." I grin. "We all have voices telling us to do things."

The clink of a marker on the tray attached to the dry-erase board resonates inside the lecture hall. "Whose mistakes caused the tragedy between Romeo and Juliet?" Professor Elliot asks, sweeping his gaze across the room but is only met by silence. He opens his arms wide mockingly. "Anyone?"

I decided to take classic literature as an elective, even though my major is economics, because I wanted it to give me a perspective that I don't have, and one of them is romance, except, Shakespeare's *Romeo and Juliet* is a tragedy, but to me, it's true love.

The professor waits impatiently when no one volunteers to answer. His eyes scan the room once more, so he can call on someone. Garret and Dravin look at each other. Reid and Jess smile when Valen blurts, "Pick someone," then coughs, causing Gia to giggle and the rest of the class to laugh. I was surprised they all signed up for this class, but here we are.

"Mr. Vikiar, since you are so inclined for me to pick someone, why don't you answer for the rest of the class."

"It was Romeo's mistakes that led to the tragedy," Valen responds.

"Good. And why do you think love is the theme? Why is it so different, let's say…than poetry about love?"

Dravin glances at Gia, Reid at Jess. I finally realized why they took this class. It's because they are in love and want to learn something more meaningful. Love is the foundation of why they are here. Valen followed along because he felt the emotion and didn't recognize or know how to act on it.

I raise my hand because I know the answer, having read it fifteen times, looking for the same thing. The good and the simple emotion of love in something. Even if you can't find it in those you want.

"Miss Devlin!" he calls on me. The whole class turns around and my gaze lands on Valen. His eyes soften. His lips twitch, forming a small grin. A direct contrast to the glare aimed directly at me from Reid and Dravin.

I lower my hand, rub my lips together, and answer, "I think it's because Shakespeare didn't want to portray life like a cheesy poem. I believe Shakespeare wanted to write about love in its brutal form.

Love is unforgiving. It's not the type of love you see in the beginning when Romeo is in love with Rosaline. It's the all-consuming kind he wanted to write about. For example, when Romeo and Juliet meet for the first time, their love is at first sight, and nothing else matters in that moment or after. Not hate, greed, or acceptance between two families. Everyone makes mistakes, but it was them against everyone, and the only way Romeo and Juliet could be together...was in death."

Professor Elliot pumps his fist in the air. "There you have it, ladies and gentlemen. Miss Devlin is a true romantic." Snorts and snickers can be heard across the lecture hall, but I ignore them. What catches me by surprise is Valen clapping with a smile. Jess joins in, and surprisingly, so does Gia. Dravin and Reid look at them like they grew three heads and have lost their minds, but I smile.

"Alright, I need your short verses for your assignment turned in next time we meet. No exceptions!" the professor announces before everyone gets up to leave.

I'm about to exit, but a hand is placed against the frame blocking my path. I recognize Valen's tattoo peeking out of the sleeve of his sweater. "Come with us."

I shake my head, stepping outside the classroom when he finally lets me through. "I don't think that is a good idea."

"Why not?"

"Because–" I trail off when the sound of my phone pings with an incoming message. I fish my phone out of my bag and look at a message from my mother telling me she made me an appointment for a wax.

"Is it your boyfriend?" he teases. I've never had one, but he doesn't know that. He must think I've had many given my reputa-tion. Sex isn't a boyfriend. It's an act. Sometimes out of choice and sometimes forced. The look on my face swipes the teasing grin off his. "Sorry, I—"

"It's just my mom. I have an appointment at the Galleria."

The Galleria is a shopping venue that also offers different

services in the office building attached to the shops, along with exclusive designer boutiques.

"Good, because that is where we are going."

"We?"

"Yeah, the Bedfords, Riodrick-Riordan's, and us."

"I don't think they would like me to come along."

"Jess and Gia want you to come. It can be a girls' thing, saving me from being the sixth wheel," he says, wincing on the last part.

I have to go there anyway. It's not like I'm going shopping there.

"Fine."

"I'll take you. We can ride together."

Walking out in the sunny afternoon toward the parking lot, I keep thinking that ever since my breakdown in the shower, he's been nice. Too nice and it feels like pity, which I loathe. I click the seat belt and sit in the passenger seat of his Mercedes sports car. "You don't have to be nice to me."

He places the car in reverse, following Dravin and Reid in their cars. "I'm sorry, Veronica."

I slide the hood off my head, combing the blonde tresses of my wig with my fingers, listening to him apologize. It's the first time I've heard someone apologize to me and mean it.

"I don't deserve an apology, Valen. I've done things and acted in ways I don't even recognize."

"I don't care about that. A-are you okay? If someone hurt you, you would tell me, right?"

I meet his eyes briefly, and he lets out an audible breath. "That was stupid. What I'm trying to say is, literally."

"No, of course not," I lie.

Why would I tell him the truth? There's nothing he could do about it. He will marry Melissa before he graduates his senior year, and I will soon be married to someone the Order still has to agree to until the next vote—which is next week. But my silence says more than words ever could. It speaks of truths left unsaid. Because we both know I'm part of a bigger game that has been being played for a long time. A game no one saw coming but me. All I can do is sit back and watch who will win or how it will end. All I know is that I will lose.

I make my way to the designer boutique where Jess and Gia are buying clothes to wear to a party Dravin is hosting. I take my sweet time so that by the time I get there, I don't have to watch them shop while I wait because they would find it odd that I can't participate.

After Valen dropped me off in front of the office building and I finish my appointment, the hour spent waxing every pubic hair on my body, I walk by the outdoor café, near the tables and chairs placed under oversized umbrellas. People are chowing down on overpriced salads, deep in conversation.

A man in a suit stands just outside a table with dark glasses and his arms crossed. I immediately recognize his stance as someone's bodyguard or maybe chauffeur because my father has both. A shrill laugh comes from behind him, causing people to stop mid-sentence and look, including me, but what catches my attention is where the laughter is directed. The man seated across from her is sinfully dressed in a white shirt, sleeves rolled up, exposing tattooed forearms, with two buttons undone at the throat, and sunglasses that cost more than my monthly paycheck at the restaurant. His straight jaw, straight nose, and perfect lips make him the complete package.

When I think of a sinner, Alaric is the first one I think about. He's the devil under your skirt. The cause of heat between your legs. The one fallen from grace. A reckoning. His name is a contradiction— Alaric means noble ruler. But even the devil was an angel, and I was his sacrifice.

The woman tries to make him laugh, telling him something, but he's looking straight ahead. You can tell by the angle of his head, he's ignoring her every word. As I get closer, I overhear her talking about a meeting and how one guy was nervous about his proposal. She must work for Alaric or with him. I've never seen her before, but where Alaric is concerned, I stopped noticing. I stopped caring and ignored his existence because I knew better. He's forbidden. The Order's esteemed member can do no wrong in their eyes.

Not being able to keep myself from looking over once more, I feel his eyes on my skin like a burn from the sun on a hot day, even with his dark sunglasses. He pushes his sunglasses on his head, and his gray eyes meet mine. The woman notices and turns to see what has his attention.

"Do you know her?" she asks, her tone dripping with jealousy.

"Yes," I hear him answer her while he looks at my black dress, pantyhose, and black boots. He looks like a model on a magazine cover, and I look like Wednesday Adams with platinum hair.

"I've worked with you for over a year and never seen her before."

She must be his secretary, and she obviously is more than that, but as jealousy creeps in, I have learned that anger feels so much better. I turn and walk over to their table and watch her mouth open like a fish on a hook.

His bodyguard steps forward. The man is built like a brick house, and I stand on the tips of my boots to say softly in his ear, "I'll be just a minute." He looks at the palm of my hand when it lands on his hard chest, and I continue, "We fucked once, but it was messy. I promise to keep things clean this time." He turns to look at Alaric, but I don't wait.

I walk over to their table, ignoring the curious stares aimed my way. "Can I help you?" the woman asks mockingly.

I nervously roll my tongue on my bottom lip, noticing the copper tones in her hair from the sun and trying to figure out why he would find her appealing. Her blouse is unable to flatter her too-small breasts. You can tell she isn't wearing a bra and her makeup is so heavily applied, it looks chalky because of the heat outside from the afternoon sun. "Who are you?" I ask, even though I already figured it out.

She glances at Alaric and places her cloth napkin on the table. "I'm his—Alaric's secretary." The way she says his first name and not his last—hyphenated name, tells me one thing: she's trying to stake a claim and wants me to know that she's fucking him. I'm not sure what my purpose of coming over here is: maybe the lecture on Romeo and Juliet got to me for some reason, or the fact that I will never know what love is truly like, let alone experience it from someone, and I'm a glutton for punishment.

"What can I do for you, Miss Devlin?" Alaric asks with formality.

I look at my short nails like I just had a manicure when I actually need one. "I came to say hi, of course. It would be rude if I walked by without greeting you and your...secretary." His phone rests on the white cloth over the table near his plate.

From the corner of my eye, I focus on the cloth napkin in her lap. She's probably hoping Alaric tells me to fuck off, or worse, that I'm interrupting their time together.

"I'm Sasha, by the way. It's good to meet one of Alaric's... friends," she says, but her eyes say it all. That I'm a threat because that is not what a typical secretary says when she is with her boss.

Her overfamiliarity with him is annoying. She is sitting out in the afternoon having lunch on a beautiful day with the one man I could see myself with when I was young and stupid and thought for one second that he could be the one person that would see me. Maybe save me from the hell I'm trapped in that wants to swallow me whole. I knew the moment I laid eyes on her that I would hate her for it.

I recognize when two people have been intimate. It's probably from personal experience or that my father fucks his own secretary regularly and isn't shy about it. My mother knows and turns a blind eye, pops the next pill to fall asleep, only to wake up, then boards a private plane to visit friends abroad for a brunch date.

A fake grin appears on my lips. I have mastered one for people who show an instant dislike for me. It's sort of an armor I have built, along with my crazy bitch attitude, to hide the way I truly feel inside, that I'm breaking and there isn't much left to ruin.

I have had sex many times and never had an orgasm that

wasn't self-inflicted. There was one time I had wanted it more than anything, but it was awful, expecting it to be magical. I was expecting it to be the kind where you have butterflies in your stomach just thinking about it, but instead, it was a horror flick, like a scene that stood out the most when you experienced it the first time, like in the movie *The Exorcist*, and her head spins around. A memory best kept buried that you can't erase because your first time is something you will always remember. The other times I had sex were because it was what needed to be done, and for others. I had no choice, but they all shared the same result. They ended the same, in pain. The only way I have learned to deal with it is acting like it doesn't hurt—like my heart isn't broken into a million pieces or that my soul isn't mine.

My eyes land on Alaric's phone when it vibrates from an incoming message, and I notice she sent him a text. I grip the napkin she placed on the table, watch her mouth open and then close when I tell her, "I think you forgot to clean up your self-worth." I toss the napkin in her lap and tune out her audible gasp when I grab Alaric's phone, toss it in the bucket of champagne with melted ice water, and watch it float like a buoy.

His gray eyes flick up, and I could swear I saw his lips twitch. "It was nice seeing you again, Alaric," I say in a sultry tone, sliding my finger over his busted knuckles, wondering whose ass he kicked or killed, watching the scab turn white around the edges before I walk away, hearing Sasha's raised voice.

"You two have something going on?"

"No, she means nothing," he responds.

The words he uttered are the truth, even if I don't like them coming from him, but it is how he sees me, and nothing I do will change that. I act out to remind myself what I am, by hearing it from his lips. Because the next chapter of my life is the beginning of my sentence.

The rest of my afternoon is spent with Jess and Gia. I'm horrified at how much I envy them that they are in love with someone who can mend them and put them back together. I watch how carefree they are. The way they smile and laugh picking out clothes. How I have to lie and tell them I already have that collection when I don't have anything from this store in my closet. But to them or their husbands, they wouldn't question it. They all believe the lies I spill. The act. Sometimes I wonder how long I can keep it up until it all destroys me.

I am frightened for myself, but thankful for the pills Dr. Wick prescribed to help me get some sleep and not succumb to my dreams. I call them *happy* pills because it's the only time, I don't feel pain. It's the first time, besides the color of my eyes, that I have something in common with my mother. My internal life has become destitute because I revert to fumbling for a token of love from someone who never offers it.

CHAPTER 9
Veronica

"Thank you for coming by...have a nice day."

I pick up my two left on the table, stuffing them in the small pocket of my apron and hear the plastic tub land on the table for the third time tonight with a loud thud. A thud louder than necessary.

"Dorothy sat the next table down in your section. It looks like they are ready for you to take their order," Adam says in a tight voice.

He's still mad about the initiation party and what happened with Melody and me showing up with her. I don't think it has anything to do with Matt because why would it? Adam never responds to my texts or phone calls so I gave up hoping that with time, he would forget about it.

"I'm on it," I respond.

"On everything apparently," he mutters.

I pause, blinking back the sting of tears, and turn to face him. "You know what, Adam."

"What?"

"Fuck you."

I push past him to wait on my next table and ignore him for the next three hours of my shift. It's Tuesday night and even though this is a small restaurant, On The Edge Diner is open twenty-four-hours and is the hangout spot for both universities when you want something to eat and everything else is closed. That is what brings it success. College kids can hang out and get a bite to eat. It doesn't matter if you're from Kenyan or Ohio State University. It is the middle ground year-round.

Dorothy was able to get the county to approve a license to sell beer and wine. Since the restaurant has a retro theme, no one questions the old cigarette machines hidden in the bathroom that sell Marlboro and Virginia Slims. There also is an old arcade game and foosball table in the back, so kids can go and play if they are bored.

It's considered a twenty-four-hour hangout mostly for high school seniors and OSU students. Privileged kids from Kenyan have their own hangouts and parties. They don't need to hang out at a retro-themed diner when they have empty mansions to use because their parents are traveling on business or pleasure.

There is a self-serve soda fountain that has all the different flavors of coke that I love. The best part of working here is that no one really knows I work here from Kenyan and I get free food Monday thru Friday. Sometimes, I bring food to the staff my father hired, knowing they are tired of working at the house all day.

When a group of girls with three guys walk in, Dorothy seats them in the back booth in my section. I can tell they are high school kids hanging out way past their curfew or maybe their parents don't give a shit if they are out on a school night.

I check the cup with extra pens by the register, picking one that still has ink when I see Adam approach. "I'm sorry," he says.

"Save it."

"I was wrong. I was mad about what they said about you and I felt stupid for not knowing how to defend you."

"Defend me against what, Adam?"

"All of them because I know that what they said about you isn't true. You're not like that and I get why you did what you did at the party, but you could have let me handle it, even though someone did."

I turn to face him now. "What do you mean someone did?"

"You don't know?" I shake my head raising my eyebrows. "Matt is out for the season— probably can never play football again...at least not at OSU. They named me QB1 as an incoming freshman and I can't be happy about it when someone is laid up in a hospital bed with both hands broken and his face smashed in."

What the hell? I'm not a fan of Matt and I get that he's an asshole with little to no regard for women, but he's hurt and his future is ruined.

"Who did it?"

"No one knows. No one is talking."

"I'm sorry, Adam."

"Is it true that you attend Kenyan?" he asks, then shakes his head. "I don't care about the other stuff. It's all rumors anyway." He smiles. "I know you...and my sisters love you. Especially Melody."

I'm not going to lie to him or keep that part hidden from him or his sisters anymore. It feels good to have friends that think differently when it comes to me.

"It's true, I attend Kenyan. I'm a senior."

He places the plates inside the plastic tub from the bar counter. "So you're friends with the enemy."

"You're still my friend?" I ask hopefully.

He wipes his hands on the towel from his back pocket. "I never stopped. Yeah, I was mad and didn't answer your calls because I felt I wasn't good enough for you to tell me and when I find out who the asshole is behind all the rumors, you can count me in to kick their ass."

I think of Adam trying to kick Alaric's ass, knowing I would never let Adam near him. Adam is a good guy. He's the reason I know that good guys still exist. Any girl would be lucky to have him.

"That would be something, but I wouldn't want you to."

He slides a strand of hair away from my forehead. "I know." His gaze shifts past my head for a second. "I think you need to get to the last booth. They're giving us death glares."

"Does it have anything to do with the girl on the left side?"

I saw the way they looked at each other when she sat down with her friends.

"You mean the one I asked out to prom but won't be seen dead with the bus boy from the restaurant?"

"She said no to you?" I ask surprisingly. He rolls his eyes. "Okay, I take that as a yes. What a bitch."

He shrugs. "It's alright, I won't go."

"Why not ask someone else?"

"Her bullshit reason grew wings and most of the girls I would have asked, felt the same, or already have dates."

I take their drink order, but I don't miss the way the girl sitting next to the one that turned Adam down to prom glances at Adam every time he has his back turned with hope in her eyes that he would pay her some attention. The bitch next to her is pretty, wearing shiny lip gloss and a short top that shows the swell of her breasts. The girl next to her is nothing compared to her with what she is wearing, but I think it's because her friend downplays her looks. Girls can be mean like that when they have competition. Senior prom is a big deal in high school and it's a tradition. Getting asked is a big deal.

I didn't go to prom my senior year because word traveled fast after what happened with Alaric. It's not that I didn't want to go because I did, but I had to turn everyone down that asked. The guys that did asked weren't genuine. You could see it in the way they approached me. It was clear they expected more than a dance. Everyone in my class went and I cried myself to sleep that night and more the next day when I saw the pictures of everyone having fun. I swore to Alicia that I was okay with not going. It was the last thing she dressed up for before she eloped with Chase.

After placing their drinks, I go to place their order in the kitchen when I hear someone from the table ask, "Who is that?" I turn and follow their line of sight behind me and my eyes land on Valen, sliding into a booth and giving me a wink. How did he know I worked here? "He's...wow."

"Hey gorgeous," he says, grabbing a menu like he's here for the food.

"What are you doing here?"

His lips lift in a grin while he scans the menu. "I came to check on you."

I step closer and take out the ordering pad to take his order. "What can I get you?"

He places the menu down and leans back. "Oh, I'm not here for food. I'm here to make sure you attend Draven's little party."

I laugh through my nose. "Yeah, nice try. They would never invite me."

"I'm inviting you and you're wrong. Jess and Gia told me to invite you because they know you would give them some bullshit excuse for not going."

"I don't belong at Draven's party."

"Why not?"

"You know why? It's…awkward."

He lowers his voice. "I think Gia is over the fact you had sex with Draven. It was before her and I'm sure you weren't the only one."

As much as Draven Bedford is attractive, I didn't want to. It was cold, rough, and impersonal. I didn't get off. I had to fake it and I was glad when it was over.

The girls behind me are whispering and giggling. I look up to see Adam and then turn to look at the girls, contemplating the invite to the party. Valen looks over and shakes his head. "He your friend?"

I slide my tongue over the front of my teeth because I hate catty bitches. Except the girl with the light brown hair is trying to hide her face so that the others don't catch on that she doesn't agree to whatever they are saying. "Yeah. He's a good guy."

"What are you thinking? Who are the girls?" My eyes slide over to his. "Do I wanna know?"

I tilt my head to the side. "If I go, can I bring some friends?"

"As long as they can play ball."

He means no one underage because they sure as hell are not leaving virgins if they go to a Kenyan party. The bell from the kitchen dings, signaling that their food is ready.

Catty bitch number one asks, "You know him?"

"Yeah, why?"

"He's hot."

Yeah, he is and also dangerous with an insatiable cock that breaks hearts.

I smile blithely. "He's a sophomore at Kenyan. He just invited me and Adam to a party Friday night, you girls want to come?" They widen their eyes like I just told them they won front row tickets at a Taylor Swift concert.

"Adam knows him?"

"Of course, he does. Adam practically knows everyone. He's got the QB1 spot at Ohio State. All the girls are going crazy over him, not just me. If you guys are down and of course eighteen, you can come since you know Adam."

"You like him?" she asks, like I know something she doesn't. "You're gorgeous. How could you like a guy like Adam?"

I do and it has everything to do with the fact that he's a nice guy and hell would freeze over before I let this bitch fuck with him.

"What's not to like...umm—" I trail off, waiting for her to tell me her name.

"Jenny."

"Jenny," I repeat. "And you are?" I point to the girl who is secretly crushing on Adam.

"Lizzy," she says shyly. I watch as Jenny shoves her lightly and gives her a what the hell is wrong with you look. *Bitch.*

"I think Adam is hot and so do most of the college girls at Ohio and Kenyan. He works here because he doesn't want his mother to work extra-long shifts so that he can attend college."

It's true, but it's also because Adam's mother doesn't earn enough to cover his expenses.

"Really?" Jenny says surprised.

I write down my number so that Lizzy can call me and I can give her the address to Draven's party. I watch her enter it on her phone, before I move away, watching Adam wipe down the table, casting a nervous glance my way before I say, "Yeah, like I said, what's not to like, I can't believe some bitch had the balls to turn him down for his senior prom. Her loss."

CHAPTER 10
Veronica

"Are you sure, Mrs... Mr. Riordan?"

Alaric's mother smiles after I butcher her name when I address her holding the outfit she bought me, after she asked me to stop by her house.

"Could you stop with the formality, Veronica? Claire is fine. Since you were in high school, I have told you to call me Claire."

I remember the first time I met her when Alicia promised to introduce me to Alaric because I had a huge crush on him and couldn't wait until I was old enough to introduce myself. I wanted a fair shot, and being underage wouldn't work in my favor. But I was stubborn and couldn't wait. I wanted to meet him, but I was more surprised to find a mother figure in Claire instead. Her son didn't notice me; I was invisible to him. But she always found a way to bring me dresses and clothes, claiming that she bought them when she was younger and never got a chance to wear them, but we both know that was a lie until she just started telling me she bought it for me. I always wondered why she was so nice to me. Maybe she heard what happened between me and her son but overlooked my behavior afterward. At one point, she thought I was into Reid, but we never had any chemistry and hardly spoke. And after Alaric and Alicia, it got worse. Like most people, he finally opened up with his total dislike for me, and it was open season.

But Claire was one of the few that didn't. Besides the hired staff at home, a few showed me kindness.

"I'm sorry, Claire."

She waves her hand demurely. "Nonsense. I want to know if you like it. I heard Draven is throwing a party and I want you to look your best. Graduation is looming, and I know...you don't have much time before—" She trails off, avoiding my gaze.

"Before I know who I'm marrying," I finish for her.

She presses her lips together, forming a thin line.

"It's okay, Claire. We all have to, right?"

She nods, but I don't miss how she won't look me in the eye, her focus on the short dress with a designer shoe bag attached to the hanger. Claire is one of those women that stays up to date on gossip. She knows practically everything that goes on at Kenyan most of the time.

"It's tomorrow at Thursday's meeting with the Order."

My chest squeezes tightly, knowing that by tomorrow, I will know where I'll be living and the monster who will be keeping me. I'm not a great catch in anyone's eyes or what the Order would consider an acceptable wife. In my case, they only care about an alliance between two families. My father doesn't care about the alliance; he cares only for one thing, power. The power to sway the vote in his favor because the Consortium is a threat to his existence. He needs more power by forming an alliance that favors his ideals.

"I'm aware," I say but don't meet her gaze, afraid of what she might see.

Fear.

"What is she doing here?" I jolt and find gray eyes flash at me in disgust.

"Alaric, you remember Veronica."

His face tightens. "Mother, I know who she is, but that doesn't answer my question. What the hell is she doing here?"

Claire straightens, holding the hanger in her hand. "I invited her here. She was just stopping by to pick something up."

He glances at the dress and then at me. "I will say this once and won't repeat it. You can manipulate and fuck everyone in Kenyan like the whore that you are." I inwardly flinch. He backs me up toward the archway leading to the exit.

"Alaric! What has gotten into you!" Claire yells. But it falls on deaf ears.

"Get the fuck out. You're not welcome here." His jaw is set in a hard line. He opens the front door and almost rips it off its hinges with force.

I should have never come. I keep telling myself to ignore her calls, but it's hard when all someone has done is be nice and give you the most beautiful things because they find they love your company. I remember Claire telling me she wished she was able to have more children. She wanted a daughter. A little girl she could nurture and dress up. Tell her stories about her days in high school and how she fell in love with her husband because she said having a boy was hard. Alaric is not the romantic type by any means. But I would listen to her because I secretly wanted a mother like that. One that would tell me I was loved and that I mattered to her. All my mother did was tell me I was a mistake she wished she had never made, but I could make it up to her by keeping Daddy happy. *Do good, Veronica.*

"I-I'm sorry," I stammer.

"Your kind is never sorry. Stop fucking with my family." He grips me by my throat, and dread fills my veins. The look in his eyes is hard and cold. "Alicia didn't deserve what happened to her. The one thing I wished for is for you to be in that grave instead of my beloved cousin. I thought you should know that."

I couldn't agree more.

"Get your fucking hands off me," I say through clenched teeth, trying to tear myself out of his grip, but he squeezes harder, leaving just enough for me to breathe.

"If you come near my family, I'll kill you, Veronica."

I blink rapidly from the cruelty of his words and begin to shut down. The need to cut taking over like an addict seeking an escape. For some, it's a high, but for me, it's a need for pain. The sting from the wound of a cut bleeding the hurt out of me. Maybe it would be better if he did it. He could finish me off.

"There is nothing I wish for more than for that to happen. I got my spot all picked out. You wouldn't even have to do it, but you see, the funny thing is, it never happens. Because I'm still here. Because they all love to watch."

He shoves me away, and I almost trip on the last step. "The fuck? You're a crazy bitch."

I laugh. It's an ugly laugh that bubbles up my now sore throat as I rub where his fingers gripped me hard and point mockingly at the heat spreading over the area. "You know, my future husband wouldn't like you to fuck up the merchandise."

Everyone will be at the Order's meeting tomorrow night, including him. All members have to attend. I don't care who they pick because it doesn't matter. I have two choices: live with it or die from it.

"I can deal with your little childish games, throwing my phone in a bucket of ice water while you ruin a lunch date with my regular fuck because you're still pissed after all this time that you didn't succeed with Daddy's bidding by trapping me. But I will not let you use my mother. Trust me, the man cursed to marry a bitch like you would expect you to be all used up. I dodged a bullet, but know that everyone who looks at you knows you're just Daddy's puppet. A spoiled little rich girl with nothing better to do than make everyone's life miserable."

I cut myself that night on my way home and when I took the bus after my shift. I had a paperclip in my purse when I received my paycheck the day before. At first, I didn't know why I had saved the silver paper clip in the little pocket next to the bottle of sleeping pills, but deep down, I knew why. It was a band-aid I needed, just in case the wound would reopen, and last night, Alaric's words triggered the wound.

Thursday night would only get worse. I cried in my room before my father was ready to take me to the church.

"I have chosen someone respectable for you, and the members will vote tonight. I'm sure they will have no issues approving the alliance. All I ask, is that you don't embarrass me or your mother. The Devlin name is part of history. You should be honored you are to represent this family as my only heir. You will do as you are told and accept the union. Understood?"

"Yes, Father," I whisper in agreement.

"Good. Don't listen to any of them, Veronica. They might have an opinion of you in a negative regard, but none of them are perfect. Remember that. No one in that room is a saint. You have nothing to be ashamed of, Veronica."

"Yes, Father," I repeat, knowing deep down that I feel ashamed but have no choice but to agree.

Walking into the church feels like I'm walking into my own funeral. All the members are in attendance, including all of the classmates I grew up with from important families. The eyes of the Bedford twins, Gia, Jess, Reid, Garret, Melissa, and the last person I want to see, Alaric, are all on me. Valen is seated in the corner; his lips turn into a frown when he watches me approach the center of the room by the altar. No one can object to the Order's decision unless they have already taken their family's place and have grad-uated. They also have to clear up any issues interfering with world leaders. Translation, they need to make sure they are mentally stable to rule in society.

"Welcome, Mr. Devlin. I see you are ready to begin. We have accepted your request and will bring it forth to be voted on. Miss Devlin, will you please remain."

I face the room like I'm in a congregation and respond, "Of course."

Everyone in the room takes in the dress my father selected for the vote. It is black lace with blood-red inserts. It must have cost him a fortune, but it makes me feel cheap with how my breasts are pushed up, almost spilling out of the neckline, and my waist is cinched. I feel like I'm being sold in an auction to the highest bidder.

Jess's eyes soften, and so do Gia's, but I look away, feeling someone's heated stare, and know instantly it's Alaric. Tonight, I'm not lucky like Gia or Jess. They got to marry someone they love and were accepted by the Order. Men that loved them back. Fought to be with them because they mattered. Tonight, my father chose because that was my fate all along. Only one man has the power to override a decision tonight, but like he said, he prefers me to be buried in the cemetery right outside this church. I won't be saved tonight.

"Veronica Devlin is the oldest heir of the Devlin estate, and so it is required, dated centuries before me, that she be married before her graduation at Kenyan University. Since she has no other prospects, it is required for her father to choose a husband so that an alliance can be formed. It has come to our attention that someone has accepted the proposal to wed Miss Devlin." My chest is tight, and I try to breathe and not collapse in front of everyone, waiting to hear my fate. The man that will have my life in his hands. "Dorian Black, will you please come forward."

No! The sound of hideous laughter begins overtaking my senses. The memory of that night and the way he began to chant the word 'whore' replays in my head. My vision blurs and then refocuses, like I'm warping between the present and the past. People are staring at me and the man I hate, as he steps forward, his eyes full of lust, making my skin crawl.

"Does anyone have cause to object to this union?" Mr. Clarence, the oldest member of the Order, announces.

My eyes quickly scan the room, hoping for a miracle, but God has always checked out, and his angels are laughing in agreement.

My eyes land on gray ones pleading, wishing for anything to stop it. For him to say something. To help me. But he stares straight ahead. The small candle of hope I kept in a secret spot in my heart for him dying forever. He could have said something because of that night.

But he didn't.

He let the sound of the wood echo as Mr. Clarence congratulated Dorian Black, telling him he was a lucky man, while my soul shattered into a million pieces when most of the room clapped.

A tiny tear threatens to fall, but I turn my head and wipe my eye like I got something in it and see Valen mouth, *I'm sorry*. Jess's mouth is pinched in a tight line, whispering to Reid, and I watch his gaze land on me, but it's interrupted by the man's voice that will use me to his advantage when the time comes.

"I'm sure you're surprised, but I couldn't resist." He lowers his voice, but I don't miss the evil glint in his eyes. "I'm going to have so much fun with you. I hear you can take pain." I swallow thickly. "It's okay, sweetheart. I can make you bleed too."

"Fuck you. How dare you. You disgust me," I hiss.

He slides his hand behind my neck and grips the skin when he lowers his lips to my ear as everyone begins to leave. "Be careful how you talk to me, wife."

"I'm not your wife," I grit.

"Yet." He chuckles. "I'm surprised no one objected. Everyone must have thought you were a bad lay, but I can work something out with you. Teach you how to pleasure me and whoever I need you to spread your legs for."

"It's gonna be hard with a small dick."

His grip tightens again, and my vision feels fuzzy, but no one can tell because the long blonde tresses of my wig cover his hand wrapped around me.

"Congratulations, Dorian. I'm sorry about your brother." I hear Alaric's voice behind me.

Dorian's hand slithers off my neck and rests on the curve of my ass, and I want to burn it off as he smiles at Alaric, but I avert my gaze. Alaric is nothing to me. Just some stupid girl fantasy that tore me apart.

"I appreciate that. My brother's accident hit us all hard, and when Mr. Devlin mentioned that he needed to marry his daughter off, I couldn't resist. She was always a pretty girl. Everyone thought so." He caresses my ass, and I want to throw up when he continues, "I was surprised she was still available, and listen, I know there is a history, and I have no hard feelings."

I push Dorian's hand off me, not wanting to listen anymore. Fuck them. "If you'll excuse me, I think my father is looking for me."

I run out of the church and notice my father deep in conversation with other members and run toward the cemetery, so I can clear my thoughts. Everything is starting to make sense. I know how my father plans to achieve more power. With me by Dorian's side, he has Dorian's vote and will counter Alaric, Reid and the Bedfords in practically everything before Valen gets closer to graduation. Everyone knows that Dorian Black and Alaric don't see eye to eye. They never have. In business, sports, or at Kenyan. They are opposites, but there is one thing they both are in my eyes, men I hate.

CHAPTER 11
Alaric

"I can't believe he can still beat you!" Garret cries, splashing water at Valen.

"What...did you think you pussies could still beat me? I'm the fucking champ at Kenyair all around. Maybe if you have a better time."

"I'll beat you," Valen says with determination.

Out of all the sons of Kenyair, Valen's time is the closest to beating mine. If he would put the work in, he might have a solid chance to beat me and every asshole he goes up against. He might also have a shot of getting on the Olympic team.

"Get wet in the pool instead of pussy, and you might have a chance," I shoot back.

"I can't believe you can still beat all of us," Dravin adds. "In the same night."

I grin. "I still swim."

"We see that, dick. You still got it," Reid says, shaking his head.

I turn when I hear giggling from the back patio, and my eyes narrow when I spot Gia, Jess, and Veronica with a couple of friends, including the new freshman replacing Matt on the football team at Ohio State.

"Who the fuck invited her to the party?" I ask in a hard tone.

They all give me meaningful looks, knowing exactly who I'm talking about, but Valen's the first one to speak up. "I did."

"Why the fuck would you invite that crazy bitch here with all of us?"

Garret wipes his face and dips in the pool. "Don't call her that."

My head whips like I've been slapped. "Oh...you're going to forget all the shit she has done all of a sudden?"

I know I'm acting childish and shouldn't care, or maybe it's because Garret slept with Veronica and is into her, and...it bothers me.

"I think you have it all wrong about her," Valen adds, looking defiant.

Reid and the Bedfords glance at each other, surprised, probably thinking Valen has gone batshit crazy.

"Let me guess, asshole. You fucked her and caught feelings," I say, leaning forward, making him step toward the deep end of the pool while Garret gives Valen a dirty look.

Garret has strong feelings for Veronica, but she apparently doesn't feel the same way. I don't understand why Valen is defending her, but for whatever reason, the monster within me is rearing its ugly head whenever it concerns her. Last night, I was about two seconds away from punching Dorian Black to wipe the smirk off his face while he pawed her ass.

"She isn't a problem anymore, so why the fuck do you care and for the—" a wave of water splashes on my face, "I've never had sex with Veronica, you jealous fuck. Everyone knows you lose your shit every time she's around."

"Fuck off, Vikiar." I growl, wiping my face.

"Leave her alone," Draven says quietly. "Gia and Jess wanted her to come, and Valen's right; she's no threat to anyone. She'll marry by the time she graduates, and she isn't thrilled about it. So you got what you wanted."

"I never wanted anything. I...she was using me. Reid called me that night—"

"I never called you," Reid shoots back.

I lean back on the wall of the pool. "You called me."

He shakes his head. "I. Never. Called. You. I was looking out for—"

Alicia. He was making sure she was okay at the initiation party. If he didn't call me to warn me about Veronica, then who did? But the text was from him. I remember.

"Stop fucking with me, Reid. You called me that night and warned me about Devlin's daughter setting me up. That asshole has wanted an in since our grandfather and Riodrick Hotels monopolized the hotel industry."

Reid scoffs. "Hey, asshole, I never called you. I knew she had a crush on you. I mean...everyone in our family knew. Your mom knew. Alicia invited her to every family function if her father allowed her to go, and Veronica begged her to introduce you to her, but you never knew she was even there. I get that she was younger than you, and you were fucking your way through college and didn't know who she was or that she existed. That night I figured you didn't like her, and the sex was shit from how you treated her after Dorian walked in on you. Shit got out of hand."

Dorian recorded her bleeding between her thighs because she got her period, her tears, and how she ran home crying after I called her out. It was fucked up, but I was pissed off, and at the time, all I wanted to do was hurt her for thinking I would fall for her mind-fuck games. I got into it with Dorian and made him delete the video and anyone who copied it. Fists were thrown, and threats were made, but in the end, we all turned on her. We fucked with her. Because she deserved it. But if Reid didn't text me that night, who did?

"Then who texted me?" I ask.

"It wasn't us." Garret chimes in. "I didn't know her like that. In high school—" Garret trails off.

Valen's mouth forms a thin line, and he pinches his brows.

They both went to high school with her, and so did the Bedford twins.

"In high school, what?"

Draven mutters under his breath, and I'm annoyed they are all avoiding telling me something. Something I don't know because I don't know Veronica like that. Dravin glances across the patio at Gia, deep in conversation with Jess and Veronica, and then shifts his gaze back to me.

"What?" I repeat with my hands spread out in frustration.

"Veronica never had a boyfriend in high school. She only hung around Alicia. Veronica was considered a prude and a stuck-up bitch that wouldn't put out. Every guy tried to nail her but never could, and trust me, they all tried. That's why everyone thought she was into girls," Dravin says.

"She turned down every single guy that tried. After that night with you, it got progressively worse. They called her names like whore, and all the bullshit assholes in high school tell chicks they pick on. It was fucked up," Valen chimes in.

Draven snaps his fingers. "I remember all the guys asked her to prom, hoping they could fuck her, but she ended up not going."

"Yeah, they said someone popped the ice queen's cherry at Kenyan," Garret says mindlessly.

A slow, nagging feeling crawls up my spine. Dread slithers through my veins, and I push off the wall. "What did you say?" I ask Garret.

"What?" he says defensively. "That's what they called her. I know you thought she was easy and was out to trap you, but one thing Veronica never was before that night *was* a slut. To be honest, I don't think it was her period. They called her the ice queen because of her colorless hair and the fact she wouldn't let a guy touch her—"

"What the fuck are you talking about? Are you high?"

Valen rolls his eyes, annoyed with me, but it can't be. I—the way I took her was rough. I—remember that she was just lying there, and then the door flew open. She was horrified to see the blood sticking to her thighs, trying to clean herself. She pleaded for me to do something, but I didn't care. I was staring at my phone with her name and the message Reid sent, or I thought it was Reid. He wouldn't lie. Not about that.

"It doesn't matter. You're off the hook. I'm pretty sure you're the last person she would want anyway," Valen says softly, walking toward the steps and tapping me on my bare shoulder. "That night changed her, but she's not your problem. She belongs to Dorian, and as much as I want to save her from marrying that asshole, I can't because believe it or not, that girl doesn't deserve the shit hand that was handed to her." His face tightens. "I can't believe I'm saying this to you, but I'm gonna say it. Leave her alone. You've done enough."

My fists clench. "You're threatening me, Vikiar?"

"What's going on?" Jess asks when she walks in with Gia and Veronica, along with the friends she invited here.

"Nothing. Valen is just pissed off. I beat his time," I lie.

"Oh. You still swim?"

I look up and smile. "Of course. Someone has to make sure they beat these punks," I tease.

One of the girls that came in with Veronica steps forward in jean shorts and a sweater. "Are you guys like vampires?"

I can see why she would think that. The Bedford mansion looks like Dracula's lair, and the red lights from the pool glow like a pool of blood. The gargoyles add to the whole effect.

"Yeah, be careful. We like to bite," Garret says, mocking with his teeth like Dracula, making her eyes widen.

My gaze lands on Veronica. "I need to talk to you." But she looks away, acting like I wasn't speaking to her. A girl with ash-blonde hair steps forward. I recognize her from the initiation party. She was arguing with her brother Adam about the guy playing her little sister with another chick. "She has nothing to say to you," she says defiantly.

"Maddison, could you take me home? Adam will give Lizzy a ride," Veronica says, clearly ignoring me.

A feeling I don't recognize stabs me in the chest. She won't look at me, and I don't know what to do. "Veronica," I call her name, but she ignores me like she can't hear me.

"Please, Maddy. I want to go home," she pleads.

"I can take you," Adam says, stepping forward, but she shakes her head and smiles.

"Take Lizzy, Adam. Maddy can take me. I have a shift tomorrow."

Shift?

"How come you work at the restaurant when you're obviously rich?" The curious one about vampires speaks up in her annoying voice. You can tell she's a bitch.

Work? Veronica works?

Veronica bites her lip nervously, trying to evade the question, and I usually don't stare at her long enough, but this time, I notice. Fear. "It's for a school project."

I smell bullshit. What is she scared about? Why would she need to work when her father is a billionaire. No school project would warrant a work-study of any kind, except an internship at the end of the semester that she needs to complete, and it's done at one of the family's conglomerates. Not at a restaurant. Adam's confused expression gives it away. She's lying, but why?

I watch Valen and Garret leave the pool, heading for the towel rack.

"Where the fuck are you two fuckers going?" I ask.

Reid chuckles. "They're leaving to make out."

Everyone laughs, but Valen glances at Veronica and Maddy, and I want to pour acid into his eyes. "I'm going to follow the girls to make sure they get home safe."

"Since when do you care if anyone gets home safe?" Draven adds, "I get why Garret is doing it."

"Relax, Veronica and I are actually friends."

"When did this happen?" Draven asks sarcastically.

"After I sucked his cock," Veronica blurts. My nostrils flare when Garret grins and points in her direction and winks. "It was good, by the way, baby. No complaints."

"I'm glad I could be of service," she purrs.

Jess claps her hands together with a grin on her face. I want to pull Veronica into the pool and punish her for giving me a visual of her and Garret, but I surprise myself by chiming in to get her attention, pushing myself out of the pool. "I can find something you can service," I tell her and then turn toward Garret and Valen. "I got her. Make sure Maddison makes it home."

Veronica's eyes go wide in panic. "What are you doing?"

I smirk, quickly dry myself off, slide on sweatpants, and grab my hoodie and wallet from the lounge chair. "You need a ride."

"Not from you."

"I'm not asking, Veronica," I say in a harsh tone. "Let's go." She stomps off, muttering under her breath, and I smile to myself because I love it when she's combative. It makes my dick hard.

"I tell you to stay away, and you do the opposite," Valen scolds.

Not caring that we are in mixed company, I look at the guys, mentally making a list of things I need to do. "Meeting. I will send the invite."

The Bedford twins raise their brows in tandem because I only call a meeting when something is off, and it is...something is way off.

I unlock my car but notice Veronica walking toward the gate. "Get in, Veronica."

"Why, we both know you don't want to take me home."

She's right. I want to take her to my home. Preferably in my bed, so I can punish her.

Walking toward the passenger side, I open the door and wait impatiently. She knows not to push me. She shakes her head, stomping toward my car in her wedge heels. "You want to take the whore home? Wouldn't you be ashamed to be seen with me or that I might contaminate your precious car?"

"How could that be? Won't your daddy be happy that I'm taking you home?" I challenge.

"I can find my way home, and no, my daddy won't be happy if he sees you dropping me off."

My gaze slides down her top, pausing at her plump breasts, remembering how her nipples tasted. Like honey. "Why is that?"

"Because I'm trying to be a good girl, and I don't ride in cars with bad boys," she purrs.

I rub my thumb over her bottom lip and imagine her taking my cock hard and deep. Her eyes focus on me like she can't believe I'm touching her.

"What makes you a bad girl?"

Her tongue pokes out and caresses the pad of my thumb, and my dick twitches in my pants, telling me to take her home, but I can't. Not yet.

"You made me a bad girl, Alaric. So. Very. Bad."

I pull her bottom lip down with my thumb and watch it part submissively, her tongue sliding over it like it's my cock.

"Is that why you bled for me?"

Her eyes flash, but I can't determine if it's anger, lust, or maybe both. Her finger slides down my chest until it rests on my rock-hard cock. She smiles, but it doesn't reach her eyes. "I wanted to know what a cock would feel like for the first time." Her finger swirls and then grips me hard, causing me to grind my teeth when she pulls on it. Then, holding on to the roof of the car, she leans in and says menacingly, "Since then, I've been trying to forget how much I hated it and the nightmares that came with it."

She was a virgin. And I took her like an animal. *Fuck.* She was tight, and she felt good, but it was all ruined by the text message and now Dorian. That motherfucker. But what if this was the plan. Dorian couldn't get me to invest, and now he has Veronica, but whose side is she on?

She releases me, and I push her shoulder, guiding her inside the car and shutting the door. I slide in, fire up the car, and lock the doors. I grip her firmly by the neck.

"What are—"

"Look at me," I demand. Her eyes are full of terror when they land on mine. Her body is trembling. "I guess I will have to change that, won't I? You don't know what's coming, Veronica."

"What's coming?"

My face is void of emotion, and I smile faintly. "Everything."

CHAPTER 12
Veronica

T aking the garbage to the back of the restaurant fifteen minutes before my shift ends, I can't help looking back. I keep having the feeling I'm being watched. The tiny hairs behind my neck stand, but I shake it off. That is what I get for watching horror flicks with Melody all the time. I'm paranoid.

Alaric dropping me off and telling me everything is coming doesn't help. It's no secret Alaric is dangerous, if not the most dangerous out of all the sons of Kenyan.

My head turns, and I focus on a dark corner. I could have sworn someone was standing there. I close my eyes and then open them so that they can focus on the dim light from the streetlights and the moon, but nothing. There is no one there, just my mind playing tricks on me.

I walk inside, sliding my sweaty hands over my apron, looking for my bag so I can head home. I have a class in the morning.

"Do you need a ride," Adam asks, looking up from wiping the tables.

"No, I'll be fine." I smile. "She said yes?"

He nods with a grin. "Yes, matchmaker—"

I play dumb. "I don't know what you're talking about."

But I do know. He asked Lizzy to prom, and she accepted. He can go with a great girl, and Adam deserves that.

"She does that, you know," Dorothy says, folding the utensils with a napkin and placing them in the bin. "She loves to make sure others are happy together."

Adam sniggers. "I see that, but who makes sure she's happy?"

"I am happy," I lie.

"Liar."

I stick my tongue out at him. "I gotta go. Bye, Dorothy." I wave and push the door open, letting out a breath and making my way to the bus stop.

There is a full moon in the dark sky, and I look down at the broken cracks on the sidewalk—the orange glow of the streetlights. Only two cars are parked on the curb, reminding me of a deserted town. I check the street to see the bus lights, but it's dark. I check my phone, and I still have five minutes until it's due to arrive.

My phone vibrates, and I check the message.

Dorian: How's my wife?

Veronica: I haven't seen her.

Dorian: I do.

My head whips around, and a wave of dread slides over me. He's watching me. I didn't imagine it.

Veronica: Fuck off, asshole.

Dorian: I'm afraid that's not gonna happen. You belong to me, Veronica. I've been waiting a long time to have you.

Veronica: Get fucked.

Dorian: Good night, princess.

Furious, I get up when the bus approaches the curb—sick bastard.

Dorian Black is repulsive. I can't imagine being married to a man like that. I don't think I can do it. Every time a nightmare ends, a new one begins.

When board the bus, I stop in the aisle and blink hard. A hooded figure sits in the center with a bird mask on. I plop down on the middle bench with my back against the huge window, looking between the driver and the masked figure. The man has his head bowed like he's asleep, but I know better. He's waiting. I look over his sweater, gloved hands, and pants but can't place him.

It could be Dorian fucking with me, or the Order sent whoever is behind the mask to kill me. Tears prick my eyes.

I don't want to die.

I've thought about it...dying or how would they do it. I think about everything, my life or lack of one. I've never been loved, and maybe it gave me the courage to try and love, but that didn't end up as I envisioned it. Perhaps I wasn't meant to be loved, or to be free, but I don't want to die.

I slide my hand inside my apron, looking for the pen I remember sliding in there and grip the top. I press on it with the pad on my thumb, so the ballpoint locks in place, watching the hooded figure. The bus stops moving, and I hear the airlock hiss and the door open.

I run out of the bus, my breath feeling like sharp glass in my throat, running down the sidewalk toward the gates of my house. My lungs burn, but I manage to look behind me. The lights from inside the bus are shining bright, and when I think it's going to shut the door, a gloved hand keeps it from closing, and the hooded figure steps out. My stomach drops, letting the dread seep in when I see him walking briskly toward me.

I turn and run as fast as I can, tears sliding down my cheeks. *Oh God, please. Please.* A gloved hand covers my mouth. I'm lifted off the ground, and the night sky feels like it dropped under me. I feel something sharp and everything goes dark.

I wake up in my bed for what feels like a split second. I look under the sheet. My mouth is dry like sandpaper, and I see that I'm naked, except for my panties. I sit up and place a hand over my forehead. Was it a dream? Am I going crazy?

I check my phone for the time and realize it's 9 a.m. and see a missed text.

Dorian: Don't be a bad girl.

Asshole.

"It is time for your internships. As you may already be aware, they need to be completed at the start of next week. All of you will be assigned a company that is part of a conglomerate to intern. Some of you need a job, and some of you already have jobs," Professor Klein announces to the class.

Professor Klein always wears a suit like he just came from working on Wall Street and fucked his secretary in the lunchroom. His tie is loose, his brown hair looks freshly fucked, and he has a look that screams anywhere but here as he paces with his hands crossed behind him, walking the classroom from end to end.

"A paper is being passed around that includes the contact information, address, and who you will be reporting to for the week. At the end of the week, I want your report on what you learned and how you could improve the company. The CEO will also report on your performance. This is necessary for you to graduate. If you don't complete it satisfactorily, you fail and have to retake this portion of the course in order to graduate."

Good. If I fail, I can buy myself time from marrying Dorian. The paper reaches my desk, and I slide my finger until it stops on my name and follow the dotted line to the company.

Riodrick and Riordan Holdings and Capital Investment.
CEO Alaric Riodrick-Riordan
Report to Sasha Barnes, Executive Secretary
216-445-3800 ext. 251
4321 N. Riodrick *Blvd*
Kenyan, Ohio, 45874

I sag in my chair and look at the paper, reading it in disbelief. He planned this like some sick joke. I don't have clothes to wear to an internship at a billion-dollar company. I've seen how Alaric dresses in suits that cost more than a used car. I only have gala dresses I've acquired for special occasions and outfits to go to parties from Claire or if my mother called the boutique because my father requested it. Dresses are always for a lavish occasion that can't be worn again—like celebrities getting criticized for wearing the same things twice. I always found that stupid, so every time I had one, I would give it away without my parents noticing; I anonymously delivered it to a female Prey that was similar to my size. No one would question a free ten-thousand-dollar dress delivered to their dorm room. Lizzy didn't when I offered to gift her a prom dress by altering it to fit. It felt good to do something nice for someone. Work clothes were never a priority because the restaurant provided the employees with uniforms, so I never had to save to buy them.

After class, I walk toward the cemetery and stop at the entrance to buy flowers for Alicia. It's a beautiful day. The sun is out, but the trees offer enough shade to sit. Springtime in Kenyan is one of my favorite times of the year because it's not too cold or too hot. It's just right.

I bend and slide my hands over the marble of Alicia's grave, removing the dried leaves. Removing a small water bottle, I fill the flower holders to place the red roses in each.

"I miss you...I miss our talks on the phone at night when I tell you everything. I miss your voice and laugh because it was the best sound." I sit cross-legged, not caring that anyone thinks I'm crazy for talking to my dead best friend. I turn my head because that feeling creeps up my neck again like I'm being watched, but no one is there, except the lady with the bucket selling different types of flowers.

Facing Alicia's grave, I sniff. "Guess what? I have an internship, and it's with your cousin, out of all people. I think he planned it to be that way, and to be honest, I'm scared," I choke out. "Every time I'm around him, it gets worse. It's like he's some curse or something, and I need saving. I've had thoughts of running away on my own. I'm saving—"

"Saving for what?" I freeze when I hear Reid's voice. I close my eyes, hoping he didn't hear everything I said.

I look up and meet his dark stare. "Nothing."

He grins, but his eyes tell me I'm full of shit. His hand slides into his pocket and pulls out a thin chain with a silver locket in the shape of a heart holding it out to me. "I think she would have wanted you to have this. I'll admit, I didn't want to give it to you because I wanted everything that was hers to stay within the family."

I squint from the sun's glare as the trees sway with the breeze. "You don't have to give it to me."

He extends his hand, and the locket swings back and forth. "I think you were meant to have this, and she didn't get the chance to give it to you. If anything, it belongs to you."

I take it from him with a smile, feeling the connection from something that belonged to her that she wanted me to have. "Thank you. It means a lot."

He looks away and is about to turn but pauses, his shoulders tensing from the effort. "Whatever you are planning to do, don't do it."

Gripping the locket in the palm of my hand, I give him a tight smile. "I don't know what you mean."

He slides his fingers through his dark hair, like it takes every effort inside him to say what he needs to say. This is the most we have spoken that hasn't included a middle finger or a snarky comment. "She wouldn't want anything to happen to you, Veronica."

I let out a slow breath because I didn't want anything to happen to Alicia and I know she wouldn't want me to suffer the same fate. But I blame myself for not asking Reid for help when I should have told him what she was planning and didn't. He could have saved her.

"I'm sorry." I look at the headstone with her name on it in gold lettering. "It should have been me in there and not her." A tear escapes the corner of my eye, and needles prick my nose. "It should have been me," I whisper.

He pinches his brows. "It's not your fault, Veronica. You didn't kill her. They did."

He means the assholes in the Order that voted for her to be hunted down like an animal and killed along with her boyfriend. Assholes like Charles Devlin who makes it his mission to rip everything I love away from me.

I shake my head with tears running down my cheeks because he doesn't know the truth. It was because of me he voted. "It is my fault, Reid." I sniff, wiping my face. "I should have never been friends with her."

"Why?"

I close my eyes, and my chest tightens. "Because people like me are not supposed to have friends like her." I stand, wiping my hands on the back of my leggings. "I'm no good, Reid. I'm nothing but a worthless bitch that doesn't deserve anything, and I think you were right."

"About what? What are you saying, Veronica? You talk in riddles sometimes, and it makes you sound—"

"Crazy." I finish for him.

"Yeah," he agrees, nodding his head. "It makes you sound crazy." He raises his hand frustratingly, making a fist. "But then there are times where there is something…something about you that is different, like it's all an act or maybe you were like that all along."

He doesn't know and he isn't supposed to know anything about me or what I do and why. "Do you know why I'm interning at Riodrick and Riordan with your cousin? Is this some sick joke?"

"I didn't know. We don't keep tabs on each other with what we do or with who unless it's important to the family business or a threat. I don't believe you are a threat, and for the reason behind you completing the internship there…" he shrugs, "it could be simple coincidence, or…he wants you there for whatever reason."

I roll my eyes dramatically. "Yeah, to finish me off before I graduate. It's not like I'm after him. I have to marry a psychotic asshole before I graduate."

"Who said Dorian Black was the psycho? We both know who is." He leans forward and says softly, "You're not married to him yet, Veronica. You're still game." He arches his neck, covers his mouth with the palm of his hand, and continues, "There is no key to Alaric, Veronica, but you are the door he needs to open."

What does he mean? I don't get the chance to ask because he walks away. All that I got was that I'm still game. It means no one is required to be faithful until the marriage takes place because it was voted by the Order, including me. But there is no end point behind an infinite game, just winners and losers.

CHAPTER 13
Alaric

"He is expecting you, Mr. Riodrick," my grandfather's secretary says, standing in the doorway to my grandfather's private offices. I place the magazine I was flipping through on the table and get up.

I don't correct her about using my grandfather's last name and not my father's because I'm part of him too, and so is Reid, and so was Alicia, but he refuses to talk about her. She was the spitting image of my mother, unlike my aunt, who was her opposite, with dark hair and eyes. Alicia and I were the only ones that inherited my grandfather's gray eyes.

Turning the door knob, I enter my grandfather's opulent office. The smell of wood, whiskey, and fine cigars permeate the room's ambiance. "You wanted to see me?" my grandfather says, sitting in his leather chair like a throne.

"Yes, I have something to discuss with you that I trust you have the answers to," I reply, unbuttoning my suit jacket and taking a seat.

My grandfather stepped down as an active member of the Order but still holds power; yet, only a few know he can overrule along with Mr. Bedford, but they rarely bother themselves with

Kenyan matters. Mr. Bedford and my father vote on issues involving world leaders.

"I trust this has nothing to do with business matters. Because the hotels and all investments are making billions in profit. You're having an excellent year, so I trust you are here in a personal capacity."

"You know me too well, Grandfather."

"I know you better than most because you think and are ruthless like me, and that is what makes a great leader."

"I want to ask you about Mr. Devlin's daughter, Veronica."

He gets up, walks to the bar, and pours three fingers of whiskey into two glasses with two ice cubes. Giving me his back, he asks, "What about Devlin's daughter?"

"She is my intern for the week before she graduates."

He chuckles and hands me the glass. "You always had a thing for the girl."

I take the glass, but he has a glint in his eyes that tells me there is more. "Thank you. It's not a thing. We both know Mr. Devlin is not our favorite."

He takes a seat. "There are no favorites, my boy. Only players. Mr. Devlin is an atheist at heart. He always hated the religious aspect and history that the Order was founded on, dating back to the eighteen hundreds. His vows on marriage are a lie. Everything he stands for" — he takes a sip and swallows — "is a lie."

"What are you saying?"

"Miss Devlin is not his daughter, Alaric." I almost drop the glass but grip it tightly, almost breaking it in my hand. My chest tightens because that can't be true. "I can tell you are shocked, dumbfounded, but really, did you think a man would let his daughter be what she is?"

I stare at the painting behind him, trying to piece things together in her behavior. "But I thought, er...I don't know—"

"I know you are very fond of the girl, but most of them are."

I frown, placing the glass on his desk with a thud. "What are you saying? Who's Them?"

"I'm not supposed to discuss this, but since you have graduated for some time now and have chosen to remain without a wife, I can discuss matters like this, and you are allowed to explore Miss Devlin, but I feel they won't approve, given her affection for you." I tilt my head to the side, placing my finger over my mouth. My mind is muddled with unanswered questions. "Dating back centuries when the Order was established, they believed in adopting a religion acceptable to conduct meetings inside the church. Rules in those days were adopted under the pretext of religion and the use of the Bible. In the library, there is a book about the history of Kenyan. It briefly discusses what I'm about to say, but Alaric, it can't leave this room."

"I understand." But I don't. What does Veronica have anything to do with any of this? "Members before us for generations still adopt these ancient rules and still manage to abide by them in modern society, claiming that they are also God's way. Like an eye for an eye and that sort of thing." He takes another sip, but that is the last thing I want, a glass of whiskey. "Are you familiar with the term sex slave or woman used to serve men in higher order just like Hebrew soldiers."

"I've heard of it, but in our case, that is human trafficking and illegal."

He places the glass on his desk with a thud. "That's not what I'm referring to in any way. There were debates in Deuteronomy in modern times, but it was adopted by the Order and still can be used before the Catholic church since it was never voted off because it didn't favor men that had to marry a chosen. It isn't a secret Mrs. Devlin, Veronica's mother, committed adultery with Mr. Bedford."

"Yeah, so. I'm not aware of the details, but they dealt with it. It wasn't like people didn't sleep with each other in college before graduation, so it didn't matter to them." Veronica was born before that, and Mr. Bedford claims his children, so I know she isn't his. She looks nothing like them. The only thing Veronica inherited from her mother were her eyes.

"That is where you are wrong, my boy. It did matter because it wasn't the first time...she is guilty of being promiscuous and a pill popper that lives in guilt with what her husband has done with her daughter."

I slide on the edge of my seat. A wave of blazing fury slides inside my veins, waking up the demon inside me. "What has he done?"

"I'm afraid, with the look in your eye, that I would need to send you to the library where you can conduct research. Brush up on your history and that sort of thing."

"Tell me," I demand.

"I can't tell you, my boy. I've said enough. You need to find this out independently because now she is under your supervision for the week. Make the most of it how you see fit and remember there are consequences for her and what she is allowed and not allowed to do."

"What does that mean?"

He downs the glass of whiskey in one go and stands. "In a few months, she will marry. Everyone else attended the vote; I recall you and everyone else didn't object. I'm sure Dorian Black feels he won something over you since you denied his business proposal when in all honesty, you could care less about the girl."

"What do you mean?" I ask. "He knows how I feel about her."

I don't want to admit I secretly objected but was too hung up about what she did that night at the initiation party. The last person I wanted touching her was that snake Dorian Black, but I kept telling myself she deserves him, but avoided admitting it to myself how I feel about her. I always blamed it on a lustful attraction because Veronica is gorgeous.

"Something you had in the palm of your hand like a gift but then you let it go like a dog, an owner doesn't want, so they put the bitch in the car and drive it to a farm or secluded area to let it out so they could drive off, never once looking in the rearview mirror so their conscience is clean. But to someone else, it seems God answered their prayers." My grandfather slides one hand into the pocket of his pants with ease. "She's not your problem, Alaric. No one cares about that girl." He pierces me with his gaze. "Especially you."

"Is that all you need, Mr. Riordan?" the librarian asks with her wired spectacles resting on her chest.

She looks like she belongs in a haunted library. Her skin is ghastly white and wrinkled, and she looks like she is a breath away from dying.

I flip the leather-bound hardcover book and respond, "That is all."

The last time I was in the library was to fuck in the back by the encyclopedia section. This is the last place I expected to spend my Friday afternoon when I should be going over my financials, but it would have to wait because Veronica is due in my office Monday morning.

It was a dick move to make sure she completed her internship at my office. I was able to override Dorian's request because she doesn't belong to him yet. Some things don't add up when it comes to her. Her eyes continue to haunt me from the minute I felt her in my arms. Her lips are a sweet poison. One look in the cloudy depths of her eyes hypnotized me after tasting her lips, loving the smell of her breath. The memory of the way her lips tasted stayed with me. It hurt to think I was being used because of my name by the man that sent her.

The history of the Order adopted certain rules in the book of Deuteronomy and in the Bible under Exodus. It reads members of the Order adopted beliefs that God could live among the people by cleansing sin and guilt when sin occurs. In Exodus 21, a man can call his daughter to slavery to serve men. I scroll down and find polygamy is allowed, and it's true, Dravin and Draven with Gia. It is all here. The rules in alliances with partners and how sex is allowed between partners.

I scroll down until I reach the term sex slaves, and I feel my blood turn cold when I read the first line.

A man can sell his daughter to another member of the Order if certain obligations are met. Once she is used when given by the hands of God. She is to be beautiful and questioned if she was born out of evil to corrupt. The law of Moses can be adopted when the woman is a virgin, but first must perform a type of ritual for purification for a life as a concubine. After her first taste of flesh, she is purified, and from then on, to serve. Purification is the pain given from the sins committed.

A man can have multiple wives if his brother dies. It also states he can impregnate a slave with no lineage (Prey).

The Prey is marked after the ritual so that there is no question about what she represents among the members. She must perform and be purified from sins committed by the flesh infinitely. She is to serve.

The man she belongs to can marry her or keep her as his concubine and do with her as he wishes until he tires of her and can set her free. If the Prey chooses a master and he has no desire for her and she is set free until she is selected by another, but this must occur before her graduation. Concubines under the rule of the Order are considered Prey and property of their master. She is to serve and obey and provide an heir. Her true master is the first one she serves with children in the eyes of the Order to be deemed abolished for her past sins. She is to serve her true master until her death. If a concubine does not fulfill her duty, she is ordered the penalty of death or sacrifice to eternal damnation, feeding the craving of flesh from man to ward off lust from the legion.

I shut the book and slide my fingers in my hair, pulling at the top in frustration. What. The. Fuck. That is what my grandfather was trying to tell me. Veronica is Prey. She chose me that night but I didn't know. And I set her free. I close my eyes. The word, *whore*, flashes in my mind. I called her a whore. The book talks about a mark, but there isn't a mark on her. I've never seen it.

My grandfather's words replay in my mind. *"No one cares about her. Especially you. He won something."* He won because no one gave a shit about her. She was acting like they wanted her too. Veronica would have never chosen Dorian that night because she chose me and he wanted her. *He played you. He knew what she was.*

Her feelings for me were genuine, and I...let her go. I—

There was no way I knew the truth.

In her eyes, I'm like everyone else in her world.

In her eyes, I'm one of them.

She couldn't be more wrong.

But I am an absolute master in the realms of greed and disgust. Beyond measure. Dorian Black wants to play a dangerous game. I going to give him a war.

CHAPTER 14
Veronica

My Docs thud on the marble floor of Riodrick-Riordan Holding and Capital Investments' top floor. I ignore the glances at my attire as I walk through the lobby and am shown to the executive offices after giving my name at the front desk. The short skirt, pantyhose, and long-sleeve fitted shirt are what I had, and I wasn't going to waste three weeks of pay on a pantsuit that I would only need for a week.

When I approach the double doors, I reach a desk with a gold nameplate that reads Sasha Barnes. Her smile when she sees me standing in front of her desk is lethal and scrutinizing as her eyes trail the length of me like I'm an insect she wants to swat away.

I give no judgment where it isn't given, but my intuition was right the first time I saw her. She still sees me as a threat, even though he treated me like I was a blood stain on his shirt. I'm not the only one she should be worried about. He isn't tamed. He runs out and picks his prey as he so chooses.

"You must be Veronica. Now that I can place a name to the face, I'll have you know that your attire is not appropriate."

I lean on her desk and tilt my head, letting the platinum locks from my wig brush the surface of her black desk. "Oh, Sasha. You should be rejoicing. You look so sophisticated and older. You can't possibly give a shit what I'm wearing." She's wearing a black skirt suit with sky-high heels, and judging from the red soles, they are Louboutin's. They are gorgeous, but the way she carries herself with her insecurities on her sleeve, they can easily pass for Steve Madden knockoffs. Her blazer is flat, desperately needing a push-up bra.

"I'm afraid it's not the standard here; this is not a college frat party."

"Why don't we let the big man judge." I scrunch my nose like I smell something rotten. "Oh, and by the way, you still smell of inferiority. It's overpowering the room."

Her eyes blaze in anger. Her mouth set in a tight line. "The five minutes you had with him is in the past. You're nothing to him."

She overheard, or he told her. Her words sting. But I'm used to the pain. I've learned to use my words as weapons and know things about Alaric. Things I've overheard pierced my heart, but some things need to be repeated so that they sink in deeper.

"Then why am I here? He has the right to send me away, you know." I turn to her and cup my mouth, lowering my voice. "You need to accept things the way they are, Sasha. You can only suck his cock so much before he gets bored, and then—" I place my finger over my lips. "He sends you home to wash your disgusting spit off his skin." I straighten and smile. "You're not the first or the last he chokes with his cock."

"It tasted great last night," she purrs.

I have a retort on my tongue, but his office door opens, and the man is lust wrapped in a suit you want to suck off. His fitted suit is a dark gray, contrasting with the light gray of his eyes. His crisp white designer shirt is open at the throat, not being bothered with a tie that screams fuck it, I wear what I want. His tattoos are like scriptures you want to read all over his skin, and you need to remove his clothes to discover the secrets of his past.

His eyes flit back and forth between his current fuck and the woman he hates. I know I look childish in comparison. I couldn't keep his attention for five minutes, but I didn't beg him to be here.

I'm unsure why I am here if he hates me so much, but I'm about to find out.

"Miss Devlin," Alaric says with formality with a wave of his hand like I'm one of his business associates and has been waiting for me to arrive. Not breaking his stare, he says, "Sasha, hold my calls."

"Yes, sir," she says tightly. His eyes, calm in their gray depths, hold a hidden warning to obey, and I must admit, her last remark stung. I'm jealous. I shouldn't be, but I am.

When I enter, he slams the door shut and pins me to it, holding me by the throat. He has to see the terror in my eyes, but he doesn't waver. He boldly stares at me, rooting me to the spot.

"What are you doing?" I ask.

"What I need to do..." He breathes heavily. "We both know I had a hand in you coming here. And do you know why?"

I shake my head.

"Because I want you to serve me." My eyes widen in sheer terror. "Shh..." he coos. "You will serve me until I decide for you to stop and, of course, before you marry the one that shall not be named because I know Veronica. I know enough."

I'm livid. *Bastard.* Tears sting my eyes as I try to regain my composure. "I hate you," I say through clenched teeth, looking deep into his eyes.

"I won't take you by force, Veronica, but I expect obedience. I won't tolerate you going against what I say. You take what I give and be the good girl I know you to be." His tongue skims my ear and whispers, "You obey, and I will reward you. I can be generous or I can punish you." He slides his hand between my thighs, swiping a finger over the pantyhose and panties covering my slit, and I mewl. "You have the right idea of what I want you to wear when you come to see me, just the wrong fabric"—he slides his fingers deeper between my thighs—"Something so beautiful shouldn't be wrapped in something so cheap."

He pushes off the door, releasing his hand from my throat and between my legs, and then walks toward his desk, picking up his phone and placing a call. I swipe the tears from my face and cross my hands over my chest, feeling humiliated by my reaction to him.

He knows, Veronica.

He knows what I am, and he did nothing to save me.

All I can do is throw him off balance.

What choice do I have?

His eyes meet mine as he speaks into his phone. "Portman, bring the car. Five minutes." He hangs up, opening his suit jacket, sliding it off his strong shoulders, and my mouth goes dry. "From the way you are ogling me, I can tell this isn't hard for you."

I look away, getting caught staring at him because the man is in perfect shape. He's pure muscle with an ideal physique from spending hours in the gym or swimming. My eyes may sell him a fantasy, but my words tell him a different story. "I have had better."

"Sure, you have. I can tell." He places the jacket on his chair. "Let's go."

"Where?" I challenge.

"Wherever I want."

"Right," I answer tightly. "Is there anything I should know? How deep do you want your cock sucked? How wide are my legs to be spread while you pound me like an animal?"

"I'll let you know when I require to be serviced."

He's throwing the same words I said the other day at Draven's party to Garret, *'Serviced.'*

That was different, and it was something horrible that turned into something two single people would do for each other as friends. Even though Garret's father is a prick, Garret isn't a creep like I thought he was.

Alaric walks forward, and I turn to allow him to pass, so he can open the door, but he pauses and gives me an impish smile. "I will be serviced, Veronica." He takes my lips in his, and our tongues meet. Hating him so much but wanting him so bad. He licks, tastes, and fucks me with his mouth, sliding his hand across my cheek, caressing my skin for a few seconds, and I bite him hard, tasting blood before he pulls away, leaving my lips swollen and my head in a daze. His lips break into a wicked smile, licking the blood off from where I bit him.

"I'm different from all the others, Veronica. I'm beyond what is deemed good or evil. You finally did it." Did what? A wave of horror causes the tiny hairs to stand up on my arms at the coldness in his eyes. I'm terrified. He has the power to kill me. "I'm going to enjoy the way you have driven me to insanity." He growls and licks me from my chin to the tip of my nose like a dog. He opens the door when I raise my hand. "Don't wipe it off," he warns.

Dropping my hand, I follow him to see Sasha widen her eyes when he heads to the elevator. "Mr. Riordan?"

He presses the button, turns sideways, and answers her question with a furtive gleam in his eyes. "I'll be out to lunch. Clear my calendar for the rest of the day."

"Yes, sir," she says flatly.

We reach the blacked-out Maybach SUV waiting on the curb. Dark and imposing like the man that owns it. The bodyguard I saw at the Galleria stands with the door open, tipping his head in my direction his eyes sliding over me, but when Alaric looks over, he straightens and looks away.

"I'm glad we understand each other," he says.

"My apologies, sir."

The man, I'm assuming is Portman, shuts the door after we are both inside. Alaric has a hungry sneer on his lips when I cross my legs, and he presses the privacy screen closed. "Take off your panties and pantyhose and put your boots back on."

When I hesitate, he reaches and tugs the pantyhose hard, making them rip. "Off," he demands.

After a few moments of staring at each other, knowing he can force me to do anything he wants, I nod and slide my boots off, not missing the shit-eating grin on his face when I slide my panties over my knees.

"Like this," I say in a taunting voice, opening my legs.

He leans closer to get a look at my waxed pussy. The pupils of his eyes darken, full of thirst. My clit is throbbing for him to touch me, but my mind is telling me not to give in to him, that he is just like all the men in my life. Evil.

He slides his finger on my thigh to my knee, making me squirm. "I want access to you at all times." His fingers grip the tips of my blonde hair. "I don't want this on. I want your natural hair."

"My father will not approve."

"Fuck your father. You serve me now, and I don't want some fake version of you."

I nod because that is the rule, serve and obey. If not, it is the same as sinning. My father will not agree with me parading around members of the Order with my natural hair. It is forbidden.

I glance out the window. "Then I won't be considered pure under his rules."

"That is pointless when I'm going to dirty you, and everyone is going to see it, but like I said before, I need consent before touching you, and I don't need your hair a different shade to think you're pure. I took what was pure about you—"

"And I bled for it," I say quietly.

"I don't regret taking it. I regret not taking it sooner."

Alaric has the driver stop in front of the Galleria, and I don't question why we are here. I also don't miss the way Alaric leans back adjusting his erection in his pants, trying to get a mental image but coming up blank. That night we went right into things, and there was no time to explore his body how I wanted to. All I remember were his rough thrusts that felt like he was splitting me in two. He has a large cock, but I want to know if it's pink at the tip or darker than the tone of his skin and how it would feel on my tongue when he slides to the back of my throat.

Then the part of me that wants to be free of this life kicks in; this man cares nothing for me. He will use me and then hand me over to a man that will make me suffer. This is just a game to him. I'm something to be used. No better than a toy for men to enjoy.

We enter a boutique called Madame with dark lace and sex toys on glass shelves. When the owner of the store notices me with Alaric, she smiles coquettishly. "Is this her?"

"It is."

She undresses me with her eyes, pausing on my breasts, waist, and thighs. "She's perfect."

"I know," he responds.

Some may think it's a compliment, but I know better. Perfect to be his whore and unworthy to be loved.

"Right this way. I have already brought some things out. I just need to take some measurements and I can make anything you wish in her size."

I'm inside the dressing room, and there are different styles of underwear and bras neatly laid out. Black, white, nude, and red. There are small scraps of lace barely covering anything. I turn when I hear the door shut, but I'm not alone. He's standing behind me and I'm in front of the mirror.

"Take off your clothes."

"Get out."

"I'm afraid that is not the way this works." I gasp when he pulls off my wig and throws it in the corner, tugging my wig cap and releasing my long dark hair. "You won't be needing that anymore." He wraps my hair around his fist and shoves my pleated skirt roughly down my legs.

"What are you doing," I hiss.

"What I asked you to, but you have a problem listening."

"I'm here to do an internship."

He laughs. "Not anymore. Your internship also involves pleasuring me."

"I'm not a whore," I seethe, my nostrils flaring.

He pulls my head back and lowers his lips, licking my earlobe and causing me to squeeze my legs. I can smell his cologne. Spice, man, and sex. "You're my whore now." His hands slide between my thighs, sticky with my arousal. "You're such a bad girl, Veronica. How are you going to try on the lingerie when your pussy is all wet? You'll ruin everything in the store." He swipes his finger over my clit, feeling the evidence of how wet I am. He lifts it up, so I have no choice but to see my arousal on his fingers and then slides them in his mouth, closing his eyes in delight.

I try to get free, utilizing the moment, and surprisingly, he releases the hold on my hair. "You're sick."

He smiles devilishly. "I know. It's what they keep telling me. Try on the black set with the lace."

Once I have the set on, I notice the panties are crotchless. I pick up the nude and the white, and they're all the same. "You realize that the panties are crotchless."

"Yes, I know. I always want access to your pussy. It also makes it easier to slide things inside." I glare at him through the mirror. "You'll thank me when you bleed." I roll my eyes in annoyance.

He opens the door, and I overhear him tell the woman, "I'll take all of it. Two sets of each. Crotchless. I also need the three-prong toys."

He's buying me sex toys.

"All of them, sir?"

"Yes. She will be taking the set she has on now. I also want multiple sets of thigh-high pantyhose."

I've never worn such expensive or intricate lingerie before. There are about fifty different sets and colors. He's gone mad. I'm sure it's not his first time buying them for a woman, and that fact alone gives me the courage to walk out of the fitting room clad in the lingerie. It's not the first-time people have seen me and I want to defy him.

He does a double take, and the woman handing him the receipt raises a brow and smirks. "Get back inside and put your clothes on." He growls.

I lick my lips seductively. "I thought you wanted me accessible at all times?"

His nostrils flare, and I know I'm like a dangling steak to a lion. He rushes me, and I shrink back in fear when he grips my arm, tugging me back into the fitting room and slamming the door shut. He pushes me against the door, breathing heavily. "You're playing with fire. I think you need to be punished."

He pushes me on the shoulder, forcing me to kneel in front of him. He unbuckles his pants, and the sound of the belt buckle causes me to wince. Images of the bathtub flash, and I close my eyes, bringing my hands together in prayer like I was taught. The memory of pain from the feeling of leather smacking against the skin when I didn't obey.

"What the fuck are you doing?"

"I'm sorry I have sinned. Please don't hurt me."

"I'm not going to hurt you, but you're making it difficult for me not to. Open your eyes," he demands. When I open them, his eyes are blazing in fury mixed with confusion. He pulls his hard cock out and begins to fist himself. "Hold on to me, and don't look away."

He strokes his cock from root to tip. I watch as he masturbates, and he's gorgeous. He bites his bottom lip but doesn't stop staring at me. "Pull your tits out of your bra for me."

I obey.

I slide the lace down under my full breasts, so he can see my aroused nipples lifted high and watch him lick his lips like an animal. He strokes faster, his bottom lip jutting out, veins from his strong neck protruding with the effort as he fucks himself faster. I play with my nipples with one hand while holding on to his hips, digging my nails, and leaving half-moon marks on his inked skin with the other. "I'm going to fuck you so hard in every hole in your body. The scent of my cum will be your new scent," he rasps. "If any man tries to smell you, all they will get is the scent of my cum, then I will kill them for trying."

The head of his cock is engorged and full of blood, but I make sure not to touch it. It would mean I'm giving in. Surrendering. And that is the last thing I will do, surrender. I'm on my knees for him because he has done what no other has done in his world, asked for consent. I could say no and I know he wouldn't do it.

I feel him stiffen, his nostrils flare, his breath coming hard, and I know he's coming. "Veronica," he moans my name. Spurts of cum fly out in his hands, on his shaved pubic area, and some even lands on my nipples.

"Lick it clean, like the bad girl you are."

"No."

I won't give in. I can't.

"Fine." He lifts me up and scoops up the cum, flicks it off my nipples, and presses me against the mirror, so I can see him. "Spread your thighs and arch your neck and give me your lips," he commands.

When I arch my neck, he slides his tongue inside my mouth and moans. My hand reaches behind me and cup his cheek, licking the inside of his mouth over his straight white teeth and tasting copper from the cut on his lip. I'm so wet I can feel my arousal sliding down my thighs. "Fuck my mouth with your tongue, baby." He breathes over my lips. It's like we need each other's air to survive.

"Yes." I moan subconsciously, and that's his cue, and I don't realize what I've done until his fingers slid inside me like his tongue is in my mouth. I try to pull away, but his grip tightens, deepening the kiss while his fingers full of his cum slide inside me. He withdraws his fingers and wipes them on my belly. "Next time, it will be my cock fucking you hard."

He puts himself away and exits the fitting room, leaving me standing confused, wet, and full of his cum between my thighs.

CHAPTER 15
Veronica

"I see you have ——————te your internship with Riodrick-Riordan Holdings," my father says, nursing his glass of whiskey.

"Yes. I was assigned to his company for the week."

His left eye twitches. "Are you fucking him?"

I lean back like he slapped me. "No."

His phone rings, he looks at the screen and answers. I watch as he listens, piercing me with a look of hatred. "I understand"—he taps the desk and looks out the window—"of course." He tosses the phone on his desk with eyes raging in anger. "You ungrateful bitch!" he bellows, his face turning red and spittle flying from his mouth, making me want to gag. I don't know why he's mad, but I sense it has something to do with Alaric. "You have no idea who you are dealing with, but I promise you, Veronica. You fuck up, and I will punish you. I will inflict pain on you that you might not come back from. You will be his little whore, but you will marry Dorian. I don't care if he has to marry your corpse. Alaric Riordan is going to fuck you like an animal and leave you like the whore that you are. You spread your legs for him, but you come here to purify your soul when the time comes."

This all because he doesn't have another heir, and could not get a woman pregnant out of wedlock, so what would be the point in that. My mother can't have any more children after me. She hemorrhaged after he beat her, and he won't divorce her because no one wants to be married to a defiling atheist. Pig.

"Since you haven't fucked him again and he is a higher member of the Order, you must go to him, but first, you must cleanse. You need to be reminded, Veronica."

I swallow the lump in my throat because this part breaks me every time. I close my eyes and wait. I pray like the priest taught me to when I need saving.

I open my eyes after a while and turn to see Charles Devlin sitting near an old freestanding tub with brass legs. Dread fills me. "You know I hate waiting, Veronica. I hear him undo his belt.

The clinging noise of the buckle assaults my ears like nails being dragged down a chalkboard. "In the tub, princess."

I flinch, hating the endearment, and step closer, looking at the hot steam rising from the antique tub and wishing something would pull me under and drown me when I step inside.

I remove every article of clothing, careful not to wet my platinum hair or the wig I placed over my head before meeting him. Charles hates my natural hair because it reminds him, I don't belong. I must have gotten the color from my real father. My heart is hammering inside my chest, scolding me for not giving in to Alaric. I want to run out of the room, but the door swings open and three other members walk in and I close my eyes so I don't have to look at their faces. If I attempt to disobey, they will just kill me right here.

Sometimes when they are circling around me, their old beady eyes look at me naked, salivating. I'm not surprised that I recognize Dorian's father. It's the first time I have ever seen him here with my father but nothing surprises me. These are the moments when I think of dying.

But those thoughts come when you want the pain to stop.

I step inside the scalding hot water, wincing when it stings my skin. I grip the soap bar, lather it in my hands, and close my eyes.

"You're such a good girl. Let me see how pretty you are while you wash away the sins you have committed from the past," he says between the clinking sound of metal from the belt buckle. "You're a sinner, Veronica. You were consummated by sin. Born out of it. An abomination no different than a bastard child in the eyes of God, and I'm your savior."

He repeats the same words, reminding me that he isn't my biological father and has groomed me to be a slave serving the higher Order. I'm a Prey born and groomed to do as they ask. I wasn't supposed to be born, so they made me pay for the sins my parents committed. My father in death, my mother in guilt, only to be kept alive if I do as they ask. I'm to be punished and enslaved until a man comes to claim me, and when he does, I have to obey or die. This is my nightmare, and I'm their sacrifice, begging for forgiveness for I have sinned.

After being dropped off by Alaric's driver the day before, I was tired from all the shopping. He picked out all my clothes like I was a toddler. The designer boutiques knew him by name but treated me with respect. The staff took measurements for my clothes and color matched my foundation, and selected makeup.

There were so many packages but they weren't dropped off when Portman took me home. I didn't bother to ask about where he was taking them because I feared what awaited me when I got home. I showered, drank some tea, and slept, dreaming of a different life for the first time since I was eighteen. It was of me and Alaric making love in a bed. The way he looked at me in my dream was how I always wished he would look at me, but then I woke up and was summoned by Charles Devlin. A man I hate with every fiber of my being. A man I have reluctantly had to call father.

I check the time and prepare for my night shift at the restaurant. I couldn't give up my shift because I desperately need the money. Being around Alaric during the day is the same as being at school, so I decided not to take the week off.

"You have a visitor in booth five," Dorothy says, giving me a wink.

I smile and lean back, waiting for Peter, our cook, to hand me the sandwich a customer ordered. As my eyes focus on booth five, the smell of French fries frying causes a cloud of smoke from the heat, making the alarm go off. My stomach drops when I see Alaric sitting alone in the booth with one hand sprawled across the red vinyl bench seat, perusing the menu.

"Why is he here?" Adam asks, standing behind me.

I play with the hem of my apron, wondering the same thing.

"I don't know. Maybe I forgot to do something at the office."

I told Dorothy, Adam, and his sisters that I was interning with Alaric, and they were all surprised that he allowed it. Him being here is for a reason, and I know it has nothing to do with the office.

"Go, I'll take the order to your table."

"Are you sure?' I ask, still looking at the booth behind the counter. I like the fact that I can watch him without him noticing. It reminds me of all the times I would stare, and he didn't know I existed. I always knew it was a pipe dream to be with a guy like him, my time with Charles Devlin and his cronies solidifying it.

"Yeah, go ahead."

I take a deep breath and head over to booth five. When he sees me approach, he drops the menu and slides his gaze up until he reaches my eyes. "How can I help you? Are you hungry?" I ask.

He smiles. "I'm hungry but not for the food. I need you. I need to blow off steam."

He came here like I'm a prostitute, and don't wait tables in a restaurant.

"Isn't your secretary available?" I gift him with a sarcastic smile. "She seems very passionate about her job...and you."

"Is she a problem for you?" he asks.

I think he's asking if I'm jealous or see her as a threat. The truth is, maybe. Do I want to be? No. Not like this. It was never supposed to be like this.

"Do you think she is a problem for me?"

"I don't know." He shrugs. "You brought her up. I didn't."

"Hmm...let me see. Then it isn't a problem with you when I hang around a guy I have slept with daily."

"Have you?" he says, looking toward Adam and then back at me with a hard glint in his eyes.

"Are you asking if I slept with anyone I work with?"

He leans back, sliding his ass half off the bench, and I wait a few seconds, making him sweat. "No," I finally say. "He's a friend, and I help his family out babysitting for his younger sister Melody, so she stays out of trouble."

He laughs, and I swear it's the sexiest laugh. His lips lift in a smile, showing those perfect white teeth, which makes my stomach flip. "You're trouble. How can you keep someone else out of it."

I fidget with the pen in my pocket and nervously click the top repeatedly, making a clicking sound. *Is he flirting with me?*

"I'm not trouble. It seems like I am or that I don't have friends because I had no choice but to alienate people. Most people think I'm some crazed bitch, and I get why they think that. But this is the only time I have to make friends and be myself. It is why I work the night shift when no one at Kenyan is around to see me because they won't be caught dead near Ohio State territory during the school year."

"Is that the only reason?" he inquires.

I'm surprised I'm even talking to him this way. Normally, people from Kenyan could care less about me, and I know why. It is my fault, but the freedom of choice was taken from me way too early. It is easy to say, *stand up for yourself. Run away.* Yeah, where would I go? They have all the resources in the world to find and kill me. My best friend is proof of that, and she simply ran away because she fell in love. Her parents loved her. Her brother and even her dangerous cousin with power and influence loved her, but they all had something in common. They loved her and none of them could stop it from happening. All those thoughts pop into my head when I want to run. The screams from my nightmares telling me to never look back is my inner weakness telling me to give up because I know the end result. It's the same as committing suicide.

"You mean the reason why I choose to work here?"

He nods.

I pull out the pad holding the pen in my hand. "People work because they need the money, and it's a way to survive. Now what can I get you?"

It's a hard pill to swallow, knowing where I live and that I have to work to pay for things I find trivial. The dresses are nice. You'd be surprised how much clothes cost when trying to blend in with rich pricks in high society. I'm Prey, which means I don't have a fat bank account like the other kids. I don't have a fancy car like Reid or Valen—I never learned how to drive. I have to take the bus or catch a ride.

Since I was best friends with Alicia, no one considered it in high school. After I was blacklisted my senior year by the man sitting in front of me and the asshole I'm now supposed to marry, no one gave a shit or looked closely. I was a nuisance. A threat and honestly, they were right. Charles Devlin made sure I was his puppet, ordering me to destroy lives.

"I'll have a milkshake."

"Flavor?"

He looks up. "What flavor is your favorite?"

Those damn butterflies are swarming in my stomach again. *Get a grip, Veronica.*

"Oreo, cookies and cream."

He taps the table with his hands like a drum. "Oreo, cookies and cream it is then," he says with a smile.

I snag my bottom lip with my teeth and write it down, even

though it is unnecessary because I won't charge him after he bought me all those pretty clothes.

"I'll be right back."

"Where you goin?"

I blush. "I have to make your milkshake."

"They got you doing that too?"

"Uh...yeah." My cheeks flame like I'm sixteen, and my crush is right in front of me. "I'll be right back."

I scuttle behind the counter to make him the milkshake. "I wish I could make you blush like that," Adam says next to me, placing the dishes in the commercial dishwasher.

"I wasn't blushing," I say defensively.

"You know he keeps looking at me like he wants to murder me every time I talk to you, but I'll die a happy man because it's about time I see you get all girly for a guy."

I pick up the ice cream scooper and slide the freezer door open to scoop the ice cream. "I'm not girly for him." I shoot back, hating myself for reacting this way when I know all he wants is...what they all want, my body.

Adam places the milk on the counter from the fridge. "Then, don't blush, and you practically ran back here like your ass was on fire after you talked to him. He wouldn't stop staring at you at the party you invited me to. I overheard some things—"

I stiffen and place the blender on the machine. "They are all true," I say, turning on the blender and drowning out the rest.

When it finishes, and I am pouring the shake into the fifty's diner-styled shake glass, Adam says softly, "There is one important part that isn't true because I know you—the real you, Veronica. You're none of those things. I hope he realizes it before it's too late."

I grab the glass and look at my friend. "It's already too late, Adam."

Alaric left me burning in the fire twice. The first time I ran, he never went after me. I stumbled, I fell, but he was never there to catch me. The second time I stood, I pleaded with my eyes, my soul screaming at him to save me. He never looked up.

My heart burned inside a church before God's angels praying for a miracle. It never came, and I knew it was because I was unworthy in everyone's eyes.

I place the milkshake before Alaric and slide a straw next to the glass. "Will that be all?"

"What time do you get off?"

"Oh, that's right. You need to blow off steam," I say tonelessly. He frowns at my sudden change in attitude, but I'm glad I found the will to remind myself that I mean nothing to this man. I never did, and my future will never change, but this is the part of my day I control. "I'm going to say this only once." He looks up after sliding the straw inside the cup with a blank expression, but I continue, "Charles Devlin has respected my time while I work in this restaurant at night, and so has everyone else. This is a time that I'm me. A time that I'm not what someone expects me to be or do. It's a time where I'm not a slave to someone's pleasure, and I respectfully request you don't come here asking for something I would never give you if the circumstances were different"—I slam the ticket on the table—"shakes on the house. You have yourself a good rest of your night. Mr. Riordan."

He looks confused when I turn away, but Alaric needs to understand that he doesn't own me or this part of my life because of who he is. I worked hard to find my identity, even if very few people see who I really am.

CHAPTER 16
Veronica

I'm walking toward the bus stop, dragging my feet down the sidewalk in my Crocs with a thousand-dollar tip in my pocket at five a.m. I wanted to give the tip back but couldn't pass up on free money when I needed it. The money would help pay for lunch for the rest of the week, and I could save the rest for Christmas to help the staff with their families at the house. They have children to feed, and every year since I was a kid, they would all manage to get me a gift, and it was the best present I ever got because it was from a special place. A place called kindness, and only some are gifted with something so precious. I was alone during that time of year. Where families would get together and go on trips and create memories.

Every year, Charles made sure he took my mother away to another continent, so he wouldn't have to be reminded of me and what I stood for, infidelity. But in his mind, I would always be called Prey. I would see the sorrow in my mother's eyes, but ignored it because she could do nothing, and there was nothing I could do emotionally. Her fate was in my hands. But I had to admit, I loved Christmas because only those who cared about me the most, remembered that the real me existed.

The smell of morning dew is still in the air, and I knew it would disappear once the sun appeared on the horizon reminding me that day is just beginning. I tried to stay as long as possible at the restaurant because of what happened last time on the bus. I still can't remember exactly what occurred; I just remember waking up in my bed, and when I asked Marilyn, one of the housekeepers, she said she was fast asleep when I came home and didn't hear anything amiss.

I'm not sure if I took one of the pills or decided to stop taking them, even if it risked me getting nightmares. That reminds me...I skipped my visit with Dr. Wick last week and need to make sure I don't miss the next one, or Charles will be pissed he didn't get the scoop.

"Do you always tune out when sitting alone waiting for the bus in the early morning before the sun rises? Anyone can just walk up and mug you."

When I look up, Alaric is in his blacked-out Ferrari, idling at the curb like last time. "I've been watching you for about five minutes, and you didn't notice me."

I didn't notice him. I was stuck in my head like I usually am when I'm alone and have time to think. His last statement reminds me of the hooded figure with the plague mask. I know it's a signature mask from the Order's secret society. Jess described it in detail, and I know they exist because of Reid, but no one questions when and if they appear. But when they do, two things happen, you die, or they want you to know who they are. If they don't, you don't. I'm unsure if he's one of them or maybe he's too close to the top to bother with mundane dealings.

"I don't have much they can take," I say, looking down the dark road to see if the lights from the bus appear.

"Why don't you have a car?"

I glance at him, holding the medium-sized bag I purchased at Target on clearance tight against my stomach, surprised he even asked that question. "You're an intelligent guy. Why do you think?"

"Humor me," he shoots back.

I slide my dark hair over my shoulder and sigh, looking down the dark road again. "Why would I need a car if my chauffeur comes to pick me up? I know when he is always coming with enough room to take all of my friends along with me," I say flatly, turning my head to meet his stormy gray eyes that look almost black under the streetlights. "On gala days or special events, I get a limo that ensures I get home. You know, so I don't look bad, given my last name."

"Is that the truth?" he asks, surprising me again because he can't be so blind. "I want to know why Veronica doesn't have a car?"

"Why?"

"Because I want to know? Why don't you come with me and tell me? We have to be at the office in about four hours. Besides, your shift is over." He came to collect me since he owns my time technically and can decide what to do with it.

Rain begins to pour in sheets without warning, like the sky just opened up in anger.

I get up without having much of a choice. I'll get wet or worse, get sick, and then Marissa would have to stay longer because she refuses to leave me alone when I'm ill. The wind blows, and I gasp when the cold rain hits my uniform. I hear footsteps hit the pavement, and then I'm lifted off the ground bridal style, wrapping my arms around his neck. When he places me in the front passenger seat, I can smell his crisp cologne mixing with the rain and the hint of leather. He leans in, not caring that his back is getting wet, and turns to face me. "You'll catch a cold in the rain." The door slams shut.

He gets in the car, running his fingers through his damp hair and wiping his face. I see the lights from the bus finally pulling up when he drives off. I shiver from the air conditioner blowing over my wet arms. "Are you cold?"

"Yeah," I admit. He adjusts the temperature of the air conditioner so that it shoots warm.

"Thank you," I say softly.

"So tell me?"

I rub my lips together and begin. "I can't afford a car, and it would be pointless to save for one because I never learned how to drive. I only have an identification card. I'm not licensed to operate one."

I hated admitting that to him. I didn't learn to drive because there wasn't a car to practice on. It wasn't like I could ask Charles Devlin to let me borrow one of his, and I didn't ask Alicia because I was ashamed of my situation. When it was time at school to get a license, I opted for ID only and took my picture. No one questioned it.

"Oh...I guess that makes sense."

I glance out the window. "Yeah, you just missed my chauffeur," I deadpan.

He laughs. "I'm sorry. I'm not making fun of you, but I must admit, I thought it was real when you first said it. I fell for it, and then I realized you meant the bus and that you were waiting for one."

"Kind of surprising, isn't it? Everyone thinks I'm this privileged rich girl with all the money at her disposal. When in reality, I sleep in the hired helps wing like a servant waiting to be summoned."

He remains quiet after that statement. I can't blame him. It's sad to be honest. At that moment, it wasn't fun thinking I was Cinderella like I did when I was younger, waiting for Prince Charming. I wasn't Cinderella and I didn't have a Prince Charming or fairy godmother. It's funny when you think you have a person all figured out, only to realize you know nothing about them.

The silence stretches in the cabin of the car. The first time I sat in it at the party, I didn't appreciate the red leather or the beautiful lines on the dash, or how the engine purrs. It must be nice to be entitled to a privileged life. When we approach the light after fifteen minutes, he takes a left turn instead of a right. I crane my neck to make sure I'm not missing something.

I hook my thumb behind me. "You missed the turn."

"No, I didn't."

"I need to get home."

"No, you don't."

"But I need my things. I have to take a shower and change my clothes."

"I have a shower and all your clothes."

The clothes are things he bought because it's what *he* likes. He never asked if I liked any of the items. Most of the them I would only see once they were delivered. He selected everything and then he pulled out his credit card, and that was it, except for Madam's boutique. My cheeks flame when I think of what happened inside the fitting room. It's not that I'm ungrateful for all the nice things he purchased. It's why he bought them— for me to be his show pony. The same way my father has me dressed up to attend his parties or when I have partaken in his games, like sleeping with Draven because my mother slept with his father and had to act like I wanted it. It's all just a bunch of mind-fuck games.

We reach a black double gate with three cameras looking down on a white pillar surrounded by tall hedges on each side. There is a screen on a call box, but it must recognize the car because the gates suddenly open when the vehicle gets close enough. When the car pulls through the long-curved driveway, there is a two-story mansion with gas-powered lamps. The house looks modern but with a hint of warmth. Sophisticated like the man.

"Is this your home?"

"Yes."

"It's beautiful."

It is. The house is white with black accents and clear glass doors that allow you to see the foyer. Seven garage doors are to the left, and each side has those beautiful gas lamps with a single flame burning.

"Thank you," he finally says, placing the car in park.

I reach the side of the door, trying find the latch to open it, but by the time I see it, the door is pulling away from me when he opens it.

Following him inside through the double glass doors, I inhale and smell the hint of spice belonging to him mixed with a vanilla scent. I imagine I'm sitting out back with the view of a cozy beach with fluffy blankets and the sun setting on the horizon.

The farther you walk inside, the vibe of the house changes. It's like the entrance and living room is a mirage, and the farther you go, the darker it gets inside the English-style gothic home with its high, vaulted ceilings and an imposing staircase that spirals upwards like a twisted spine. Opaque, polished oak panels line the walls, contrasting the pale marble flooring beneath. An oversized, ornate chandelier hangs above, casting dramatic shadows across the room. A massive antique mirror dominates one wall, its tarnished surface reflecting the past and the present.

When we reach the master bedroom, it's a sanctuary of luxury and gloom, with a four-poster bed draped in rich velvet curtains and a canopy of dark lace. Moonlight filters through the draped windows, casting a silvery glow on the inky walls. A glimpse inside the en-suite bathroom features a claw-footed tub and a vanity adorned with antique mirrors. A shiver runs down my spine when my eyes linger on the bathtub.

"The bathroom is through that door," he says, but I stay rooted to the spot and gaze at him with wide eyes. "What's wrong?"

"D-do you have a shower…please," I stammer.

He looks in the bathroom, where the tub is trying to lure me in to remind me of how I could pay for my sins, and slides his gaze back to me and nods. He walks inside, and I'm relieved when I see the modern rain shower with a digital screen mounted on the tiled wall.

"Towels are in the towel warmer."

I wait until he leaves and place my bag on the counter, looking at the smudges under my eyes from my mascara running and stringy dark hair badly in need of a wash. Wiping my face with a tissue, I turn the shower on, press the buttons on the screen, and look up when the water comes down like rain. It must have activated the music to turn on because "Concrete Jungle" by Bad Omens begins to play softly, and I smile.

I pour shower gel into my palm from the dispenser nailed to

the dark tile and wash my body, basking in the warmth of the water and the clean, fresh scent of his soap. *How could anyone skip a shower?*

A breeze of cold air slides over my skin, causing my nipples to pebble, and I turn to Alaric walking naked inside the expansive shower. "I expected you to use the tub. I always use the shower, but I don't mind."

I want to scream at him and tell him to get out and give me privacy, but I can't. I have no choice but to eventually be his until my time is up and I graduate, or he tires of me. Usually, I play a game my father wants me to star in, and since Gia and Jess showed up, I have turned over a new leaf and prefer to play a game where the innocent win. But this is different.

I stand against the wall watching him under the spray while "Concrete Jungle" by Bad Omens gives way to "Bad Decisions" by Bad Omens and finish washing my body slower than necessary.

He plants his hands above his head on the tile, leaning forward and letting the water run down his perfectly muscled back and trim waist, his tattoos glistening under the bathroom's light. He has ink everywhere, in places I've never seen before. On his neck and shoulders, it stops on some parts and begins on others. Some are scriptures from the Bible; others are skulls and angels. I pause and linger on his impressive cock between his muscled thighs. He's long and thick with a barbell through the tip. I don't think he had it before, or I would have felt something like that the first time.

I have to admit that I'm aroused. I'm wet and want nothing more than to slide my fingers between my thighs and pleasure myself. *It's been a while since I touched myself.*

"Do you like what you see?" he asks, bending his elbows and turning his head to look at me.

I slide my hands down my stomach slowly until I reach the lips of my pussy, washing myself with my eyes closed, letting the water rinse me off. I moan while I rub my clit, not caring if he's watching. It's bold, but this is all I could do without walking over there and touching his thick, long cock, stroking it in my hands, prepping myself for when I take it inside my body. How well will it fit now? I was an inexperienced virgin the first time, but now I could take him fast and hard.

"Do you like what you see?" I say breathlessly, throwing back his own words. Taunting him. I don't know why I say it. Acting like a different person for so long just stuck and became as natural as breathing.

I suddenly feel heat, and something soft touching me. My eyes pop open, and he's so close I see the tip of his hard cock on my lower belly. He pins me to the shower wall with his body, and my fingers stop rubbing myself, staring wild-eyed into the storm of his gray eyes.

"Don't stop," he rasps, his forehead touching mine, water sliding down the sides of his face to his lips. "Don't be scared. I won't hurt you...I want to watch you come." He grinds the length of his hard cock against my stomach, his chest heaving, breaths coming quick and shallow. I can feel his piercing rub against my skin. It must feel good for him because his bottom lip is snagged between his teeth.

I continue to play with myself.

My mouth parts when I hit the sensitive spot I like. The place that will bring me over the edge. He lowers his hand and fists his cock to the same rhythm. I moan, and he grunts, but his forehead never leaves mine.

"Faster, baby. Show me...fuck—" He strokes faster. His eyes pin mine. His pupils are full of something dark and powerful I have never seen or felt before. I can feel my heart pounding inside my chest. His jaw flexes, and I keep rubbing and flicking my clit on the brink of a powerful orgasm. "The day you let me slide my cock between those lips again, I'm not going to stop," he says breathlessly. "If I were to drown, I would want to drown in you." He takes my lips in his. I swirl my tongue, matching the rhythm of my fingers. The pressure begins to build, my orgasm coming hard and fast. He breaks the kiss and whispers against my lips, "I won't stop until you give me the real you, Veronica." I swallow hard and moan when my orgasm crests, and I come sliding two fingers inside, feeling my walls clench. I arch my back as he takes one nipple into his mouth and sucks hard.

I gasp. "Harder." He sucks harder, and I come, stars exploding behind my eyes. "Yes!"

The sound of my moans reverberates off the tiled walls. My fingers grip the strands of his hair hard when he holds me and I must admit, my orgasm felt like the best high.

Alaric is a dangerous drug everyone warns you about. The one that makes you forget that your shitty world exists. A drug that is hard to shake once you're on it. The one that you always end back on because it consumes you and your entire world, promising to make it better, not caring that it could kill you because you know, deep down, you would sell your soul to the highest bidder just to get one more taste of that high, and that is what I just did. I sold my soul, not caring what happens because I am an addict. And he is the drug promising me rapture in my hell.

I slide up the tiled wall, releasing his hair and holding on to his shoulder, my head looking down, watching his thick, hard cock swell, getting ready to spill his release while he fucks himself. His sweet words replay in my head. A dull ache forms in my stomach, shooting up to my head, telling me to ruin them—that they're a trick. To him, I'm the whore they made me out to be. The one with no choices. *Ruin what he said! Ruin them, Veronica. He doesn't love you! Whore! Whore!* The chant goes on inside my head.

My eyes flick up to him like they're possessed. I grip his cock and stroke it faster, making him grit his teeth when I take over. His nostrils flare until he gives a loud grunt, and cum spurts in strings landing on the tile, my stomach, and fingers.

I tilt my head with a sultry smile and reach for the bath gel to wash his cum off my hands and give him my back. I close my eyes. "I'm glad I could service you in blowing off steam."

I turn, widening my hand full of soap and his cum under the spray of water, letting it wash away like it was something grotesque I touched and wanted off my skin. "Don't worry," I purr,

"I won't take what you said to heart. Some things are said in the heat of the moment." *Ruin it!* He blinks. His skin is flushed under the spray. Silent. *Good Girl, Veronica.*

I slide my hair over my shoulder, revealing the mark behind my neck. Small but unmistakable. The mark of Prey belonging to the Order. A skull with a small rose. A cross and an inverted cross right under it. I hear his breaths short and fast. Turning my head over my shoulder, his eyes are hard, and his jaw is tight.

I plaster a fake grin and then lick my lips. "You could whisper sweet words, tell me you like what you see, or how I make you feel, but there is one word I always hear when I look at you or when you look at me. The one word I will always remember. Whore."

He slides his fingers through his wet hair. "Veronica, I–"

I turn around, cupping his cheek and feeling how hard his jaw is set. *Tell him!* "I thought a girl's first time was supposed to be special. If it's her first time or first time with someone she thought was good enough. A crush—girls have those you know—I know for some guys they don't— guys like you. The popular, rich ones." I drop my hand and continue, "My first time was…unforgettable. It reminded me what I was worth to you and every guy I would meet." I audibly swallow and laugh, so I won't cry in front of him because I could never sink so low. He took a lot away from me that night. I wanted that moment to be something to remember—to help drown out the bad that would come. The one thing I begged for when I would look at the stars in the sky. I drove Alicia crazy that summer, trying to be anywhere he would be. I would have accepted him to kiss me goodbye and for him to never talk to me again. I didn't expect a phone call or a repeat. And right now, the last thing I need is for him to see my tears. He wants me here, then I will take what I can from him—time. But I will not give him any more pieces of me.

"Veronica, I—" he tries again.

"I want to go home," I say quietly. I look around the shower like the walls are closing in on me. "I don't want to stay here with you."

I cross my arms over my body, like he didn't just watch me finger myself and see me fall apart. I wait, hoping he agrees, watching the water slide down the drain like the moment never happened.

He opens the glass door and relief floods me when he says, "I'll take you home."

We drive in complete silence. My purse clutched to my chest, and a designer shopping bag between my feet with an outfit he picked out that's suitable for the office and some other items he expects me to wear. I was surprised he didn't end the arrangement right then, or maybe he will when he drops me off. He could call someone in the Order who would then call Charles.

Since my hell with Dorian Black is soon to begin, I would have to first purify my soul like the sick bastard he is, and maybe it would be a good thing. I could think of a way to leave and change my identity, like those witness protection programs where people adopt new identities and move to another country where no one can find them.

"Are you okay?" he asks. "You're very quiet—"

"I'm fine."

I keep cutting him off because I don't want to hear his lies, so he can convince me to fuck him. He might say how sorry he was or he didn't know, but he had plenty of time to find out. He's Alaric Riodrick-Riordan. He managed to convince the whole Order for him not to marry and to immediately take over for his father. I am here with him because of some sick joke or game they put him up to or that he wants to be a part of. *He did nothing, Veronica. He watched and did…nothing!*

He pulls up to the driveway, and I'm glad I figured out how to open the door from inside his Ferrari. I step out, closing the door before he can say anything, and walk toward the servants' side door. The front door of the house gives me flashbacks of that night with him and what had happened when I made it home. That was the first time I had to pay for my sins. It was the first time I knew the reason for my existence as a Devlin. Charles would tell me things I didn't understand, but I did—that night.

Since then, I have used the servants' door, which is also closer to my room. He waits until I'm inside and drives off. When the door closes behind me, I let the sobs and tears come. I almost don't recognize the shrill sounds coming from my throat, wishing the words he said to me were true and hating myself for having to ruin them, but knowing I wouldn't forgive myself if I didn't. What I hate the most is that I want him when I shouldn't. After everything he's done, I'm scared I'm still in love with him.

CHAPTER 17
Alaric

I frustratingly grip the strands of my hair, pulling and ripping a couple out as I watch the side door shut and drive off. I was trying to tell her that I— what. That I've never felt so ashamed of anything I've done, but I'm not just ashamed, I'm disgusted with myself for treating her like a prostitute. The solemn look on her face when she told me what I reminded her of, what I said to her that night at the initiation party, she gave me what I just asked of her so freely that night. She chose me.

In her confession, she admitted what I meant to her in the beginning and what I mean to her now. It was heartbreaking to see her fall so beautifully in my arms, only to break seconds later. The words I said hearing her beautiful moans were true. If I were to drown, I would want it to be in her.

The mark on her neck sent a ball of fury inside me, wanting to rip it off or cover it so no one could see it. How could Charles Devlin be such a bastard to an innocent girl? But I know the answer. Because he can. She is nothing to him but a poisonous thorn to his ego. Something he can torture and use to get more power because he is a failure as a husband and a lover, so he wants Veronica to pay for it all because outing his wife would draw attention to his inadequacies as a man. He prefers to cover it up by being ruthless in the eyes of the Order, all to inflate his ego. *Piece of shit.*

I slam my hand on the steering wheel because I know I haven't treated her any better. I saw the look in her eye. I'm one of *Them.* Just another sick bastard using her, watching her like a creep in the diner. I'm not going to lie, what she said, it messed with my head and the way she talked to Garret fucked with my head even more. *Serviced. That fucking word.*

I'm at a red light and I'm still gripping the wheel. The sun is rising, blinding me with a stream of light. Placing my sunglasses on, I turn the wheel, put the car in gear and hear the tires squeal when they kiss the pavement followed by the engine roaring through the loud exhaust.

After the ten minute drive, I reach the bronze gate and it automatically opens because his parents are rarely home and the last four years all the Kenyan parties have been here like his own personal playground. Not giving a fuck that I'm going to be late to the office— I'm never late, I open the front door, letting myself in the grandeur of the mansion, reminding me that vampires must live here because you never see people inside the house during the day.

I walk through the house like I own it, knowing the piece of shit must still be in bed, and take the stairs two at a time. I reach the landing and push the door open with a slam, causing Garret to bolt out of bed. His eyes widening like he just saw a ghost.

"What the fuck man! Really?" he says, sliding his hand over his face like that's going to make me disappear. "You scared the shit out of me?"

That's the idea.

"Why did you sleep with her!" I growl, walking over and grabbing him by the neck.

He holds his hands up in mock surrender and I look down, noticing he's naked and the fact that he does have a small dick winking at me. *Pathetic.*

I must sound like a crazy, deranged asshole, but I don't care. I'm going to dig out the truth and kill who ever fucks with me.

He blinks rapidly, probably trying to wrap his head around who I'm talking about, but he knows because he begins to shake like a dog when it does something bad and its master walks in.

"I–"

"Now is not the time to lie to me, Garret." I squeeze harder, causing him to turn red.

"Please." He struggles, but if I want to know, I can't kill him.

I release him, and he begins to cough in a fit. When he finally gets himself under control. I throw some shorts at him.

"Put those on. I can't take it anymore."

"Fuck you," he chokes out. He slides the shorts on and shakes his head. "I knew it. I saw the look in your eyes when Veronica said it, but it wasn't like that man. I'm in love with her." My fist flies, connecting with his left eye. The sting in my first two knuckles a welcome feeling, telling me it hurt him even worse.

"Ow, man! What the fuck!" he yells, placing a hand over his face and doubling over.

"Wrong fucking answer." I grip him by the hair, lifting his head and watching the swelling get worse around his eye. *Good, I hope it hurts.*

"Speak."

"M-my father arranged it. I had trouble getting girls in high school and after–" I glare, tightening my hold on his hair and causing him to gasp and close his eyes. "Please man. I didn't know you felt anything for her. I thought you hated her because she was trying to get you to marry her or some shit. Every girl wanted you. When I started Kenyan, I had trouble getting girls and Veronica knew. When I tried to go after Jess, Melissa stepped in because she has a thing for Prey because she likes women." He opens his eyes, and I release a bit of my hold, so he can talk. "I didn't hurt Veronica, but she made it seem that Jess was just Prey and we needed to fuck with her like we all do to Prey so she—" he looks away with a pained look in his expression, "I couldn't believe she wanted me like that. She's beautiful and I fell hard for her. My father laughed at me when I told him...I still don't know why she did it, but the next day, she made it known on campus that we slept together and then all the girls wanted me. I threw parties and it was like my flaws were suddenly overlooked, but I didn't want them. I wanted her. Reid and Valen thought I wanted Jess, but in the end, it wasn't her I wanted. Veronica made me feel like I was a man. When I told her how I felt, she didn't laugh—" he looks up at me, scared that I'm going to go after his good eye, but he swallows— "she said we could be friends and that was all. I never touched her after that and I am—"

"What?"

"I'm her friend and if she needs anything I would...do anything for her."

I smile manically. "How charming," I snarl and shove him on the bed.

"I'm sorry, man. I really am. I didn't know and she really isn't what people make her out to be, but I don't know why she doesn't change the way she acts or stop playing these games messing with people's heads."

I have an idea why. He doesn't know what she is to the Order. But I don't tell him that. I pin him with a hard stare before walking out of his room and growl. "Touch her again and I'll kill you."

I pull out my cell phone once I'm in the car and dial Portman.

"Sir?"

"I need you to pick up Miss Devlin at her home and take her to my office as scheduled. Please have her breakfast ready when she arrives in my office."

"Yes, sir."

"Tell her I will meet her there and to wait for me. Understood?"

"Y-yes, sir."

"And Portman?"

"Sir," he responds warily.

"Keep your eyes to yourself."

"Yes, sir. Understood."

I hang up, giving him the only verbal warning I will give when it comes to her.

CHAPTER 18
Veronica

The elevator doors open, and I ignore Portman because every time he speaks to me, he stares at the ground like I'm going to hit him, only giving me curt answers. I'm wearing what Alaric picked out for me. A beautiful black silk wrap-around dress and underneath is some type of undergarment. There are actually strings that look like rubber bands made into a monokini with a crotchless panty paired with over-the-knee suede boots by designer Gianvito Rossi. Little lace petals are intricately sewn into the bands that cover my nipples, but the single string that goes between the cheeks of my ass is uncomfortable because it rubs when I walk, making me wet.

I pause at the desk right before the double doors to Alaric's office, and I'm greeted by a man. I expected Sasha and her ironic smile to greet me, and he must know because of the surprised look on my face.

"You must be Verrronica," he says, rolling the Rs in my name. His voice has a feminine tone and you could tell he was gay. His suit is perfectly tailored with a pink flower on the breast of his pocket and a little LGBTQ pin with a rainbow on the collar. It's so cute. To me, a gay man is a girl's best friend.

I smile. "Yes."

"Mr. Riordan hired me to assist you in whatever you wish because I can tell"—he winks—" you will be assisting him with everything he needs."

"Where's Sasha?"

He raises his brows and shakes his head from side to side in a rhythm and lowers his voice. "Sasha, who? This is an opportunity of a lifetime. Please, if I did something wrong—"

My eyes widen in horror, hoping I didn't offend him. "Oh, no. You're perfect." I smile, calming him down.

He places a hand on his chest in relief, breathing dramatically, like he just ran a marathon. "Oh, thank God," he rushes out. "He gave the agency I work for specific instructions when selecting the perfect candidate on short notice and I promised I could assist you with anything you needed."

"What did he do with Sasha?"

He cups his hand over his mouth and whispers, "He fired her." I step back, looking at Alaric's closed office door and then back at him. *Why would he do that?* "I'm Sergio, by the way," he says, holding his hand out for me to shake, and I do. "We're going to get along fine. I see a spark in those beautiful eyes." He lowers his voice again and whispers, "He must go crazy looking at you."

I snort. "You will understand when you see me and him in the same room."

"Well, he's not in yet, but there is a delicious breakfast waiting for you in his office," he says, sashaying toward the door and holding it open so I can walk through.

After eating a sensual breakfast of fruit, eggs, and coffee, I wait for the man in question to appear. My phone goes off, and I look at the incoming message.

Dorian: Is he bored of you yet?

Veronica: What do you want, stalker?

Dorian: Is that any way to talk to your fiancé?

Veronica: You are nothing of mine, and you know I would never choose you. I'd rather die.

Dorian: That can be arranged.

Cold dread sits at the bottom of my stomach, making me nauseous.

Dorian: What's wrong? Afraid, princess. I have so many fun things planned for you.

"Is everything alright?" I drop the phone on his desk. Alaric is standing in a tailored blue suit, freshly-shaven, with a questioning look in his eyes.

I swallow thickly, realizing I'm in his chair like I own the place. "Oh...um...I'm sorry." I stumble blindly, getting out his chair, careful not to drop the plastic-covered plates and trying to clean up the mess.

When I toss everything away and move so he can sit, I notice he's watching me like a lion waiting to pounce. He's quiet, his hands are in his trousers pockets, waiting. For what? I don't know.

"I hire people to clean," he says, before taking a seat. "I had a meeting this morning."

I sit in the chair in front of his desk, and when he places his hands on the smooth glass surface, I notice the first two knuckles are red and swollen over white spots of skin from the scabs I saw at the Galleria that were almost healed. He stares at me when he notices me looking at them but doesn't say anything.

I find the courage to gently reach out with my hands and gently caress the red skin, leaning across his desk. "Getting into trouble," I say in a soft voice. His lips twitch, and I know he wasn't at a meeting.

He probably beat the shit out of someone, and it isn't the first time. When I learned that he existed, I was consumed with wanting to learn everything about him, like every girl does when she is crushing hard on a guy. I wanted to know what he was into, what he liked, where he hung out, if he was single or had a girlfriend—so I could hate her because she was with the guy I considered mine when I would daydream about him in class. In those dreams, instead of him kissing her and taking her out on a date, it was me. I overheard Reid one time complain about Alaric's character but what stood out the most to me was Alaric's bad temper. He would fight with anyone who got in his way or wronged him.

He's as violent and as lethal as they come when you think of the sons of Kenyan. The villain of all villains. The one you don't cross. He is heartbreak guaranteed, but it doesn't keep the girls away; it attracts them even more, even if they know there is no future. Alaric doesn't have a girlfriend or plan to get married like the rest of his generation, but that didn't stop me when I turned eighteen and wanted something bad enough, having waited so long to get it. You don't care. You go for it.

"I caught my hand on a door."

"Did it hurt?"

"You should see the door."

"What did the door do?" I ask playfully.

"It got in my way." He looks behind me, and his gaze slides back on mine. "Lock the door."

I get up and do as he asks, hearing him move around the room behind me. Once the lock is in place, I see hooks on the wall with chains I hadn't noticed before because a wall slides up, hiding the toys hanging behind it. He must not like to take his women home. He pulls the chains, the sound clicking against each loop. There are leather wrist cuffs on each end as he holds them in each hand.

"Come here." I hear the chains rattle. "Take off the dress and leave everything else on."

I untie the dress, letting it fall in a puddle of black silk at my feet. I watch his pants tighten between the space of his suit jacket, right under his belt. *I hate belts.* "Hold both wrists out."

I hold out my hands and watch him fasten the cuffs on each wrist chained to the wall. "Why are you cuffing my wrists?"

He looks up. "I want to ensure you don't leave my office until I tell you to." He leans in close. "I want to see you dressed like this and watch you come."

"What if I need to use the bathroom?"

"Then you'll go, but if you run, I'll punish you."

A chill runs down my skin, my nerves on end, and I look away. "W-with what?"

He lifts my chin with an index finger so I can look at him and frowns. "I would never physically hurt you, Veronica." He cups my pussy, pulling me toward him. "This...is mine...I'll punish you, but I'll make sure you like it."

Mine. I know he means I'm his for as long as he allows it. There is no way he means it permanently. He must see the confusion mixed with the look of terror on my face. "This is not a game." His red knuckles slide up my stomach and stop at the side of my breasts, causing the nerves to tighten all over my skin. My nipples are hard underneath the lace. He stares at my heavy breasts for a couple of seconds and asks, "May I?"

I nod, watching his head dip as he flicks his tongue over the lace petal. Arousal grips me, sending intense pleasure between my thighs. My breath comes in quick when he moves to the other breast. I squirm and it causes the elastic string to tighten, causing heat between my legs and around the lips of my pussy.

"Mmm..." My fingers pull his perfectly-combed hair. "If you're going to cause the mess between my legs, then it's only fair everyone knows what you've been up to." He grins, flicks the lace to the side with his tongue, and holds my breasts with both hands. He traces the area around my nipple in tiny little circles, and when I think I'm going to scream from the intense pleasure, he flicks my nipple with the flat part of his tongue, sucking it inside his mouth and then the other. "Oh, God." I moan, holding his head, so he won't stop. "Please," I beg.

"What do you want?"

"Your fucking tongue, everywhere."

His eyes flick up, and his hand shoots to a button on the wall I didn't notice before, causing the chain to retract. "Stand with your back against the wall."

The cuffs have rings that allow free movement, so I can turn without crossing the chains. When the chains shorten, giving me no choice but to stand with my back against the wall, it causes my arms to spread like open wings at his mercy.

He removes his suit jacket and walks over to a box I hadn't noticed sitting on the couch on the far wall by the bar. He opens it and removes a black leather rabbit mask with a silver metal cross in the middle. "I bought this for you," he says, holding it up.

He walks over, places it over my head, ensuring it fits securely on my nose and the openings around my eyes. Once it's on, he steps back. "It looks gorgeous on you."

"Does it?" I purr.

I step to the side, widening my stance. My pussy is hot and throbbing, wanting his mouth to lick and suck. "I like it on you, but I like that you're at my mercy more." I pull on the restraints, but they don't budge. I can't move my arms down. The chains that have retracted have my arms pinned to the wall by the cuff on my wrist, not letting me pull to release them. "I can do whatever I want to you."

"I can scream."

He shakes his head with a devilish smile. "They can't hear you." I begin to panic. My body feels flashes of hot and cold. He steps closer, giving me enough room so I can knee him in the balls, but what would that do but piss him off. He leans in, and I feel the heat from his chest through his shirt on my wet nipples. "I'm going to make you come, and that is the only scream I want to hear." His lips brush against mine. "Your screams belong to me. Your pain belongs to me—" his hand slides over my throat, cupping my cheek, "your fears...belong to me."

Every breath I take, I take in his scent. The vibrations of his voice embrace my skin, awakening a deep desire. A pleasure he can only give me. I've never had a man give me an orgasm. I tried, but I knew why I couldn't. It wasn't because I was a sinner like Charles said I was. It was because of the man in front of me. He took that from me. Taking it only allowed me to have one if I gave it to myself. It felt like a cruel punishment for what he thought I did.

I want to kick and scream at him for always having power over me.

Over my body.

Over my mind.

The punishment I took for him wasn't why I hate him; it's because it was for nothing. He still thought of me the same way. He could have anyone—any woman he wanted like this, so why me?

"Why me?"

He doesn't answer but takes my lips with his and my face in his hands, sliding his tongue over the delicate skin of my mouth. He pulls back lazily. My eyes follow the backs of his fingers sliding between the valley of my breasts. I bite my bottom lip when he reaches my wet slit, spreading my arousal over my clit in circles, causing a little cry to bubble from my throat. I arch my back against the wall while he plays with me. His other hand lifts my leg over his hip, placing kisses on my throat, not once pulling his hand from between my thighs. The wet sounds of his fingers rubbing my clit are the only ones I can register between the sounds of our breathing.

"When you look at me, and I look at you, and that word possesses your mind—" he slips a finger inside me, and I gasp, "the word whore." My half-lidded eyes widen. "You forgot the rest—" The dark pupils of his eyes darken. "You're *my* whore."

The phone rings and my eyes shoot to his desk, where it's going off, but he ignores it. I'm disappointed when he pulls his finger out and licks it clean. My leg slides off his hip, and I watch as he slowly drops to his knees surprising me. I thought he was going to answer the phone but instead, Alaric is on his knees, lifting one leg over his shoulder and pressing his mouth over my opening and fucking me with his tongue.

"Mmm..." I moan, hoping that the office is soundproof and he isn't messing with me because everyone on this floor will know what the CEO is doing to his intern, and it's not going over financials.

He hums while he takes my clit in his mouth, the vibrations from his throat making me wet, teasing my pussy as he moves faster. "Fuck, yes," I say breathlessly. "More, don't stop...Alaric." I push my hips forward, wanting more and hoping he won't stop when I grind my pussy on his mouth. His lips make kissing sounds with my pussy, and the phone rings again.

"Are you going to get that?" I ask breathlessly.

"I'm eating," he murmurs. "They can wait."

He slides his tongue and fucks me with it. In and out, he sucks and twirls his tongue until I can't take it anymore and come, making a desperate, dirty noise. My pussy pulses in his mouth, but he doesn't stop, causing my leg over his shoulder to shake but not caring if the heel of my black suede boot digs into his back. My breaths are coming out faster than the last as I try to calm myself by closing my eyes.

"I love the way your pussy tastes and your skin smells." He places stray kisses on my inner thigh, my pussy, and my stomach. He rises on his feet and undoes the cuffs on my wrists. The ache from having them up causes tingles that feel like tiny needles. I rub them, watching him walk back from the bathroom to hand me a wet cloth. "Put your clothes on, we have a meeting."

My eyes almost bulge. That is why the phone was ringing, we're late. When we walk in, they will all know or have an idea why and all I can think about is that he didn't stop. He didn't care.

He hands me the dress, and I glance upward to see his reaction from what we just did, or rather...what I let him do. Taking it from him, I hand him the washcloth.

"We're late," he says softly with a grin, causing me to blush. "But I'd do it again."

CHAPTER 19
Veronica

We walk into the board meeting, relieved Sergio is behind us, covering for us. I'm sure Alaric could care less what people may think, but I'm here as an intern, and deep down, I know I'm not doing anything related to school.

"Sorry we're late, gentlemen. My lunch ran late, and I have to eat," Alaric announces with a smirk. All the men seated at the boardroom table glance at me and Sergio as we take our seats, while I'm wishing the floor would swallow me whole. Alaric walks to the head of the table and takes his seat.

There are six men in total besides Alaric, Sergio, and me. The first one eyes me with curiosity. He's wearing a brown suit with a pink pinstriped shirt that clashes with his red facial complexion. He reminds me of a pack of Starburst, the pink and red pack where pink and red are the only colors inside. The man seated to his right, who keeps scrutinizing my long dark hair, reminds me of a guy trying to sell a pyramid scheme on an infomercial with a bad haircut because he doesn't want to face the fact that he is balding. The one to the left of Starburst gives me a knowing grin, and the way his eyes linger on me longer than necessary, I know he knows my father, which means he knows who I am.

"You're Devlin's daughter, right?" he asks.

"I—"

"She will be addressed as the Intern in our office and be called as such," Alaric says curtly.

"Oh, well now, Alaric, we can also just call her Veroni–"

"Call her by her first name, and I'll cut out your tongue," he says icily, pointing at him.

The man's face turns white, then gulps and looks away.

"Oh my," Sergio whispers.

"That goes for everyone except Sergio. He will guide my intern while she's here, assisting her with everything she needs. She will be addressed as the Intern. Not her first name or her last name."

Starburst clears his throat. "Intern it is," he says, giving me a nervous smile.

"Veronica, look over page five and give me your analysis," Alaric says.

I turn over the prospectus in front of me and turn to page five. I quickly scan the line items and immediately notice the issue as to why EBITA is higher than in previous quarters. I clear my throat, trying to calm my nerves about being put on the spot, before I respond. "Direct Labor was higher than normal because...um, there are more employees but no reason as to why the company is top heavy when development hasn't commenced to expand for a full quarter in the same positions. When everything else was the same the previous —"

"She's not making any sense," the asshole to Alaric's right interrupts me in a raspy tone. I can smell the stench of old cigars permeating around him like a cloud. I can tell he has something to do with the company's financials because I know I'm spot on. A wave of annoyance causes me to drop the paper from the folder in my hand on the table.

"Interrupt her again, Gino, and I'll pull the funding from your next build."

Alaric is a capital investor and lends money to companies, then takes a percentage of the profits. Page five is a huge problem with a certain investment. But knowing how smart Alaric is, he already figured it out. These men are the ones needing money to fund different projects for companies that Alaric is investing in.

I wanted to avoid coming in with an attitude since I'm just an intern. They know I'm just a senior at Kenyan with no traditional work experience.

Alaric glances at me and says, "Continue."

I lick my lips, pick up the folder, and turn to page five, glancing at Gino. "Your company has hired employees that work in the same capacity, causing the direct labor to increase; therefore, increasing your EBITA instead of decreasing or at least staying the same in the last quarter. There is no reason to increase overhead when you are seeking capital funding unless there is a loss, but clearly there is nothing reported. Increasing your direct labor hurts profits. Is there a reason for the increased overhead when the project hasn't broken ground? It would be detrimental to the company when you do have to hire the employees for the new project after it commences, putting the company in the red and risking not being able to pay back the loan, leaving with interest-only payments."

Gino's face turns a different shade of red. His jaw clenches in anger because I figured it out and it doesn't take a genius to know he's funneling money out in case it goes belly up or he already knows it will. The employees probably don't exist and are ghosts on paper. He would file bankruptcy, and then lenders would get pennies on the dollar when he has to restructure. He will then open another company while he has loads of liquid cash stashed somewhere.

"You're wrong," he barks. He looks at the rest of the men. "She's wrong."

"I'm right, and you know it. I bet those employees are ghosts on paper."

"What would you do, Veronica?" Alaric says in a soft voice. "If you owned my company?"

I stare Gino straight in the eye. "I'd pull the fucking plug on his whole operation and leave him having to get a loan at Wells Fargo, but that wouldn't work because I would place liens on his assets, causing the banks to pay you out before he files and they place it in a REO."

Sergio inhales air next to me, covering his hand over his mouth and stifling a smile as he looks away.

"Congratulations, Veronica. You passed your first test. My senior advisors couldn't find it, but you did in five minutes." I grin, and Gino looks like he's about to blow a gasket glaring at me like I'm the devil that fucked up his plan.

He pushes the chair back and stands up with a snarl. "You bitch. You're nothing but a cunt."

I flinch because I hear the sound of his belt buckle, triggering the mental image of an antique bathtub and the sound of hard breathing. My palms are sweating, and my heartbeat is pounding in my ears. I feel hot, imagining the steam from a hot bath.

"Are you okay?" I hear Sergio ask.

"I need some air," I whisper.

Sergio looks behind me and nods, getting up and guiding me outside the boardroom. The door shuts behind us, and I know I messed up in lashing out at one of Alaric's business associates, but I wanted to tell Gino to go fuck himself, the lying, stealing prick, but the sound of his belt buckle and him calling me a bitch and a cunt triggered the memories I try to forget every day. It also doesn't help when Portman shows up so he can take me home for the rest of the day when it's the last place I want to be.

"How is your internship going? I heard you are interning with one of the most prestigious family's companies," Dr. Wick says with a cold smile, reminding me of Maleficent. The tone of her voice sounds regal. A bitch with a chip on her shoulder because she was fucked over by a man and wants to make other people's lives just as shitty.

"It couldn't be better. I watch old men in suits with a lot of dough, listen to their refined voices, and watch their hard cocks swell every time I walk by in heels. It's quite entertaining. You should talk to the board and get the male doctors to wear suits. I promise you, Dr. Wick, you won't be disappointed."

Her eyes narrow when I pull out another Virginia Slims and light it up just to piss her off. She takes a deep breath before the smell of smoke reaches her.

"How's Mr. Riordan treating you?"

My eyes light up because I expected this question. My father must be curious. I take a drag of the cigarette and exhale, wetting my lips. "He's riding me hard," I say in a sultry voice. "Making sure I get the work done right. I COME...in every day by 9 a.m."

She swallows because I think she gets aroused when I talk about men insinuating how I use their appendages. How hard they get when they see a woman. I don't care if my father takes it out on me later. I'm used to it after so many years and this is where I can vent. When I started seeing Dr. Wick, I secretly hoped she would find me crazy enough and put me in a room in the ward for a couple of days so that I didn't have to go back home and deal with Charles and his rituals.

"What else do you do for Mr. Riordan?"

I snuff out the cigarette, adding to the holes in the carpet under the chair. "Oh, a lot of things. The first week, I had orientation." I lick my lips seductively. I inwardly laugh when a flush rises on her cheeks, and she shifts in her seat. "Does Mr. Wick...fuck you hard. Not those lazy fucks, you know--" I wink, "a good solid hard fuck. The kind that makes your toes curl?"

Her face turns red in lust and anger. "Leave."

"Just tell him, Dr. Wick." I lower my voice. "Tell him to fuck you with his tongue. You won't be so uptight."

"Leave!" She raises her voice, pulling the neck of her blouse, and I notice she isn't wearing a bra. Her nipples are hard, and she's aroused. Good.

"I need to change my medication. The one you gave me messes with my memory."

She tears a script off the pad after she scribbles something on it the way doctors tend to do, like five-year-old's writing in a notebook, and only a pharmacist understands.

The door opens, and another doctor walks in with dark hair and a medium build. "Excuse me, Dr. Wick?" The color in Dr. Wicks's face turns pink. Her eyes widen. The pen falls from her fingers, and I smile when she smooths her skirt and rights herself.

"Yes?"

"I need you in room four," he says.

"I'll be right there," she says softly, but I don't miss how her eyes betray her.

She's fucking him.

She hands me the script and turns toward the hallway but then turns with her hand gripping the door. "Same time, Friday."

Turning in my seat, surprised she still wants to see me after she asked me to leave. I give her a knowing smile. "Remember, what I said."

"I gotta go."

She closes the door, and I hear her heels click-clack on the floor heading down the hallway, then, "You needed to see me, Dillon…" The sound of clothes being shifted, heavy breathing, and a grunt fill my ears until the closing of the door shuts off the rest, so I turn and make my way out to the receptionist.

"Is that all?" the receptionist asks.

"I also need my monthly birth control refilled."

She looks at my name, and she freezes for a moment. She looks up with wide eyes and smiles. "I'll be right back. Let me fill those for you."

Weird.

She comes back after five minutes and hands me both filled prescriptions. "Did Dr. Wick need you to come in again?"

"Yes."

"Date and Time?"

"Friday at Four."

"Perfect."

"Let me get her to sign off, and you should be all set." She moves to get up, and I don't stop her when she walks down the hallway looking for Dr. Wick.

I walk out, not feeling bad about her getting caught fucking Dillon. Bitch fucks with plenty of lives.

CHAPTER 20

Alaric

I'm brooding in my office, seated at my desk, contemplating after I let Sergio escort Veronica out of the meeting and had Portman take her wherever she needed to go. He notified me she wanted to be dropped off at campus. I could get the traumatized look on her face out of my head when Gino called her a 'bitch' and a 'cunt.' It was as if she shut down entirely, her body tense and voiceless. It was also as if an invisible curtain had fallen over her.

Something triggered it, but I couldn't understand what or why. People have called her worse, but I've never seen her shut down like that. I expected a fast retort on her end but nothing.

She was magnificent in there. She is brilliant, with her sharp mind and astute responses. She knew what the right decision was. It was spot on to what I had concluded myself. After she left, I pulled the plug on Gino's' funding and terminated all his contracts with my company, but I wasn't done with him. I wanted to go after her, but I had something to take care of. Something that couldn't wait. My phone buzzes on the glass surface of my desk from an incoming message.

C: Ready when you are.

A: On my way.

I rise from my desk, casting my gaze at the wall to where I had her restrained, recalling the taste of her on my lips. Yet, an invisible chain bound her to a hellish realm—a nightmare created only for her. An inferno where she remained ensnared, devoured from within, and I couldn't reach her.

Once on the highway, I accelerate the car, hurtling into the darkness for the twenty-minute drive. Drizzling rain obscures the illuminated streets as I reach the ancient house nestled in the woods. Concealed behind trees, the house appears abandoned, deliberately crafted to avoid attention. Only a barely visible black road hints at its presence, either concealed by the speed limit or by those already acquainted with its existence. Only the Consortium visits this place. The house has a wood wrap-around porch missing two slabs of two-by-fours and an old, rusted swinging bench. The house might look abandoned to some, but out here, that's the look we were going for, so it's not easy to find.

There are sixty-six members, but only ten I truly trust concerning Veronica.

I walk up to the door, and it opens with a scream from the hinges. "Where?" I ask.

I follow him inside, where the old fireplace is burning, casting the only light in the room. Ten cloaked figures with plague masks encircle a man confined to a chair.

A cloak and mask are promptly placed in my hand. I quickly pull it over me, ensuring my anonymity as I step into the circle. Gino is bound and gagged, attempting furtive glances and struggling against his restraints. Faint red marks on his wrists reveal his prior struggles. His muffled screams fill the room as I near.

Extending my hand, I receive a pair of black leather gloves. Slipping them on, I permit the removal of the gag, granting him speech. "Who the hell are you?" he gasps; voice hoarse from his screams.

Dressed in his work attire, his shirt stained and evidence of incontinence at his feet, he trembles in fear. His panicked eyes dart

around the room, his demeanor a stark contrast to the arrogance
that once resided in them.

"Gino, Gino, Gino," I echo mockingly. "What shall we do with
you?"

"Alaric, you son of a bitch! I—"

"I would watch your tone and choice of words. Such impu-
dence led you to this predicament like calling someone a bitch and
a cunt."

"You can't be serious!" He laughs hysterically, but I see the fear
in his eyes. I'm feeding off of it.

"I'm afraid not."

"She's just an intern! I get it, you're sleeping with her, but she
ruined my company—"

"You did that all on your own. I'm not here because of your
company. What your company is worth is nothing to me. Her actions
in those five minutes surpassed your two decades in this business.
The issue, however, is your blatant disrespect for what belongs to me."

"I-I didn't know," he stammers. "I heard she's nothing but a
bitch and a whore."

The contemptuous words kindle a fiery rage within me. Valen
hands me a sharpened butcher knife, and the man's eyes widen in
horror. "P-please. I'm sorry," he pleads. "P-please, please. I promise
not to say anything. I saw nothing. Just…release me."

"My concern for your future utterances has waned, Gino."
Raising the knife, its gleaming blade catches the firelight. "Your
fate was sealed the moment you insulted her."

I bring the blade down repeatedly; each strike a visceral mani-
festation of the trauma she endured. The splatters of blood deco-
rate my mask and gloves, echoing the rhythm of my swings. The
memory of her face, that vulnerable expression, fuel my unre-
lenting fury. I continue until my arms can no longer bear the strain.

"Jesus," Draven says when I'm done.

"Jesus isn't going to help anyone that has hurt her. I suggest
you spread the word. Veronica is mine."

Returning to the campus library, I delve into the history of Kenyan and the Order. Victoria's induction into the Order wasn't due to birthright; I look up and stare at the old wooden shelves. The library is dark except for the light in the hallway and the small lamp I have on by the brown desk in the corner, casting shadows on the leather-bound books, their words akin to scriptures. I recognize how history underpinned governments and beliefs, ours veiled within cryptic texts penned by the privileged. Countries adopt them to create a way of life, but ours is a secret, hidden in riddles inside books penned by assholes with fat bank accounts. Temptation, greed, gluttony, and sin. A way to cover it all when it's committed. It's all a prophecy, you're born or married into it.

Charles Devlin adopted Veronica because she isn't his biologically, so that means she is no different than Prey. Only children fathered by a man born into the Order are members automatically and the ones that are not mentally stable attend here. The question is, what is her mental instability that was strategically put in place to be accepted here as the heir of the Devlin estate? It had to be manifested. She has to see a doctor on the fourth floor to be screened. Dr. Wick is the only shady bitch that's heartless enough to have medical notes of her patients' progress, offering band-aids to the problem Veronica would have.

I sit back in the uncomfortable wooden chair, scanning the gold spines before me. *She's Prey,* I think to myself. Prey chooses. I read that she was enslaved as Prey and she must have gotten the mark when initiated. I close my eyes, trying to remember what she said in the shower. Her gaze lingered on the claw-footed bathtub. That same fearful expression returned in the boardroom. She didn't have the mark when she chose. She chose me that night at the initiation party.

The spine of a book with three words in Latin catches my attention, Praeda Litatio Captura. They all mean Prey in Latin. I know that because my grandfather made sure I learned Latin. Turning its pages, dread tightens my gut at the sight of the mark—the same one I saw on the back of her neck. I turn the page, and I want to throw up. Disturbing images fill the pages, depicting ritualistic horror. Illustrations of a woman standing in a Victorian-era bathtub with men around her. They have whips, and she's naked. *Do you have a shower?* The way she looked at the claw foot bathtub. It was the same look I saw in the boardroom. Fear.

The bottom of the picture reads Peccator (Sinner) Rituale (Ritual). Not being able to read more, I close the book like it's the Antichrist. I slide my chair back with force, causing it to fall back, wanting to kill them all, but knowing I can't. There's more of them and not enough of us. The Consortium knows there are sick bastards at the top, but this is some archaic sick shit that they have done to her.

I pinch the bridge of my nose and close my eyes. *Oh, baby. I'm so sorry.*

I need to get her out of Charles Devlin's house. He delivered her on a platter because of his bitterness. His hate. The purpose behind all of it, is for her to find the realization that she is fundamentally animalistic, repulsive, and putrid. Unworthy. Cleansing herself under the pretense of abuse and repeating the same thing over and over until ultimately, she gives up.

I look around and place the book back on the shelf, knowing I can't come back. They will know because someone is always watching and you can't trust anyone. I'm walking out to my car and dial Portman.

"Is this a new thing?" I look up from the menu when I hear her voice. "Spying on me while I work?"

My gaze returns to the menu. "I'm here for a cookie and cream milkshake. I liked it the last time I was here."

She shakes her head and writes it down. "Anything else I can get you?"

"Yeah, when can I take you out on a date?"

She takes the menu from my hands, and I meet her clear blue eyes when she says, "I think we're past that."

I shake my head. "I don't think so...no...not at all. Have you ever been on one?"

I watch her swallow when she looks out the window with an expression between doubt and uncertainty for a few seconds. "No," she finally says.

"Me either. It will be both our first time then."

Her gaze shifts to mine. "Why?"

"Because I never got the opportunity to ask you."

"I think that ship has long since sailed. You don't need to take me on a date or go through all the trouble. Under the circumstances, I'm a sure thing."

"See...that's the thing. It's not what I want."

She places the ticket on the table. "Stop it...stop playing games with me." Her eyes get glassy. My stomach turns into knots because I'm not playing a game with her, but in her mind, I am not to be trusted. I get it. I've been an unredeemable asshole to her, and I don't deserve her. But fuck I want to make it right. "I'll be right back."

I'm about to go after her but don't want to push her. I don't want her to go back home after her shift, so I wait. I hear the blender turn on, and when it stops, it's not Veronica but Dorothy bringing me the glass with a straw. She looks older than I remembered. She has wrinkles around her mouth from years of smoking. Her skin looks like paper when it's been in your pocket too long. Her hair is dull and stringy with streaks of gray, but she's a good woman and stays on top of all the gossip from both schools. Last I heard, she was friends with Mrs. Bedford before she died. I've overheard my mother mention her once or twice. Her father left her this diner last year after he passed away, and she made it into a retro restaurant open twenty-four hours.

"Funny seeing you here, son. I'm surprised to see you in this neck of the woods," she says in a raspy voice, placing the glass on the table.

"I came to see someone."

"Ahh, Veronica. She's a looker, but I gotta say...you're wasting your time."

"Oh, yeah. How's that?"

I'm curious. I want to know what she thinks of her and the reason behind saying that to me. I'm sure Dorothy can tell me more about Veronica than her mother ever could. The only person that knew her was my cousin—her best friend, but she is dead. I think she was the only person who knew Veronica inside and out. I wasn't very close to Alicia, but I respected her and thought if she was best friends with Veronica, there was a reason.

That night at the party, I tried to blame Veronica, but the reality was, I wanted a reason. A reason not to feel a certain way for a girl and I used it. It was easy to accept the worst and not fight the feelings with my inner self so I could open my eyes and see her for what she really is, an innocent woman.

"She doesn't give any of the boys that come in here the time of day. They come in here like hound dogs every time they see her. Adam is always giving them looks when they give her a hard time."

"Who gives her a hard time?"

She snickers. "The boys. Why...you goin' kick all their asses? I see the way you look at her. You're Claire Riodrick's boy." I'm not surprised she recognizes me. "A Riordan because of your father." She leans her hip on the table and lowers her voice, making it sound raspier. "I know who you are, and I can guess why you're here, but I do know that girl isn't for the likes of you. She's kind. Whatever business you have with her, leave it at Kenyan or at work where it belongs. This is the only place I have seen that poor girl smile and be herself. So don't you come in here messing with her head," she warns.

"I think you got it all wrong. It's not like that."

She scoffs. "Oh, you goin' to marry her?"

My eyes widen in horror at the sound of the word marriage. I don't believe in it.

Is she insane?

"That's what I thought. I know about your little deal with the big dogs. I got ears. I've heard plenty about you, Alaric. I know she is interning at your company because she told me but refused to give up her shift here at the restaurant. She likes working here. She works hard and I'm tired of her getting treated like a piece of meat all the damn time. I'm sure you have plenty of women that would love to play games with you, so you can toss them aside when you're finished, but Veronica isn't one of them," she says morosely. She's about to leave but pauses. "Say hi to your mom for me. She's a real nice lady." And then walks away to take other orders, leaving me stunned by how she defended Veronica.

I cast my gaze toward the kitchen, where a hand can be seen banging a silver bell, and watch Veronica prepare her orders. She said she would be right back but sent Dorothy because she's afraid. I know I get under her skin and don't care if I look like an idiot staring at her. She's a mystery I want to unravel. She's too smart to be working in a restaurant, and most people from Kenyan wouldn't be caught dead working here. It's obvious she's different and has learned to play both sides, but this is the side she prefers because it's where she feels important, valued and loved by the people working around her. I don't want to take that away from her. It's humbling, but I'm determined to get my date with her, and I won't take no for an answer.

CHAPTER 21
Veronica

After my shift ends, I find myself walking the familiar path toward the bus stop. An unsettling sensation of being watched clings to me like a shadow, causing my nerves to prick. I can't shake it off, even though every time I glance around, the empty streets at four in the morning reveal no one lurking in the shadows. I could've stayed at the diner until five, but I'm tired, and the thought of a hot shower followed by a brief nap is all that fuels me, especially when I'm done at his office at nine-thirty. I didn't expect him to see me at the restaurant after I told him not to go there when I was working or that he would ask me out. He, of all people, dared to ask me out on a date. I can't deny a small blossom of hope unfurled within me. The way he looked at me when he posed the question was a puzzle—a mixture of sincerity and confusion.

Alaric Riordan is a man who doesn't bend, who doesn't apologize or acknowledge regret for any of his actions. And certainly not for the torment he subjected me to. If there's anyone on this earth for whom he'd reserve even a whisper of remorse, it's not me.

I hear a purring of an engine, and from the corner of my eye, I spot his Ferrari, but I ignore it and keep walking to the bus stop.

"So, what time do I pick you up on Friday?"

I stop and turn to face him. "You don't take no for an answer, do you?"

"No. When I want something, I get it."

"Of course, money is no object to someone like you, and because you have so much of it, you get what you want. It doesn't matter what anyone thinks. Money…power and all that."

"This has nothing to do with money or power. Just a man asking a woman out on a date."

"What for? You've already had me; the last time I checked, I didn't meet your standards. If you want a date so badly, ask Sasha or Tara. Last time I checked, you were fucking her and did your cousin a favor. Go ask them; I'm sure they will oblige. Maybe both of them at the same time. It all depends on your kink."

"I don't want them."

"I don't think you have trouble finding a woman, Alaric. After all, you have me for your little sick game for a while. The only reason I talk to you is because you have the decency to give me a choice and don't have to fake it."

"Did you the first time?"

I pinch my brows together, rub my arms, and stop walking to face him. He applies the break, and I ask, "First time?"

"The night at the party. I'm not talking about sex. Did you fake it?"

My instinct is to tell him yes, but the truth is, it would be a lie because everything I felt that night was real. It was the last time I felt like myself. It doesn't matter if I tell him the truth because it's too late. "No," I say and keep walking on the sidewalk.

"Get in, Veronica," I hear him call out. "You're not going back there. You're staying with me."

I pause a step. "But–"

"Don't piss me off," he warns. "Get in the car."

He jumps out and walks around, opening the passenger door, and waits for me to enter. I could run, but what would be the point. He will find me; the last thing I need is a pissed-off Alaric.

In my mind, I want him to get annoyed with me and end this little game. I would go back, and the real nightmare would begin, but deep down, I want him to keep me like this, belonging to no one. Dorian can only interfere if I'm playing a game with Alaric, but how long? A cynical voice in my head drowns out the faint hope. *This is how to get back at you*—a strategic move to infiltrate my thoughts and emotions. If he had truly cared, truly understood the depth of that night, he would've seen through the lies they said about me. He would've sought me out and attempted to hear my side of the story. But he didn't. His inaction spoke louder than words ever could.

The drive to his house is silent. We don't say a word to each other the whole way.

As we pull up, he graciously opens the door for me, and I step into his home, mirroring the scenario from the first time. The opulence of the surroundings is as overwhelming as before, everything unchanged except for one conspicuous detail: the bathroom. Its centerpiece—the bathtub—is now conspicuously absent.

A cold tremor traces its way down my spine as I catch sight of the pipes, now tightly sealed, starkly reminding me of what used to exist there. A mixture of relief and unease washes over me. While seeing it is a chilling reminder, I'm grateful I don't have to look at it.

"I had it removed last night," he says, standing behind me. "I'm sure you would prefer the shower." He knows. I nod and look away. "I'm not a fan of them either, to be honest. It's like bathing in your own dirty piss."

"Is that supposed to be funny?"

He shrugs. "It's the truth. I never used it. It came with the house."

"So you're just going to leave it empty like that?"

"What would you like me to put in its place?

I look around and notice the shower has glass doors—"What if the entire bathroom was an open shower. No glass doors but had an area to sit and lie down like you were bathing in the rain."

"Is that what you would like to do? Bathe in the rain."

"If it was warm with the sound of thunder minus the lightning," I say mindlessly. He steps close behind me, and I can feel the heat of his body. I must smell like food. "I should take a shower. I must smell like fried food," I add, changing the subject.

"I don't mind. I'm kind of hungry," he replies. All I can think about is yesterday when he ate my pussy in his office, and we were late for his meeting. The sounds that escaped my mouth. I always thought that women sounded like that when they had an orgasm because they were faking it or it was staged. I guess not all the time. He places his hand on my waist and pulls me toward him so my back can feel how hard he is for me. "Are you hungry, Veronica?"

My thighs clench. My pussy throbs hearing the timbre of his voice. The heat from his hand on my waist. The scent of his cologne. "How did you know about the bathtub?"

His lips are close to my ear. "You said you preferred a shower?"

He knows, but he won't admit it, and I'm unsure if I'm grateful or upset. He brought me here to show me. My head is pounding at the same time my body is aroused. Confusion, indecision, and want swirl inside me.

He turns on the shower and slowly unzips the back of my uniform. "Let's take a shower. You look tired, and you've had a hard day."

He faces me naked in the shower, and I can't keep my eyes from wandering between his legs. His dick is perfect. It's thick and long, even when it's not hard. His stomach is chiseled, and he has those deep V's that disappear like deep valleys. When my eyes trail up, he has a gleam in his eyes; he places gel in his palm and begins to wash, stroking his long shaft.

He turns around, and I can't help but admire his ass and strong legs. There isn't an ounce of fat on his frame. He looks perfect, and he knows it. The water slides over his muscles, and the smell of his shower gel permeates the air. I place shower gel in the palm of my hand and take the opportunity to wash myself, closing my eyes under the spray and wetting my hair.

The third time I close my eyes to rinse the conditioner from my hair, the energy inside the shower shifts like an impending storm, and I know he's right in front of me. When I open my eyes, I can't help how he stares at my body like a piece of art.

"I love to taste you, but I want to be inside you." He pulls my bottom lip, pressing his thumb into my mouth. "I want you to suck my cock."

This is what he wants, but secretly, so do I, and there is nothing more satisfying to a woman than when she enjoys the man she has sex with. He pulls his thumb out, and I drop to my knees, slowly noticing his jaw tensing in anticipation. His nostrils flare when I touch his shaft, feeling it rapidly growing in my hand. I stroke it once, then twice. I lick my lips, look up, and slide his engorged cock into my mouth. I hear him hiss through his teeth when I take him deep, hitting the back of my throat. I relax and breathe through my nose, trying to accommodate his size.

His hands slide to the back of my head, threading his fingers in my wet hair. I dig my nails in his thighs when I bob my head. Faster and faster. "I love the way you take my cock. I'm going to fuck your throat hard... until you give me that pussy."

I want him to, but I know, deep down, why I won't give in to him so easily. My mind can tell me otherwise, but I know. I fear he will end this, and I don't want it to end. I want to stay with him. I prefer him to punish me than to return home to what awaits me. For the first time, I have to admit I am scared. I am afraid I will die in Dorian Black's hands.

I take him deep, loving how his length feels in my mouth and throat. He fucks my mouth hard, almost choking me, but I love it. The feel of him and the power I have to make him lose control. I almost can't breathe, but he's close, and I want to taste him. I grip his ass, pushing him deeper into my mouth.

"Take it, baby. You're so good." He growls, biting his bottom lip and holding my head, moving faster. He's panting by the time he shoots his cum down my throat. I sputter, trying to swallow it. It drips down my chin, dropping between the valley of my breasts. When he pulls out, and I shoot him a glance, he cups my face. "You're mine," he says breathlessly.

He lays me on the soft bed after we dry off, hovering over me between my legs. His elbows are resting on the mattress on both sides of my face. My eyes are trying to adjust to the darkness of the bedroom.

"Are you okay?" he asks, his eyes trailing my mouth, and I respond with a simple nod. My jaw is a bit sore, but I liked it. "When you decide to let me have you, and only when you decide, I want you to be sure. I want you to want me because it's what you want." He presses his warm cock between my legs. A whimper escapes my throat at how good it feels, and he looks down where he's pressed against me. "Because I'm not going to stop once you let me, but I do like that sassy mouth."

I place my palms on his chest, lift my chin, and whisper, "Are you telling me you want to be friends?"

"Are you being funny?" I giggle, and he smiles, placing a kiss on my forehead. "Let's sleep; I have a meeting in a few hours."

CHAPTER 22

Veronica

After waking up in the most comfortable bed, I take a shower and notice everything he picked out that day we went shopping is in his closet. All the clothes take up residence on an entire wall. He has a note on a black double-breasted blazer that reads, "Wear this."

When I open the bottom drawer where the shoes are neatly placed, there is a lingerie set, also black, and a note that reads, "I want to see how bad you are."

No, you don't, I tell myself. He doesn't want to see how bad I am because every time I have let that side out, it has been because I have had to act that way. At first, it was hard, and I felt a certain type of guilt that always came after every penance in the form of a ritual. It always boiled down to that event, like a turning point. I was now one of them. A hypocrite. I hated how they began to make fun of me everywhere I went, at school or a party. It became easier after Alicia passed. There was no one to talk to or trust with all my secrets. That side of me became a weapon, and Alaric wants to see it in its pure form.

The elevator doors slide open. "Twentieth floor," the voice from the elevator announces. When I walk toward the reception area, Sergio practically jumps out of his chair and rounds his desk. "You look gorgeous," he says, clapping his hands excitedly and checking out my outfit. "Dolce & Gabbana blazer dress and those ankle boots are perfect."

"Thank you."

"He's in his office. He's in a meeting, but I think they should be wrapping up," he says, but I don't miss the way his lips turn slightly into a frown when he finally says, "Go on in."

I stare at Alaric's door, the butterflies in my stomach dying slowly. He left early for a meeting. The alarm I set on my phone is what finally woke me up.

I turn the handle on the door without knocking, and the sound of female laughter hits me like a slap in the face. "Alaric, it was just breakfast–"

Tara is sitting with her legs crossed in a short skirt. She crosses and uncrosses her legs to attract his attention. Her blouse is open, revealing the top of her bra, screaming I'm a desperate bitch and want to fuck.

My eyes lift and land on Alaric. He looks relaxed without his suit jacket, sporting a blank expression, and I instantly hate that I'm wearing the outfit he picked. My eyes flick back and forth between them. How comfortable they look sitting in his office. He must have taken my advice and took Tara out for breakfast.

"I trust you had a good meeting or…breakfast. Is there anything you need me to work on?" I ask formally.

"Veronica, I heard about your internship here," Tara says in a catty tone.

"I'm sorry about your engagement with Reid."

She smiles dryly. "It worked out alright, I guess. I was dating Alaric, if you can call it that. I think we were better suited than Reid and I were. Arranged marriages work out like that sometimes, and I guess me and Alaric have something in common. We aren't committed. I did hear about yours. Dorian Black. Congratulations. I'm surprised he hasn't swept you away yet."

Bitch.

Tara's father was brought into the Order years ago, but they didn't require Tara to attend Kenyan. She inherited her father's company and has been doing business with the Riordans for years. It was the reason behind the initial arrangement that she and Reid were supposed to be married. Tara has been dying to be tied to one of the sons of Kenyan. She failed with Reid and is trying to get Alaric to commit.

"I'm hard to please," I reply, giving her a closed-lipped grin. My gaze lands on the time from the phone clasped in my hand. Five hours. Five hours and I can get the fuck out of here, and then there is one day left, and I don't have to step foot in his office again.

"I trust you already had breakfast. Ours was great. We went to this little café down the street after our meeting," she drones on, my gaze now locked on Alaric. "The pastries are so good—"

My gaze serenely swings to Tara. "Are you trying desperately to tell me you two are still fucking?" I walk slowly toward the corner of his desk and lean on the edge, watching her raise a brow. Alaric is silent. I swing my long hair to the side, letting the side of Veronica that everyone expects to show up. "Let me guess, he chained you to the wall over there." Her eyes shift to the wall where the chains and different cuffs hang hidden from view, and I know I'm right. "You sucked his cock; he may have...sodomized you, breath play, or chained you." Her eyes light up in recognition while she relieves those moments with Alaric. I hear him clear his throat, but I ignore it. "He does that to every woman, and you're no different. You just...think you are."

"How would you know?" she asks cynically.

I lean close, placing one hand on the arm of the chair she is sitting in, my lips inches from her ear, and say in a soft sultry voice, "It sucks to suck, doesn't it? It must be exhausting trying to fuck your way into an alliance."

I lean back, and her lip curls in a snarl. "Funny coming from you because everyone knows you're a twisted...sick whore probably on meds. I'm surprised Dorian agreed to marry you when no one wants you. You crazy bitch."

"That's enough," Alaric barks.

I let out a sardonic laugh. "It's okay, Alaric. She's right. She's just mad that so am I. The only difference is, I don't give a fuck, and she does." I push off and walk toward the door.

"Where do you think you're going?" he asks in a hard tone.

I ignore him, walking out his office door, my skin on fire, wishing it would melt the clothes he bought me and, like an idiot, I'm wearing. I close the door and meet Sergio's surprised expression.

"Is everything alright?" Sergio asks.

I walk to the elevator pressing the button repeatedly. "Everything is fine."

"Of course," he mutters.

I pull out the Uber app and order a ride, not caring if I don't complete the internship. What are they going to do, fail me? Alaric would give them a bad report, my professor will fail me, and I won't graduate. Who gives a shit. It's not like I have a promising job when I graduate. It will give them all something else they can criticize and use to make fun of me.

"You know I don't need babysitting anymore. I've learned my lesson from Zach," Melody says, plopping on the couch with a bag of freshly made popcorn. It's Friday night, and I shut off my phone and asked Dorothy for two nights off, promising her I would take the late afternoon shifts to make it up to her, avoiding contact with anyone at Kenyan.

"I know, but maybe I needed to be around a friend for a change."

"It's Friday night," she says, while I'm scrolling through the streaming apps, looking for something to watch. "You're over twenty-one. You could be at a dance club with a hot guy or on a date. Yet, you're holed up here with me. Maddison said you have hot friends."

I pause my fingers on the remote. "Trust me. You are better company...and...those aren't my friends."

I hear the front door open and slam shut, but I continue scrolling, looking for something to watch in the horror section.

"Of course, they are your friends. Maddy said they want to hang out, but you always refuse their offer."

I cringe inwardly because Jess did point that out the night of Draven's party, but I shrugged it off and changed the subject. Melody has no idea about Kenyan or the things I've done.

"They aren't,"Adam says, plopping beside me on the couch.

Melody gives a side glance. "How would you know?" she asks between bites.

"Because I know, and that is all I'm saying. I've worked with Veronica for almost a year and have never seen them show up until recently. Take her word for it"—he leans forward and snatches the popcorn from her hand—"we are more her friends than they are."

"I was eating that," she snaps.

"Sharing is caring."

"Why are you here and not on a date with Lizzy?"

"Because I wanted to hang out with my friend Veronica. Besides, Lizzy can't go out tonight. Her parents are a little strict." He hands me the bag. "Why did you take two days off?" he asks me.

"I needed a break."

He nods. "How is the internship going?"

"I wouldn't know because I left Thursday morning and haven't returned."

"Is that why you have your phone off?"

I haven't told anyone what happened or how I felt seeing Tara in Alaric's office or the fact that he took me up on my advice and went on a date with her after his meeting, like those cliché dates where a guy asks the girl to go out with him for coffee. What's worse, I lashed out and acted like a jealous idiot when there was nothing to be jealous of because I was there for two entirely different reasons, and none of them had anything to do with dating or a serious relationship. I turned him down when he asked, but seeing and hearing about it by the horse's mouth hit home. *"You're getting married to Dorian Black in two months, Veronica. You never meant anything to him, and you never will."*

I scroll and land on *Nightmare on Elm Street*. Perfect.

"Really, that one?"

"Yeah, why not."

"It's scary and messes with your head."

"That's exactly what I was going for, and it's not scary."

"I heard it was based on a true story where the guy couldn't sleep, and he checked himself into a psychiatric ward and was found dead, clawed to death or something."

"He must have fucked up somewhere."

Adam laughs, but then there is a knock on the door. He glances at Melody and then at the door when the knocking becomes louder.

"Are you expecting someone?" Melody asks.

"No," Adam responds, getting up to open the door.

Boom! Boom!

"Shit."

Adam opens the door, and I hear a familiar voice. "Where is she?" Alaric's voice sounds like he wants to murder someone and is on a rampage.

My heart hammers inside my chest, and my head pounds from how much I have hidden my emotional torment for the past two days. I haven't slept. I took an Uber to campus, then sneaked into the dorm room showers, slept last night in an empty dorm, took the bus to work, and ended up here after calling Dorothy and Adam. I never went home. I stopped at Target on the way here to buy some clothes from the clearance rack so I didn't look like a homeless person that hasn't changed their clothes. I learned what it felt like to air dry your underwear after hand washing it in the dorm room shower sinks.

"She's on the couch," Adams says, eating popcorn like nothing is happening. "We were beginning to watch *Nightmare on Elm Street*." He moves past Alaric and sits right back next to me, holding the bag of popcorn out to me so I can have some.

I avoid meeting Alaric's gaze, slide my hand, and grab popcorn while the opening credits roll up. "You're going to sit there and ignore me. I've been looking for you. You didn't come back—"

"You were busy, and I didn't want to interrupt your date with Tara. You two had a lot to catch up on. I ate breakfast on my own and figured out why should I go back. The internship was over anyway."

"It wasn't like that, Veronica. It wasn't a date."

Melody shakes her head in annoyance and mutters, "Guys are so stupid."

"Some...not all," Adam points out.

Alaric snorts and plops himself down between Adam and me, pulling me toward him so I have no choice but to lean on his side. "You didn't come home. You don't answer my calls because you shut your phone off, and you are not working at the restaurant. I had to beg Dorothy to give me Adam's address to find you."

"So," I quip.

"So...I was worried you didn't come home."

"Your home is not my home. What do you want?"

"I want you."

"So," I repeat.

Melody raises her brows when Alaric gets up, and when I look up, arousal spreads through me. He's wearing a fitted black hoodie that reads Saint across the front. His tattoos on his neck give him that bad-boy sex appeal he knows how to pull off when he is not in the office.

"It was nice seeing you and your sister again, Adam."

He picks me up and throws me over his shoulder, holding me by placing his palm on my ass.

"What the hell, Alaric!"

I watch Adam, the traitor, open the front door for him. "See you later, Veronica. Looks like you have a date for Friday night, after all."

"Traitor!" The front door slams shut.

CHAPTER 23
Veronica

"I kind of like you like this," Alaric says, palming my ass. "Feisty."

"Fuck off. Put me down."

"In a minute."

He walks over to a black Bentley, which unlocks when he places his hand on the door. He finally puts me down and slides into the driver's seat, pulling me in his lap. "What are you doing?"

"What does it look like? I'm driving."

"But I'm on your lap."

"Because you are driving with me."

"Are you crazy?"

"I don't know." He fires up the car and buckles us both in the seat. "That's what they say, but who knows, are people that kill others crazy?" He adjusts the mirrors. "Let me know if you can see through the rearview and side mirrors."

I nod. My hands tremble slightly because he is pulling out onto the road, and I have never been behind the wheel of a car before.

"Relax. I will never let anything happen to you. I've been worried about you. I thought—" he trails off.

"You know where the gas and the brake are?"

"I know the basics, just never been behind the wheel."

He maneuvers the car to an abandoned lot. "Alright. Try it out."

"I–I'm going to mess up your car," I say, stammering nervously.

He slides the palms of his hands over mine and rasps against my neck, "I have more." He slides my hair over the opposite shoulder. "I picked this one because it's a smoother ride and not as intimidating."

He removes his hands, and I panic. "No...no...put them back."

I hear the smile in his voice. "Alright." I close my eyes when I feel the heat of his hands over mine.

"Don't let go."

He kisses my neck. "Never." His mouth wanders over my skin, causing a chill to slide down my back. "Relax, baby. I'm right here. You scared me. I couldn't find you, and what you saw wasn't how it was made to be. I had to get rid of her and sever ties with her company."

"Why?"

"Because she was a game, Veronica. It was the only way Reid could marry Jess."

That is probably why he didn't interfere in her little jealous rant in his office or didn't go after me when I walked out. Reid wanted Jess but was betrothed to Tara since they were in high school, and Alaric was the only way he could sway the Order and blackmail her. Since her father wasn't initiated into the Order by birth, his daughter had no freedom to sleep around before marriage. That was only reserved for offspring born into it.

I press my foot on the gas, and the car lunges forward, and I laugh when he grips my hands tightly over the steering wheel, the car picking up speed. "Slow down, you little speed demon." I let my foot off the gas as we come up on a turn. "Okay, slow down." I apply the brake harder than necessary, and he holds me so I don't fly forward. "Not so hard. You're doing good."

"Liar."

"You are. Turn the wheel to the left and let your foot off the brake. Don't press the gas until you get the hang of it."

"I want to go faster."

I did. Going slow is like sweet torture. I want to feel the rush of being scared but knowing he won't let anything happen to me. I love feeling safe in his arms.

Once I straighten the wheel, there is nothing but an open parking lot about a mile long. No car in sight. Just the moon in the dark sky and the yellow-orange glow from the streetlights.

"Alright. Press the gas."

"Hard?"

"However you want."

I press the gas and floor it, hearing the engine rumble and the tires screech on the pavement. My heart is beating so fast as the car picks up speed. Adrenaline surges through my veins, putting every cell in my body on alert, but I know nothing will happen— nothing will happen as long as he is with me because I know, deep down, he won't let it. The lights fly by like straight lines, and I can't see the end of the street.

"Let go of the gas." I do. "Now Brake!"

I brake, and his arm feels like steel wrapped around me, holding me to his chest. The seat belt locks us both to the seat. The screaming sound of the tires fill my head. I'm panting by the time the car makes a complete stop.

I lean back and feel him kiss my head. "You did well. Did that feel good?"

"Yes."

I have to admit that it felt good. I felt like all my problems faded in those seconds. In those seconds, Alaric found a way I could feel free.

"Let's do it again."

We do. He teaches me how to turn the car around and apply the brake in different scenarios. How to park and parallel park for the next five hours.

"Thank you," I tell him, seated in the passenger seat.

"Anytime. We'll come out here whenever you want, and I'll teach you."

I look down at my hands and slide my thumb over where he

held them on the steering wheel, wishing his words were true because I know there wouldn't be a whenever.

"Hungry?"

"Yeah."

"I know this place that makes a great sandwich, and they have ice cream shakes."

I smile. "Okay."

We pull into an All-You-Can-Eat diner the next town over. The Bentley sticks out in the parking lot with the regular working-class cars like Hondas, Toyotas, and Fords. The place is really half diner and half gas station. When you walk in, three aisles have quick essentials like a convenience store. The rest of the place is a diner with eight booths, four on each side. They have a soda machine like in Dorothy's diner, but this place has a jukebox that you don't have to pay to play a song. You can send a text, and it will give you a list of songs you can play.

When we walk in to be seated, some kids, who look like they're still in high school, are sitting in two booths next to each other.

After we place our order, I ask, "You come here a lot?"

"When I want to think. When I need to get away from it all. I come here and eat like the common folk."

"I never would have thought you ate at a place like this."

"I did in high school and freshman year of college."

I imagine him sitting here like those kids in the back booths laughing and making jokes with their arms around a girl. How I wished my life were so simple.

"That must have been fun."

"Not really. Not when you were destined to be the first of your generation to be the greatest. Reid, Alicia, Valen, and the twins. They were all younger than me. I had to prove to everyone that I was better and that the other members attending Kenyan weren't. No sweat."

"That must have been...stressful."

"Yeah, and then the whole marriage thing didn't appeal to me either. Everything was thought out and chosen to benefit others;

you were just created to follow it. I honestly thought I had it bad. Until..." The waitress sets our meals along with our cookie and cream shakes on the table and walks away. "Until you.

He means finding out that I'm Prey and the shit I was forced into.

"There is nothing I can do about it. It's done. In two months, I belong to a different type of monster."

I slide my phone on the table with the text message open, letting him read Dorian's texts. He picks up my phone and scrolls through them, and his expression turn furious.

He places the phone on the table and slides it back across the table. "I'm sorry."

I lock the screen on my phone, wondering if he's sorry because I have to marry that asshole Dorian or if he's sorry about that night. It doesn't matter; nothing does. But I am grateful that I don't need to go home. That act alone is worth its weight in gold.

"I'm sorry about everything, Veronica."

"Is this your 'I misjudged you making your life miserable, and I feel sorry for you' speech."

He shakes his head after placing his shake down. "No, this is a I know I fucked-up speech, and I want to fix it."

There it is. The guilt and the pity.

"There is nothing you can do to fix it. Some people are destined for a great life, to fall in love, be happily married or happily single, and have gorgeous children. I'm not one of those people." I look at the high school kids laughing like they're in slow motion. The helpless feeling I hate making its way under my skin. "I've tried everything, and it all boils down to what I'm destined to be... unworthy of having anything good."

"I don't think that."

A laugh bubbles out of my throat, causing me to drop the sandwich. "A few days ago, I found that highly unlikely. You threw me out of your mother's house because I was there when she called me, so I could pick up a dress she bought, saving me from having to buy one because—" I trail off.

"Because?"

Rolling my eyes, I finish what I was about to say, "Because I'm broke. I make twelve bucks an hour plus tips. Do you know how much they take out in taxes or how much one of those dresses costs when you make peanuts?"

"Charles Devlin doesn't buy you clothes?"

"Ha! Unless it's out with him for some stupid ball or to sell me off. Oh...I can't wear the same thing twice because, God forbid, I embarrass the sick bastard. The only thing I do have is a roof over my head with utilities included."

I don't tell him I shower in the dorms because Charles found it amusing to install only bathtubs in the entire mansion to punish me.

"Stay with me."

I lift my gaze and see in his expression that he's serious. "Why?" I shake my head. "It won't change anything."

"There is something I want to change."

What would he want to change? In my mind, there is nothing that could, except my existence.

"What is that?"

"Our first time."

CHAPTER 24
Alaric

Relief settles inside me, seeing her in the passenger seat of my Bentley. I went crazy looking for her since yesterday, after telling Tara to never contact me again and that I was terminating any business we had from her father's company. She accused me of using her, but the truth was she had an expiration date, and it was passed due. What I fear happened when Veronica walked in. I couldn't panic, but I did after Tara stormed out.

I looked for her everywhere. I even called Valen, who told me to check the dorm showers, but I couldn't. It was too early, and I was not a creep looking in the women's showers, knowing they would be occupied. I decided to give her a day and would try again today until I had to bribe Dorothy to redo her kitchen so she would give me Adam's address. I swear that woman hates me.

"I missed you," I tell her.

I did. I couldn't sleep last night. I never thought I would ever need a woman to fall asleep, but I find that I need her. I want the warmth of her hair and the smell of the shampoo I bought her. The feel of her skin on mine, her lips parting when she is in a deep sleep. Lips I kiss when she isn't aware that I'm doing it.

After we shower, I drape a towel over my neck and notice her splayed out on the bed in one of the sets I bought her.

My cock instantly goes hard when my eyes slide over the slit between her legs from the crotchless panties that attach to the lace pieces on her hips. She's holding herself up with the palms of her hands behind her as her dark hair falls like a waterfall down her back.

I swallow hard. "You're gorgeous."

She always was. I walk over to a drawer and open it, pulling out the thigh-high socks similar to the ones she wore that night.

I watch her eyes widen when she spots them in my hand. "You weren't kidding."

"No. I'm not," I answer, handing them to her, so she can put them on and I can watch.

I wish I was a superhero with powers that could take us back in time. Because that night was a setup. They ruined us, and I was too blind to see it. I can still see the terror and horror in her beautiful innocent eyes replaying in my mind on repeat. The look she gave me screamed for help, but all I could see was betrayal. Her father had people watching her every move, but so did I. Except yesterday, and I was terrified. Sometimes it takes a person to disappear for a moment, knowing you might not get them back to realize what the mystery of death means. The end of the world you're currently a part of.

When she slides the last sock over her soft thighs, I kneel on the bed, feeling it dip with my weight. "Is this okay?"

She knows what I mean. I want her to want this as much as I want it. I slide the towel off my neck and kneel, completely naked, between her thighs.

"Hard or soft," I ask.

She smiles, and I think I just saw what an angel would look like. It would look like her. Because God could have only been the one to create something so perfect.

"How would you have wanted our first time to feel like?"

I knew the answer before she asked, but I wanted to ask her anyway. It's because the more I hear her voice, the more I can tell myself this is real. It isn't another woman touching me, so I won't have to close my eyes and imagine it's her.

She's here.

In my bed.

With me.

I slide my hand behind her neck and pull her to my chest. I kiss her, taking my breath away like the air thinned and I need oxygen. Our tongues search like they're seeking each other's secrets, and there is only one way to hear them, to consume them. I've never made love to a woman before, and now I know why. It's because of her.

If there is one part of my life I would redo, it would be the first time I looked into her eyes because I could convince myself to never let her go.

She pulls away, panting, her chest rising and falling. She lies back on the bed, her legs open wide like the first night. I dip my head, sliding my hands under her legs and gripping her hips, then lick her clit.

"Alaric...mmm." She moans.

Her sweet little cries slip through her lips every time I lick, careful not to suck. I want her to want me as much as I want her.

I slide my tongue and suck the soft skin of her inner thigh and notice the faded cuts she tries to hide. I lick and suck them, hearing her gasp. She arches her back, causing her full breasts to push out. She holds my head when I slide my tongue to her clit and finally suck, holding me to the spot she loves. I slide my tongue inside, fucking her pussy. She grinds her hips, fucking my mouth.

"Mmm...yes..." She mewls. "I need more, Alaric." I pull the crotchless panties open, hearing them tear. "Please."

I glance up, and the pupils of her clear eyes darken, following me when I hold myself over her, stroking the tip of my cock over her clit. "Right there?" I ask, playing with her clit with my piercing.

She bites her lip, gripping my shoulders. "Yes...more."

I tilt my head, holding her gaze, and push the tip inside her tight pussy. I almost bite my tongue at how good she feels. She falls back on the pillow, and I slide the rest of the way inside her in slow, smooth thrusts, holding her gaze and getting lost in her.

"I'm drowning," I whisper.

That is the most I have ever said to a woman, and I mean it. It's my first time—our first time. I slide all the way out and push in as deep as I can, filling her, stretching her.

Her hands slide down my back and grip my ass, pushing me deeper. Her legs are spread wide. I hook each of them over my arms, holding her, and I watch as my cock disappears inside her in measured thrusts. My cock swells with each thrust. My balls draw up, and I know I'm about to come, but I hold out for her.

"Come for me, beautiful."

Her hands slide down my chest then back up to my neck as she pulls me down, taking my mouth with hers and whispers, "Fuck me...fuck me hard, Alaric."

My nostrils flare, and I place one hand on the mattress and the other around her neck. "You don't know what you just asked for."

Her lips lift in a seductive smile. "You're the only man that can make me come. Now make me come," she says, licking her lips.

She whimpers when I enter her again. Over and over. Harder and harder. Holding her neck in the palm of my hand, I squeeze, allowing her just enough space to breathe.

"Harder." She moans.

I go even harder, fucking her like an animal. She comes with a scream, her pussy contracting, but I don't stop impaling her. It spurs me on, and I go harder, gripping her throat, my hips move faster and my ears ring, warning me that I am going to come hard. I know I'm constricting her air, but she keeps meeting my thrusts, and when we can't take it anymore and it becomes too much, she comes a second time. When I ease my grip on her throat, I come on a roar, watching her take gulps of air. We're exhausted and spent, her beautiful dark hair sticking to her neck. I push it away, still inside her, filling her with cum, licking and sucking her neck, leaving marks.

My tongue traces her ear as I slide out of her and whisper,

"Turn around, beautiful. I'm not done."

She turns around with her ass in the air on her elbows, and I slap her hard on her ass, making her yelp. My cum leaks out of her swollen pussy lips with every slap. I grip her by the hair hard and slide my finger up her slit, lubricating her tight hole with my cum. "Can I have it?" She mewls when I play with her tight hole. "Is this your first time?" She nods. "Good, I want all of your firsts and I'll take your lasts too. They think they have you but they don't know that you have always belonged to me."

"Alaric," she calls out my name breathlessly when I push in the tip of my finger, stretching her little by little. She's so tight.

"Play with your pretty pussy and lick your fingers." She slides her fingers inside her pussy and a sweet little cry escapes her lips.

"Mmm…" She moans when she slides them out and puts them in her mouth. "Your cum tastes so good in my pussy."

My fingers slide and entwine with hers around her clit, and I push them together, fucking her pussy and pressing my cock into her tight hole. She is so wet and swollen, but that doesn't stop her from pushing my fingers inside her cunt. Squeezing my cock deeper into her tight ass, she whimpers.

"Breathe, baby."

"You're so fucking big, and I feel so full." I push deeper, holding her by the hips and matching the speed of her fingers playing with her pussy. "It feels so good." A filthy noise escapes her lips. I pick up speed, ruthlessly fucking her in the ass. I pull my hand away and grip her by the hips, our skin slapping against each other, making clapping sounds. My heart is beating fast, and my chest tightens when I begin to come.

"Oh God…Alaric…I'm coming."

"Me too, baby." I pull her by the hair and lick the mark on the back of her neck while my cum fills her tight hole. "Mine." I growl.

CHAPTER 25
Veronica

After class on Monday, I head over to Babylon, the bar across the street from campus. Alaric is at work, and I want to avoid showing up at his office and raising questions. The rest of the weekend, we spent in bed, ordering takeout and watching horror movies. He told me about his childhood and the pressure his parents' expectations put on him. He showed me how sorry he was by worshiping my body.

The change in his behavior toward me could be because of guilt. His possessive words and how he brands my body make me crave him more than I should. My heart is reckless in holding on to the attention, enjoying the moment, knowing that it will all end at one point. *It will end, Veronica.*

I'd heard about life's guilty pleasures and thought they never existed for me, but it takes one person to show you everything you're missing. Then you realize how wrong you were and that it was because you were in the wrong room at the wrong time. If someone were to tell me that I could be set free but that I would never experience what it was like in his arms, I would prefer to be chained in a life of sin, suffering penance, because my life wouldn't mean anything without being in the arms of the man of my dreams.

My eyes adjust to the bar's darkness when I walk in from the afternoon sun, hearing the jukebox blare Nirvana's "Heart-Shaped Box." My eyes scan the pool tables, and I find Garret, Jess, Gia, and the Bedford twins, along with some of the guys from the swim team gathered around the table while Valen and Reid play a game of pool.

Jess waves at me from across the room to head over.

"Hey, I heard the big bad wolf has you holed up in his lair."

My cheeks heat, and I roll my eyes, trying to play it off. "I've been studying."

Gia bursts into laughter. "Is that what you call it, studying."

"Higher learning," I shoot back.

I walk over and grab a pool stick. "I got next."

"We were just finishing a game, and Valen lost."

I jut my bottom lip out when he grimaces a bit. "Poor baby, you lost to the big boys." He hates losing.

"I wouldn't necessarily say they're big," Valen teases.

"We are all bigger than you ass-wipe," Dravin chimes in, and I laugh through my nose.

"You should ask Jess. She knows," he retorts.

"Fuck you, dick," Reid barks.

Gia is trying to calm the situation down because Garret is also within earshot, and he is really quiet, while Jess nervously chews on her lip. "I can attest to that. He can hang," I add, setting up the pool table and lining up the break. He does have a bigger-than-normal cock.

Everyone swings their gaze to Valen with a questionable expression. Looking up at Reid, his dark eyes meet mine, surprised that they're not full of contempt. "Ladies first," he says.

I smile, lining up the shot; carefully, so my ass isn't hanging out of my pleated skirt.

"Hey, just because she's seen it doesn't mean she's touched it," Valen defends.

I feel a warm hand slide up my thigh, causing the nerves in my heart to tingle. "Seen what?" I hear Alaric's deep voice behind me.

. . .

I almost drop the pool stick between my fingers when I feel the hard ridge of his cock pressed on my backside through his pants.

"Nothing," Valen responds.

His lips skim my ear. "Are you being a bad girl, baby?"

Electricity runs over my skin, causing me to look up at our audience nervously. He's here. "We were discussing how big Valen's dick is compared to the twins and Reid."

"Hmm, is that so," he says with an edge in his tone.

With a smile, I line up the ball to break and shrug. "I've only seen it. I've never touched it." I shoot the ball, hearing them hit. I straighten, but his hand is under my skirt and over my panties, holding me against him.

Reid proceeds to line up his shot.

"It's okay, baby. I think everyone has seen Valen's dick." Jess and Gia laugh, and the twins snort. How he calls me baby makes me dream and wish that this is real, and I'm truly his girl.

When it's my turn, he lines up with me on the pool table, but I feel something soft and rubbery between my legs. I pause, and then I feel the vibration of a vibrator. My mouth drops open when the first wave of arousal slides between my thighs. My eyes widen. "Take the shot," he whispers.

I can't without missing the ball entirely. It feels so good, but I can't grind my pussy against it without everyone noticing. I shamelessly widen my stance and hear the small chuckle from his throat. I grind my teeth every time he circles my clit, stifling a moan. Gia and Jess are watching with raised eyebrows. Reid is smirking, and I want to flip him off. "I can't," I whisper.

"Mm...yes, you can."

I'm about to face plant on the pool table as a moan escapes my lips from the sweet torture. I wiggle his hand away, but his finger slides the vibrator inside me.

"I'm—I'm," I stammer, pressing my lips together, trying to focus on the shot.

Reid gives me a sly grin, dark eyes pinning me to the spot. "Take the shot. We're all waiting, "he says.

Time seems to slow down. The music fades in the background. The sound of Nirvana makes its way to Bush's "Glycerine." All I can feel is his hand fucking me with the vibrator. My chest rises and falls, pushing against my bra. Gia leans back on both twins, her lips mouthing, 'She looks so hot.'

Alaric's lips brush against the spot under my ear, and the pool stick almost slips from my grip. My eyes roll when Bush's "The Chemicals Between Us" begins to play. The little voice in my head whispers, *Play with him, Veronica. Be a bad bitch.*

I blink, gaining control, and when my eyes flick up to everyone watching me, my lips curve in a sultry smile. I slide the pool stick back and forth between my fingers like I'm stroking a long cock. I push my ass out and grind my hips against him.

"Deeper," I moan, not caring who's watching.

"Oh fuck," Valen says softly. "That's so hot."

I push the end of the pool stick while Alaric slides it deeper inside me, my climax building, and I'm about to come. I feel his other hand grip my hip. I shoot the ball in the corner pocket when I fall over the edge, coming on the vibrator around his finger. I bite my lip, and a little mewl crosses my lips; I drop the pool stick on the table. Alaric pulls it out of me and lifts me so I'm sitting on the edge of the pool table, wrapping my legs around his hips. He lifts the small vibrator on his finger, pushing it past my lips. "Mm..." I whimper, sliding my tongue and sucking it into my mouth, tasting my arousal. He pulls it out and slides it into his mouth with a groan.

"You two are so hot," Gia says.

I smile, resting my forehead on Alaric's black dress shirt. The first three buttons open at his throat. I close my eyes, breathing in his spicy scent.

"Fuck the game. It's more fun to sit and watch them."

Alaric raises his hand, flipping Draven off, and I want to die of embarrassment. I still feel awkward in front of Gia when it comes to Draven.

After the game of pool is over and Reid lets me win, I'm sitting in the booth with Jess and Gia, nursing a beer with a plague mask on it.

"It's good, and…it's cheap," Jess says with a smile.

Word must have gotten around about my money situation. Alaric must have told Reid. I heard that Jess and Gia didn't come from money, but Prey usually don't because they get in through scholarships, and they don't live in fancy apartments or mansions, except me. Since they married, their money problems evaporated like a cloud of smoke. There is nothing their men wouldn't buy or do for them, and they deserve that.

"It is," I say, taking a pull.

The back door by the exit near the restrooms opens with a screech, followed by a slam when it closes. My eyes swing toward the hallway, and my stomach flips with dread. Dorian walks in, eyes scanning the entire place until they land on mine with a malicious gleam.

Jess's gaze swings over, watching him approach. The guys are still playing pool in the back, and I want to jump over the booth and run toward Alaric, but that's what he would expect. Me to run away like a helpless animal.

"I thought I might find you here," he says, sliding in beside me.

"Why is he here?" Jess asks in a snarky tone.

Dorian looks between Jess and me in mock surprise. "She hasn't talked about me?" Gia shakes her head, glancing at me. "My name is Dorian…Dorian Black. I believe we haven't been formally introduced. I'm Veronica's fiancé."

Anger spirals underneath my skin at that word. It is the last word I want to be associated with when it comes to Dorian Black.

"I missed you in your class. I wanted to take you out to lunch."

I inch away, sliding farther into the booth. "What for? You know the rules, Dorian."

"I don't think it matters, princess." He lowers his voice. "It wasn't like lover boy over their objected to the vote. He couldn't care less. After he's through fucking you out of his system, you belong to me. In sickness and in health."

I'd rather in sickness so I can die.

"I think you need to leave," Gia snaps.

He slides a black box on the table, and I look away. "In a minute, Mrs. Bedford, I want to give my future wife her engagement ring. She will be mine in every sense of the word in two months."

"What the fuck are doing here, Dorian?" Alaric asks in a harsh tone.

"I came to see my future wife and..." he flips open the black velvet box, revealing a black marquis cut engagement ring on a platinum band, "surprising her with her engagement ring."

My lips form a thin line. The ring is hideous; it reminds me of him, fake with no class. The center diamond is huge and oppressive. I remember seeing a pin on Pinterest of ugly engagement rings, and I saw one similar to this one.

Reid leans on the table to take a look. "Dude, that shit's ugly."

"I agree," Dravin chimes in, leaning over. He glances up at me. "It looks like a ring you find in a 'This shit is ugly store,' and no one wants it."

Jess looks away in disgust, and Gia blows a puff of air out of her mouth when she takes a look. "Who would wear that thing?" Jess says repulsively.

Dorian takes it out, and I hide my hands under my thighs. "She will. Because she will wear whatever I tell her to. In two months, she's mine." He turns to Alaric. "It wasn't like you cared so much about her. I didn't see anyone lining up to take her hand. They do like to have fun with her, though." I look away because as much as I hate him and want it to be a lie, it's the truth. But right now, he can't do shit about me being with Alaric, and I'll die before wearing his ring or going anywhere with him before I have to.

Alaric's jaw is set, and his eyes are full of rage. The little muscle in his jaw ticks rapidly back and forth. "You're just mad because I would never choose to be with you. I'd rather die than spread my legs for you."

Dorian's lip curled. "Too bad, I'll enjoy spreading them for you."

"Touch her, and I'll cut off your hands. I would be careful what I do next if I were you," Alaric warns.

Dorian leans back in the booth, as my eyes dart to Alaric. His gray eyes provoking Dorian. You couldn't see a crucial flicker that he wasn't serious.

"You're gonna threaten me for touching my wife."

"She isn't your wife, and I've done worse for much less."

Dorian smiles. "Like Gino? I heard he went missing."

Valen clears his throat. My stomach rolls over thinking about that day when he called me a bitch and a cunt. What did Alaric do?

"I don't know what you're talking about. I...canceled his contract."

Dorian moves to slide out of the booth. "Canceled his contract." He repeats like he's thinking it over. "I like it. Well, I gotta go. I have a business to run." He glances around until his eyes reach me. "My lawyers will be in touch, princess."

Dorian starts to move away, but then turns and comes back. I reach for the ring and throw it at him, causing him to flinch when the ring drops to the wooden floor like a nickel. "I knew you were coming back because you forgot something."

He knows I would never want to marry him after what he did. He made sure kids in school would put tampons in my locker. I overheard Crystal Mathison say it was Dorian Black that told the incoming freshman football players going to Ohio to do it. I thought Alaric was behind it, but Alicia said he wasn't. He just wanted nothing to do with me. Dorian never had a reason. When the Order voted for him to marry me, I knew something was behind it because I would never go out with him or give him the time of day. Dorian Black and his father are like a disease. There is no cure for their form of cancer. They just keep coming back.

Dorian's eyes are slitted, unemotional, aimed right at me,

promising me that he will make me pay. He doesn't bend to pick up the ring; he simply smiles. A smile that doesn't reach his eyes. "You're mine, Veronica. And deep down, you know it."

"Yeah, I can tell she is ecstatic," Draven says morosely. "Get off of it, man. Everyone knows she wouldn't look at you if things were different. It's bad enough we have to listen to you. Take your ring and get the fuck out of here before we all lose our patience."

Alaric slides into the booth beside me and cups my cheeks, bringing my lips to his and kissing me savagely. "Let's get out of here."

When we leave Babylon, it is already well into the evening. Stars are in the night sky, and half the moon shines brightly. The guys, Jess, and Gia are all heading home, and it's just me and Alaric alone in the parking lot.

"It's been a while since I've hung out at a college spot."

I'm surprised he doesn't mention Dorian and his delusional behavior, but I feel he held himself back. I know how angry he can get. Then what Dorian and Alaric said about Gino and canceling his contract tumbles into my head.

"What did you mean when you said you canceled Gino's contract?"

He opens the passenger door of his Ferrari, and his eyes touch mine. "I severed business ties."

I slide inside the car. Before he closes the door, I notice him ogling the exposed part of my thighs between the hem of my pleated skirt and the tops of my thigh-high socks. "Really?"

He shuts the door and rounds the car sliding in, thinking that is the only answer I am getting, but he surprises me when he says, "You were exceptional at the meeting, and I would never let someone get away with disrespecting you. You were right, and I was the only person that caught it. No one that worked with me was able to, but you did. In five minutes."

No one has ever praised me. Not my parents for something I did. No one has ever thought I was smart. I just trucked along and went from graduating high school to beginning college. No one cared about my grades because no one asked. It feels good for someone to say that I am exceptional.

I blush and look straight ahead. "Thank you."

"I think you're very smart. I have looked at your essays on financial analysis, and they are good—really good."

"Thank you. It means a lot coming from you," I say in a very low voice, my heart fluttering in my chest, hoping it doesn't fold in on itself from falling deeper in love with him.

I recognized the feeling this morning when he kissed me passionately and then had Portman drop me off at school before he dropped him at work. The butterflies take flight when I think of all the dirty things he's done to me. How sore I am between my legs. The delicious sting I'll feel when he takes me again.

"I forgot to ask how your little hole is. I know I took you hard."

"It's sore but in a good way."

He glances down at my thighs and places his hand over them. "Why aren't you wearing the clothes I bought you? I love the socks, but I mean the other stuff. It's been more than a few days since you touched anything in the closet. "

After the incident with Tara, it reminded me why he bought me the clothes, and I didn't want to spoil what was blossoming inside me for him. I didn't want to cloud it with negative thoughts from my subconscious. I wanted him to desperately see the real me with the little time I had left.

"I didn't pick them at the store, and you always left a note telling me what you expected me to wear that day."

"That's because I thought it was better to buy you everything in the store so you could choose whatever you wanted."

Dumbfounded, I reply, "Oh."

I didn't see it that way. I just thought he wanted to control what I wanted to wear. Like Charles did.

"I only said that I preferred the crotchless panties because all I could think about was being inside you. I didn't want to shred every piece of lingerie you wore."

"You were so sure I was going to give in, huh?"

"Honestly, I have never been rejected before." He glances at me briefly. "You're the first."

After having dinner at an Italian restaurant and making it home, it's already nine-thirty, and I'm following him out to the backyard to the oversized swimming pool, glowing like a pool of blood.

"What is it with you guys and the red light in the pool?"

"It's a Kenyan thing. A signature for the team. Our logo has red in it, and the color of blood is red and rich."

"Like the sons of Kenyan."

"Yeah, like us."

He slides his shirt off his shoulders and removes his pants and boxers, standing completely naked at the edge of pool and facing me. His naked body is sculpted like a perfect statue. His strong arms and thighs, chiseled abs, and his large thick cock hanging between his legs.

"Swim with me."

"I'm super slow. All I can do is keep myself from drowning."

"That's okay. I'm a good swimmer."

He swims competitively and has a spot on the Olympic team, but he refuses for obvious reasons. Do I want to get in his pool with him? Of course, I do. But I'm scared. Scared that when this is all over, I won't be able to breathe without him. He is becoming the air I need so I can live another day, so when I fall asleep in his arms at night, I can wish for it to happen all over again. To be consumed by him.

I nod and slowly remove my clothes until I stand naked before him. He calls me over with his finger.

"Look at me," he says, touching my shoulders. I raise my chin up, and he kisses me fully. It is desperate but soft, full of a promise I can't figure out. Something is happening between us, or maybe it was already there waiting for us. For the right time.

I shiver when a light breeze hits my skin when he pulls away. His gray eyes hold mine when he whispers, "Swim with me. The pools warm."

He swims laps for the next twenty minutes. He's like a machine, his arms perfect, cutting through the water with measured strokes. I sit on a built-in ledge watching in fascination how perfect he is. His back muscles bunch with the effort. The temperature has dropped because a light fog is coming from the pool's heat, skimming the water's surface.

In the springtime in Ohio, the days are hot, but as night falls, so does the temperature, especially when you're naked in a pool. He stands between my legs while I'm seated on the edge of the pool's built in sun deck, sliding his hands over my thighs and stopping at my waist.

My head tilts, and I look up at the dark sky, watching the stars wink at me from above. If I could look up at the sky every night, I would want it to be with him.

Sometimes you wonder how someone you love could hate you. How could they hurt you or break your heart when you only wanted the opportunity to love them.

"What are you thinking about?" He rasps into my skin. His lips wandering down my throat.

"How much you hate me."

"Does it look like I hate you?"

"I don't know. Do you?"

His tongue slides up my chin, his lips ghosting mine. My nipples pebble from the breeze. "Let me show you. It's why I took you to my favorite place...a place I love the most. You can look at the dark sky you love so much," his thumb caresses my cheek, and he's staring deep into my eyes, "and let the angels and Gods watch us from above while I make you mine."

His hard cock crowns my opening, the air thickening around us with every breath I take. We're in a bubble, and nothing can break it. He slides inside me, stretching me inch by inch, never breaking eye contact. His soft lips skim mine in sweet torture. Tears prick my eyes at how smooth and gentle he is with his words, like a balm to my inner wounds. "I love you," he says softly.

A single tear slides down my cheek, hearing him say it. Those three little words mean so much.

"You're on a mission."

"How is that?"

I blink the tears away. "To steal all of my firsts," I say softly.

He nods, the skin between his brows pinching together like he's struggling with his emotions. He slides his fingers into my wet hair, holding me, sliding deeper inside, moving slowly.

Under the stars, we make love, but I can't say the words back. In my mind, it is too late. He...is too late. But those words have never been said to me before by anyone, and I want to savor them. Because I know what my future holds, and love isn't part of it. But I feel it, and that's all I ever wished for.

CHAPTER 26

Veronica

Dorothy places a rack of clean plates on the serving counter with a clink. "You have a visitor in booth eight, Veronica."

I look over and notice Dorian seated in the booth, watching me with rheumy eyes, reminding me of his father. "Yes," I say faintly.

"I got to tell ya, Claire's boy is better looking than that piece of work right there. Alaric's a ball buster, but the way he looks at you…ain't no man ever looked at you like he does."

"Are you sure it isn't because you got a new kitchen out of it?" I tease.

She leans close. "Nah, I would have told him where you were. It helped that Alaric's a tycoon. He could help an old lady out. Now that animal seated in booth eight gives me bad vibes. I think I heard about him a few years back when he was still in college. A few guys came here one night and said he was a real asshole. It's a shame he was like that to the girls too. He's a looker, but you can see it in his eyes when he looks at you."

"Me?"

"Oh yeah, I see it. I'm not sixty-eight for nothin'."

"What do you see?"

"Desperation."

A feeling of cold dread creeps down my legs because I can see it.

"Let me go see what he wants."

"Scream if you need anything. He looks the type."

If you only knew.

"What are you doing here?" I ask angrily.

He just wants to annoy me by showing up here.

"Is that any way to talk to your husband?"

"You're not my husband," I say through clenched teeth.

I hate every time I look at him; it reminds me of that night he flung the door open at the party. He had no right. It doesn't excuse Alaric for how he treated me, and I get that he's apologized, but what was Dorian's excuse? I never did anything to him.

He straightens the salt and pepper shakers, but he's trying to get under my skin. "Not yet." He slides his gaze over my uniform crudely, and I want to rip his eyes out. "You know, you don't have to work here. I think it's a waste of your time—"

"Save it."

"I can find other things you could be useful in doing. I have learned a lot of things about you, Veronica."

Creep. I don't miss the meaning behind his words, and I can't stand him. The way he looks at me makes my skin crawl. But the apple doesn't fall too far from the tree. Does it?

"How creepy of you. I'm sure you learned a lot from your father. He's disgusting and pathetic, just like you."

He smiles, but it doesn't reach his eyes. "I would be careful if I were you. You should be nice to me because *he* won't be able to save you. Once he is done with you, you must be cleansed of the filth." Fear sneaks its way in when I'm reminded of how this ends. The bathtub and the sound of water haunt me, no matter how hard I try to escape it and the memories it keeps. The heavy breathing… the pain from each strike, enough to hurt but not enough to leave a mark. He chuckles. "What's wrong?"

"Leave me alone." I turn, but he grips my wrist hard. I can feel my bones grind. I try to rip my wrist from his grasp, but he pulls me toward him. "You're hurting me."

He loosens his hold a bit. "Not yet. Soon. But I forgot to tell you, my secretary was upset."

"And? What did you do to her? Fuck her without asking," I retort.

He laughs, but it falls off. "Oh, I fucked her, but so did Alaric. I guess he can't help himself. He fucks everything that moves. She was upset he was a little rough on her throat the last time. The chains in the office didn't help either, but none of that surprises me. He did however tell me he doesn't give a shit about you before he turned down my business proposal. He's just using you to get to me because I'm marrying you. See, I always wanted you, Veronica. No guy could get the high school senior, but everyone with a dick wanted it. I admit I acted childish when I saw you two that night. I wanted to hurt you." I snatch my wrist from his grip in hurt and revulsion. "But when my father told me how special you are." My blood turns cold, and my skin feels numb. "I knew you would be perfect."

My jaw hardens. "You're sick, just like the rest of them."

His eyes gleam. "But I'm the only one that will fight to keep you. They...just use you, Veronica, but they have no plans to keep you. No one wants you but me."

"I hate you."

"I'm going to make you my whore, and you'll like it."

My hands shake.

"Is there a problem here?" Adam asks, walking up to me with a rag in his hand.

Dorian turns his head to look at Adam. "Hey, man. I was just here to check on my girl."

Adam swings his gaze between Dorian and me with a confused expression, and I shake my head slightly. Dorian slides out of the booth. "I'm trying to convince her to stop working here. She doesn't have to, but you know how girls are. Stubborn. I can provide for her, but she stuck in her ways."

"She likes working here," Adam says in a serious tone.

Adam would know if I was seriously dating someone, and the only guy he has seen me with is Alaric. I look over when a couple walks in, needing to be seated.

"Dorian was just leaving."

Dorian winks at me, and I want to throw up. "I'll see you later, babe, and remember to call me." He gives me a peck on the lips before I can turn my head, and I wipe my mouth in revulsion. "You'll owe me for that one," he says through his teeth.

"Have fun jerking off," I snap back. "I'm sure you're used to it." He grins and points at me while walking backward toward the exit with his jeans and sweater, looking like a trust fund reject.

When he walks out, I watch him cross the parking lot to his ostentatious-looking car, a gold McLaren sports car that looks like a shiny easter egg. Hideous, just like the owner.

"Who is that guy, and why did he say you're his girl?"

I glance up after peering through the window, making sure he leaves. "I'm not. Not yet."

"What do y—"

"Long story. If he comes in again, let me know so I can hide in the bathroom and tell him I'm not here."

"Want me to kick his ass?"

"No!" He raises his brow at my outburst. "Look, he doesn't play by the rules, Adam. He's well-connected and has all the money and resources in the world to—" I trail off.

"To what."

I sigh in defeat. "To make shit disappear like rich people do. He hates Alaric. He's trying to mess with him by using me," I lie.

I'm not sure about anything. I don't know what to believe, but what Dorian said about his secretary and what Alaric told him about me felt like getting stabbed with a hundred knives. They all burned because the truth hurts. I have to marry Dorian.

"Fine, if he comes back. I'll make sure to tell you and ask him to leave."

"Thank you," I say nervously.

"No sweat."

After my shift, I take the last trash bag on my way out. I texted Alaric and told him that my shift would run a little later and not to pick me up. I want to confront him, but what would be the point? He would continue with his life, and I would be trapped in my hell or...I could run. I have money saved. They would vote, and all would be in agreement to end me. I've thought of it a lot this past week. I could just take a bus, leave and go somewhere far away, and not tell anyone. It would give me time. I always wanted to leave Kenyan and go somewhere warm like California. Maybe Texas.

I toss the trash bag in the huge bin and freeze. I blink hard a couple of times. The exit to the left and right are blocked by three men, all wearing plague masks. The first time I saw one on the bus, I thought I was dreaming, but it was real because six are standing right now like the people in the movie the Purge. Disturbing.

It's still dark at 4 a.m. Two lamp posts are the only lighting in the back of the restaurant, and no one comes back here. I look to my left and right, backing away toward the door. "What do you want?"

My palms are sweating, and my hands are shaking. I clutch my bag under my arm, knowing they are not here to mug me. They stand rooted to the spot, looking like human-sized birds. A spine-chilling fear grips me as they move forward in unison like walls closing me in. I can't see their eyes. The eye sockets on the mask shine with the reflection of the lights. The black cloaks conceal their bodies. It could be anyone under those masks. They could kill me, and no one would know who did it. Tears prick my eyes.

"What do you want? I repeat.

Silence.

"Stop fucking with me!" I yell.

They shake their heads slowly, and my fear contorts to anger. "I'll fucking scream, and everyone will come out."

They don't respond. *Bastards.*

They keep walking toward me like they don't care if I scream for help or call 911. I reach into my bag, searching for my cell phone, trying to unlock it before pulling it out and dialing 911 while I scream at the top of my lungs. There are six of them and one of me. There is not much of a chance, and the back entrance to the restaurant is behind me. I would have to run screaming and dialing 911 all at the same time to give me a fighting chance.

My heart is beating wildly in my chest. My fingers are trembling, and the hair is sticking to the back of my neck. There is a sheen of sweat on the top of my lip. I'm terrified, but I can't show them fear.

I turn to run with my phone in my hand, trying to dial for help and screaming.

"Adam!"

I hear the sound of heavy footsteps as a gloved hand covers my mouth, and I'm lifted off the ground. I struggle, but whoever it is, is too strong. I hit the side of the mask and hear a loud grunt. I try to kick and scream, but it's no use. A large blacked-out SUV pulls up, and I'm shoved inside.

"You son of a bitch! Adam! Adam! Help!" I scream. The door slams shut. They place a dark hood over my head, and I try to kick and push when they tie my hands and feet together.

"Help!" I'm breathing fast, and my chest hurts. My voice is hoarse, and my throat burns. I feel something hard being stuffed in my mouth and a piece of rope tightening across my face. I have no choice but to breathe through my nose. I can feel the car moving and rustling on the road.

Tears prick my eyes when "Closer" by Nine Inch Nails begins to play. Tears crest on my lashes because I can't undo the ties from my hands or feet. I panic trying to slide my hands free. When I see that it's no use, sobs tear through my chest.

I can feel a hand on my shoulder, and I jerk away and bump

into something hard and solid to my right. It takes a moment to realize that I'm sitting in between two of them. They were sent to kill me. Tears are falling with every sob that bubbles up, muffled because of the ball of fabric in my mouth. I think of Alaric, hoping he finds out that I was taken by the Consortium. I feel stupid for telling him I would get off an hour later.

I close my eyes and pray.

After twenty minutes, the SUV stops, the engine cuts off, and I hear doors open and close. I try to jerk away when someone's hands touch my shoulders. Then I'm grabbed. It's dark, but whoever is carrying me is strong. To him, it's as if I weigh nothing.

I try to see through the hood over my head to find out where they are taking me, but it's too dark. No light filters through, and when they put me down, I try to take a step to see if I can run, but it's no use; I fall hard to the ground and hit my shoulder.

It was stupid, but I had to try.

I'm picked up and carried, hearing his footsteps. I hear a door swing open and more footsteps, and I'm placed on what feels like a bed. Dread snakes through me, wondering what they will do and why.

After ten minutes, the rope around my head is removed, releasing the gag, and the hood is snatched off my head. My eyes try to adjust to the gloom of the room. I blink a few times, trying to acclimate my eyes. There is only a stream of light from the window coming from an outdoor light, and when my eyes finally focus, a cold knot forms inside my chest, sinking to my stomach.

The six men in plague masks and cloaks are standing at the foot of the bed, watching me. I'm not one to beg, but right now, I can feel panic gripping me in its clutches, telling me to plead.

"Please," I whisper. "If you're gonna kill me. Make it quick," I say in a shaky voice. Tears slide down my wet cheeks, mixing with the ones dripping from my nose.

They all shake their head. Sobs begin suffocating me. One of them reaches out with a gloved hand, and I shrink back in fear.

"No, don't touch me." I sniff. "Please...leave me alone."

Five of them walk out, closing the door. Now there is just one standing in the middle of the room at the foot of the bed. He reaches out, grips my ankle, and pulls me so I slide down to the foot of the bed. I can scream, but they will re-place the hood and gag me again. When his gloved hand slides up my leg, I kick out with both feet, hitting him in the chest. I hear him grunt. He removes his mask, and relief, mixed with a new fear, causes my blood to turn cold and my face to drain of its color. I wipe my face with both hands tied together.

"Why?" I ask.

"Because I'm one of them."

CHAPTER 27

Alaric

"Y ou can go right in, Mr. Riordan," my grandfather's secretary says when I walk in.

"Thank you."

When I walk in, my grandfather is seated at his desk smoking a cigar. A plume of smoke hovers around his desk, nursing a scotch in his right hand, the gold ring from his pinky finger catching the light. The same one that is given to all the sons of Kenyan. The same one was given to me once I graduated with the Order's crest engraved on the top.

"You wanted to see me, Grandfather?"

"I did."

My grandfather called me while I was in my office, and there are only two reasons my grandfather would summon me here, death or money. No one has died in our family, so I will choose option two.

"Have a seat. We have much to discuss."

I sit and unbutton my suit jacket as he taught me as a formality. My grandfather preferred to teach me how to be a ruthless businessman. He didn't let my father teach me because he considered me *his* apprentice. The oldest Riodrick-Riordan had to set an unprecedented example for this family. One person to look up to, including my cousins and the other families.

"What do we need to discuss?"

I watch the ash fall in the ashtray from his cigar as it burns. The smell permeates everything it meets. Cigars in my grandfather's world signify power, success, and wealth. The more expensive, the better.

"I trust you went and did your research because I have found that you have terminated contracts. Tara called her father, and her father called, but I wasn't surprised since Reid refused to marry her because he grew a conscience and fell for Prey. The other," he smiles with the cigar between his teeth, "disappeared."

"He did."

He means I killed him, and he fell from the face of the earth.

"Did this have to do with Miss Devlin?"

"I would prefer you not address her by that name, but yes, sir. With all due respect."

He chuckles. Takes a sip of his scotch, setting the glass on his desk. "They think you are fucking her under the pretense of her belonging to the Order for some time before she marries Dorian Black."

I blink. "I am."

"She's your whore."

"She's mine. Period."

The glass clinks when he slams his hand on his desk. "Do you know what you're doing, Alaric! You took an oath to not have a wife. You can't keep her."

"I am, and I will. Whore, wife, slave, or whatever the fuck they want to think of her as. She's mine. Besides," I undo the buttons on my wrists and roll my sleeves up, "they broke the rules. She was mine to begin with. Before."

"You figured it out."

"I did."

He rolls the cigar between his fingers, lost in thought. "Then I have to give you something that arrived today from the Riordan estate under Alicia's last wishes before she died."

I take a deep swallow because out of all of us, Alicia was the most doted on by my grandfather. She was the apple of his eye. The one that could do no wrong, and like all of us in our family, we couldn't save her.

He takes out a folder and slides it across his desk. "Open it."

I open it, pulling out two sheets of paper addressed to me and one to Veronica Devlin in Alicia's handwriting.

Alaric,

Every language is silent.

Every prayer is heard.

Love, Alicia

Confused, I turn the sheet of paper over. Nothing, that is all. Two fucking lines.

I read the second one, not caring that it's addressed to Veronica, and it isn't for my eyes. Still, I read it before giving it to her because I want to know everything.

Veronica,

If you are reading this, I am dead. I gave specific instructions to have this delivered to you before your graduation. You entrusted me with your secrets and gave me your love unconditionally. I am forever indebted to you for always keeping mine and giving me your promises. The world needs more people like you. Strong, full of love, and witty. You are the best friend I could have ever wished for. The greatest love I have ever seen and felt in someone's heart was yours. It was a shame having to watch something so precious not be embraced by others around you. They judged when what they needed to do was save you.

I'm so sorry for failing you and for not telling my promises to you when I should have. I wrote you this letter to be handed to you before your graduation because we both knew what would happen. What they did to you. I'm sorry for not letting you leave with me when you begged me to, but I want to remind you that I love you more than you would ever know, and please don't cut that pretty skin when you feel nothing. I bet you have a grave all picked out next to mine because I know you. You believe in love when others think you believe in hate. That's because they don't see the beautiful person you are. The one screaming on the inside to be loved. To be saved.

I promise to keep a petal for every flower you leave on my grave in my magic garden. I know you want to lie beside me, but there is someone who needs you more. He just doesn't know it yet, but he will. I promise. He will see what I see, and when he does, God help them.

I love you, Veronica.

Till death do you part, I will forever be in your heart.

Until we meet again,

Alicia.

I slide the paper inside the folder.

"All is well?"

"No. I need to hurt some people."

"You have my support."

"I need your vote and Mr. Bedford's."

His eyes flick to mine when he snuffs out his cigar. "Done. I trust you need time to put everything in place."

"I'm working on it. I just need time before she graduates."

"I'm going to warn you. There are things you are going to see. Things that have circulated, but you can't lose your head. You can't kill everyone, Alaric."

"Just a couple."

"Alaric," he warns.

"It's about time I take out some of the trash."

"What are you going to do with Devlin?"

I glance at my watch and get up to button my suit jacket. "She doesn't belong to him. Veronica belongs to me. Rules are rules."

There is a gleam in his eyes when I throw their words right back. "Yes, they are. You know what this will mean for her. Don't you?"

"Your granddaughter made her a promise."

"I see that. And?" he says promptly.

He's asking what I plan to do with Veronica. The truth is, I don't know exactly. But I know one thing...

"I'm in love with her."

He looks at me steadily. "You have always been in love with her, son. It's why you never took another to be your wife. Show her. Even if it's too late and she won't believe you, like I said. There will be things about Veronica you need to be prepared to deal with. Remember, even the devil knows the Bible."

"It's a good thing I know both."

It is nine at night when I walk out of the Riodrick building. The yellow streetlights flare on the pavement when I pull out of the garage. I smell like my grandfather's cigars, and I'm starving, but I need to see the Bedford twins, and it can't wait.

I'm at the Bedford estate after the twenty-minute drive from the city into Kenyan. Draven still lives here, and Gia and Dravin live in a modernized mansion behind it. It makes sense, I guess. Gia is the mistress of both properties, and the twins share the same woman. I always wondered who got Tuesdays and Thursdays but to each his own.

If I think of sharing Veronica with another man, rage filters inside me, and the only thing I can think of is killing someone. It's bad enough I have to stomach her fucking Garret and Draven, but I would be a fucking hypocrite because I have slept with other women. One of them, in fact, hated Veronica, and she walked in on me at a Kenyan party. Thinking about it makes my stomach turn cold in shame, making it seem she wasn't special. The words I said and the things I did to her.

"I hope you didn't come to see me so you can punch me in the face like you did, Garret," Draven says when he opens the door.

"Do you love her?"

"Hell, no. I'm a married man. I love one woman."

"Then all is good. I'm sure Veronica feels the same way."

"Trust me. It was weird, and now that I know the truth, I get why it happened. No offense, but at the time, I'm a man, and she is a beautiful woman. I don't think you could blame me if she had come on to you the way she did. Fucked with my ego."

Draven is a confident guy. I'm curious at what he meant about her messing with his ego, so I ask, "Ego?"

"She didn't get off, dude. It was like a switch," he snaps his fingers, "Just like that. It was over. It was weird. That is all I'm gonna say. It was a game, and she plays it well, but I must warn you."

I slow down in front of his father's office door. "Warn me about what?"

He pinches his nose like I've seen his brother do countless times. It's like watching a clone but with a different demeanor.

Draven looks grimly at me. "What I'm going to show you, all I have to say is…I'm sorry."

A feeling of unease sweeps over me. It feels like I am looking down, and I'm not sure how hard the fall will be if I jump or if there is another way down, so it doesn't hurt as much when I fall. Whatever it is he needs me to see, I am not going to like it.

It is mainly the reason he wants me to come here. He said he needed to show me something when Reid dug into Veronica's past. Whatever it was, Reid couldn't show me. He said he couldn't, meaning…it's bad.

"Alright."

He opens his father's study door, and Mr. Bedford sits behind his desk. He has a sharp look in his gaze when we both walk in.

"Alaric."

"Mr. Bedford," I say, shaking his hand.

He takes a deep breath and I take a seat, but I don't miss how he moves irresolutely back to his desk, like he isn't sure if he should leave me with Draven and let him show me what I need to see or if he should stay.

"I'm going to make this quick. I have never seen this before because I don't partake in these things. This is more for the generation before me."

He means my grandfather's generation of sick fucks. Our generation fucks girls in college, knowing our lives after we graduate are to serve the Order with a wife in our arms. Chosen by us or not. We play games and don't take them seriously, but who in college does? Frat and college parties are full of college kids, getting drunk and high, having the occasional coke habit, and fucking girls. Not these guys. They're more sadistic and take shit to a new level of fucked-up. I read the book on their history.

Mr. Bedford glances at Draven and then at me. "I'm sorry, Alaric."

He turns the screen, and I see her, and my blood turns to ice. My eyes sting, and I suddenly feel hot. I see the men around her, their faces, and what they are doing, and I imprint it into my memory. The ritual. But I can't get the image of her face out of my head. The look of agony. The pain, her skin and the way they touch her, the way they masturbate like the sick fucks they are.

"It started—" He trails off because even for a man like him, it's difficult to watch an innocent woman being treated that way. "After the night with you. This is nothing compared to the so-called sin she committed. It was never supposed to be you she ended up with. Everyone knew how she felt about you, and the only reason it's allowed now is because they know she can't marry you."

I swallow the lump in my throat. "I can only use her."

"Right," his father says. "You have to let her go, Alaric."

"I'm not."

"Do you know what you are saying, Alaric? She belongs to the Order and to Dorian Black. I hate to say it, but he played you. He played the game and knew where to aim. He wants her and has her."

I glance at Draven as two tears escape down my face. "I need all the names and locations of those men in that video." He nods.

"Are you out of your mind?"

I turn to Mr. Bedford. "Shut it off," I demand.

He turns the video off and says, "You can save her from them, but you can't erase the damage that was done, Alaric."

"We're all damaged, Mr. Bedford. Fucked-up even."

"You're just going to find and kill them, and then, they will vote to kill you too. The higher Order. I can't vote against it, but—"

"They were all dead the second they touched her. They made a promise to themselves the second they looked at her."

"Well, you won't have to worry about her mother. Obviously, Devlin isn't her father, unless he's a really sick bastard and jerks off to his own flesh and blood, but we both know the truth because I slept with her mother. More than once, in fact. I knew that girl wasn't his. You could see it in her mother's eyes when she looked at Veronica that she was a mistake. A mistake she wished she could erase. A beautiful mistake."

"Father," Draven scolds.

"I'm not going to hide that that young lady isn't beautiful. Everyone knows it, you did, too, and I think that saucy bad bitch attitude only adds more to her appeal. Now that we know the skeletons she hides underneath. She's Prey."

My Prey.

CHAPTER 28
Veronica

"How does it feel," I ask, watching him untie my hands and feet.

"How does what feel?"

"To be a lying sack of shit."

"Go take a shower."

I pull my hand back and slap him hard on his face.

He covers his cheek with his hand and grimaces. "What the fuck, Veronica!"

"You lied!"

"I was protecting you."

"From what?"

"Them!"

"Aren't you a little savior!" I marvel.

"Look, I'm sorry."

"Whatever, Adam."

I can feel my cheeks flood with color at how angry I am at him for lying to me this whole time.

"Was any of it real?"

He sighs, and I watch my handprint turn red on his face. "All of it was except that I needed the money to work at the restaurant. I was sent there because of you. I'm attending OSU, and everything else was real. I'm still your friend."

"I was screaming for your help," I say, trembling. I feel so stupid. I feel betrayed. They are always two steps ahead. "I'm going to die, aren't I?"

"People are going to die; you're just not one of them."

"Where am I?"

"Somewhere safe."

I look around and see that the room's walls are painted black with wood furniture. There are three floor-length mirrors. A chandelier over the four-poster bed with wood carvings in intricate designs. "What the fuck is this place?"

"Rich people have more than one house, I guess."

"Who?"

"I am not allowed to say, but you will find out."

"Just please go take a shower. I hate to say this, but you look like shit."

"Gee, I wonder why."

"Bathroom's that way." He points to the left, and a door leads to the bathroom, and the light is already on."

"Where's Alaric?"

"On his way."

My heartbeat begins to calm down, but my legs feel like rubber when I try to stand. My throat is still sore from all the screaming, and my chest hurts when I take deep breaths from all the crying. I'm going to kill him.

When I walk into the bathroom, I sigh in relief when I don't see a bathtub, and it's just a shower with no doors. The dark porcelain tile is everywhere. A white marble vanity is to the left on the walls and floors. I notice a red robe placed neatly on the side with shampoo, conditioner, and bath wash in clear bottles with red bows.

When I look at myself in the mirror, I see that Adam wasn't kidding. I look like shit. There are dark circles under my eyes. I'm a mess. I can't stop shaking, and I know what is to come. The numbness. The need to feel. I look around and notice a razor. I pick it up and take it with me.

The steam comes from the shower like a sign that I'm home. A shelter to drown my pain of being alone, but I learned that sadness needs company too, and depression is its best friend. The pain is its food and tears its ocean.

The waterfalls are like acid rain on my skin. The steam is a storm cloud of my emotions, taking away cold air to breathe. I wash my body. I wince at my wrist. There are fingerprints under the redness from the rope where they tied my wrists together. My fingers grip the razor. It's new, and I know it will cut if I angle it just right. I crouch on the tile and let sobs rack my body. The sound of defeat echoes in the shower like a warning. I angle the razor on the inner part of my ankle.

"You shouldn't damage something so pretty." I jolt, dropping the razor, hearing it clink on the tile and watching him pick it up. I didn't notice him come in. I was so lost in my head.

"Give it back," I croak. "I need you to leave me alone."

"I can't do that. If you need to cut, you cut me." I glance up, confused. My eyes trail down his naked body. "Here," he holds the razor near the skin on his chest, "cut me." He wipes a tear from my cheek with his thumb. "I'll bleed for you." My bottom lip trembles.

"Why are you doing this to me?"

"I'm not. I'm saving you."

"I can't be saved."

He steps forward, throwing the razor on the ground until we're inches apart. In a split second, Alaric lifts me in his arms, his hands gripping my butt and wrapping my legs around his waist. I have no choice but to wrap my arms around his neck. "I'm sorry. I had to have them take you the way that they did."

"Why? I was so scared."

He looks down between us and feels it. "You're trembling."

"I can't make it stop. I need to—" I trail off.

I hate admitting to him that cutting makes it stop, but my whole body is shaking. "Fuck. I'm so sorry. He was watching you, baby. Dorian was watching you after he left the restaurant, and Adam told me what he did. What he said. I'm so sorry you had to find out this way. Look at me, Veronica." I pull back and see pain mirrored in his eyes. "I know this sounds fucked up, but I need you to trust me. Can you do that?" I look away. Every time I trust someone, they fuck me over, or they die. "You're going to stay with me. You're not going back. Ever." I nod because I don't want to go back. "Answer me."

"Y-yes."

He pushes me against the shower wall, my legs slide down, and I wait until I can stand. He wraps his hand around my throat, and arousal shoots between my legs. "Let me wash up."

He washes us both and it soothes me at how gentle he is. He makes sure the shaking stops, warming my skin before rinsing us both off.

After he dries us both, he carries me bridal style into the bedroom and places me in the center of the bed. "You have a thing with chains."

There are chains anchored to the wall. Three separated inches apart.

"I do. I like them, but I like them better on you." He pulls the middle one, with a leather collar attached, and fastens it on me. He slides his thumb over my lips and whispers, "Beautiful."

"Where are your chains?"

He smiles, lifting an eyebrow. "Is that what you want? To chain me."

"I would. Naked."

"That can be arranged, but I think you would like it better when I do it to you."

"Why is that?" I purr, arching my back on the bed.

When I turn my head, his eyes never leave my body. "You're not trembling anymore."

How could I tremble when he is more dangerous than anything I have seen or felt. Nothing can hurt me when the man holding me in his arms has no fear in his eyes - only fury and desire.

"No. Not with you."

He kisses my lips, pulling the chain behind me, causing my neck to arch. "You'll tremble but for a very different reason."

"Do your worst."

The light filtering through the window is bright enough that I can see his body. Perfect with his hard cock jutting out between his thighs, kneeling on the bed.

"If I touch you right now, I won't stop. I'm going to fuck you. Hard."

Our eyes battle between lust, control, pain, and pleasure. "Then, fuck me. Make me sin."

"Then we are both going to hell." He grabs my legs, pushing them apart. My pussy dripping wet for him. I arch my back, waiting for it. The pleasure of pain. He warned me that it wouldn't be soft, which is the last thing I want. I want it fast and hard.

He strokes his cock, gripping it at the root, watching my pussy. When my fingers trail around my clit, his nostrils flare, knowing that is all it will take. He rams his cock inside me, hard. I gasp, and he freezes while holding me by the hips. My hands are holding me upright behind my back. The collar pulls tight around my neck, and he pushes into me and then begins to pound me harder. Faster and faster. It is raw and powerful.

The chains rattle, and I let out a high-pitched moan. "Mmm, yes!"

His hand grips the leather collar, and his eyes blaze like he is possessed. You can hear our skin slapping between the rattle of the chains in a series of claps. My tits bounce with every hard thrust. It feels like he is splitting me apart, and I know that I won't be able to walk when he's done. I want more.

His chest heaves when he pulls out and then slams into me again. I fall on the pillows, my hands unable to hold me up. He pushes my legs over his arms and clings to me. My legs are shaking. His hands span my waist, pushing me toward his hips with every thrust.

"This is mine." He growls. His jaw is clenched hard. "Come on my cock, baby."

I can feel how hard he is inside me. "Mmm, harder!" I scream, losing my breath.

"You were made for me. This is the only pussy that can take my dick."

My orgasm is cresting and coming in fast from his words. "You're about to come. I can feel it."

I claw at his chest when I come, my orgasm exploding like a storm destroying everything in its wake. He pushes harder, and I feel him come on a roar, filling me with his cum. We are both sweating, but he makes no move to get off me. He stays inside me, gripping my thighs and lifting them over his shoulders, pushing himself deeper.

"I love you so much," he says.

The words don't cross my lips, but I hope he can see it when he looks at me. I just can't say it. I need him to feel it. The way I feel it when he's inside me.

"I'm sorry for everything I have ever done to hurt you. You deserve all the beautiful things in this world. If you don't have them, I will swim in the stars to find them for you if I have to."

I slide my fingers over his cheek, pulling him down for a soft kiss, our foreheads touching. "I have only ever wanted…just you."

He looks down at my wrist and sees the fingerprints. His mouth pulls into a frown. "What's this?"

"Adam told me—he hurt you."

"I'm fine. It's just a little red and sore. The ropes—"

He nods, but I see the little muscle in his jaw tic. His gray eyes go dark. He pulls out of me and undoes the collar on my neck, lifting me off the bed and taking me to the shower.

"Alaric?"

Silence.

CHAPTER 29

Alaric

Walking out the back patio, I reach the fire pit out back. Garret is the first to spot me. "Dude, this house is sick. You slaughter anything, and no one would know."

I had it built on the edge of Kent and bought the land as an investment. No one knew this house existed until now. It was the best place to take Veronica from the diner. Adam texted me what happened when Dorian showed up.

"That's not why I bought it, but if you're thinking like that, I suggest getting checked out with Dr. Wick."

"Touché."

I notice Valen rubbing the side of his face. I smile, having a good idea. "What happened?"

"I think the blind date was a bad idea," he grimly says.

Draven chuckles. "I told you not to grab her like that. She packs a punch."

"At least I didn't play Closer like a psycho in the car on the way here with a hood on her head. Way to go, dick. You fucking scared the shit out of her. She's a cutter."

"She hit you?" I ask Valen to change the subject. I don't want anyone to think she is weak.

"Yeah, man. Look!" He points to the side of his face, moving into the light of the fire. It's red and will leave a bruise.

"He got slapped," Garret says, pointing to Adam.

I glance at Adam; sure enough, he has a red handprint on his face.

"That's what I get for lying to her."

I feel bad for him because he is a good friend to her, but he's one of us. My mother and grandfather's idea. I wasn't surprised my mother set that up. She was always fond of Veronica and Alicia's relationship. I was just too stupid with my head up my ass regarding Veronica. I wanted her but hated what they made her represent, and it was all a lie.

"We had to come out here," Valen says.

"You needed to come out here. I was fine hearing them go at it," Draven says.

Veronica is very vocal in bed.

"Dude, is it always like that?" Adam asks.

"No. Only with him," Draven replies.

Good. At least Draven stroked my ego burning with curiosity.

"Where's Reid and Dravin?" I ask.

"With the girls."

They got Adam up to speed on most of the details with Veronica. He's aware of my plan. They all are. I get goosebumps thinking about her.

"You finally fell, huh," Valen says with a smirk. "You're in love with the little hellfire."

I am, but the look in her eyes tells me she can't say the words back. I don't expect her to for all the reasons she shouldn't. Sometimes damaged people can't feel how you want them to because you have to put them back together differently. I have to be patient with her, and I'll do whatever it takes.

Draven scoffs, rolling his eyes. "It's about time. You always carried a torch for her."

But I don't miss the hurt look on Garret's face when he looks around and licks his lips, avoiding everyone's gaze. He'll get over it.

"We stick to the plan?" Adam asks.

"Yeah," I reply.

Veronica is no longer working at the restaurant, and Adam is only too happy to quit. I ensured Dorothy would be okay, and she was relieved Veronica was taken care of. She said she would get a shotgun and shoot me if I hurt her. I let her slide because she cares for Veronica and sees her like a daughter.

The next day, Veronica has class. I already sent the report to her professor, who agreed she is an exceptional student, but I didn't miss the little gleam in his eyes when I first mentioned her name. I threatened him that if he looked at her in any way that wasn't customary for a professor, I would end his career. He thought it meant he wouldn't teach at Kenyan and would get fired. He didn't know what I planned to do with his eyes for looking at her incorrectly. He still sputtered his way out of the situation like an asshole that got caught with his pants down.

I have eyes watching her. Dorian is a threat, but he doesn't know I know his sick game with Veronica or what I have planned for my girl. She is sex in a pair of heels, and I am crazy about her.

It is three in the afternoon on a Wednesday, and I am waiting for my girl in the quad with a basket. College students are milling about talking shit. For a moment, I wonder if things were different. If I was four years younger and attending Kenyan. Would I kiss her before and after class? Make sure my schedule was aligned with hers? Live off campus with her, share a house, and wake up with her in my arms?

"She doesn't come out here, you know." I glance up and see Jess standing with Gia.

Dravin walks up, slides his hand around Gia's waist, and places his hand over his lips, trying to stifle a smile when he sees me with a picnic basket. *Dick.*

"Try the cemetery. It's her favorite place."

A sense of fear grips me when I think about what Alicia wrote to her in her letter. She knew exactly how Veronica would take her death. It's what I'm afraid of, her not wanting me enough to stay around. I grip the handles and stand.

"Thanks."

"She likes red," Jess says with a smile. "She's always wearing it somewhere."

"Yeah," Gia swallows, then rubs her lips together like she just remembered something. "She loves those black Docs, and I notice they have little red beads through the laces. Simple stuff like that. She only acts sassy when—she has to, but she is always in the cemetery with her best friend."

A woman sells flowers at the entrance, and I pick out two bouquets. One with different colors and another with red roses. I spot her immediately. Sitting on Alicia's grave, the letter clutched in her hand, tears falling like rain, and my heart breaks for the first time. Her pain is the only thing I can feel. I'm afraid she will give up, and I can't live without her.

She looks up, her beautiful clear blue eyes like water from the cleanest ocean. She is gorgeous, with her long dark hair catching in the wind. Those ridiculous old boots that belonged to my cousin.

"I bought you new ones, you know."

She knows I mean her boots when I place the basket on the ground and sit beside her.

"You're going to ruin your dress pants."

I shrug my shoulders. "I have a lot of pairs."

"Sure, you do."

"Shorts and shirts, too," I tease, handing her the colorful bouquet. "Those are for Alicia." I give her the red roses. "These are for you."

She grabs them, sniffing the scent of the rose petals, trying to compose herself and wiping at her face. "They are beautiful. I would have thought you were the black roses type."

"I like them red. It reminds me that you bled for me like I would bleed for you."

A pink stain appears on her cheeks when she blushes. I turn, opening the basket. "I brought you lunch," I say, pulling out expensive cold-cut meats and cheeses. A bottle of sparkling water and two glasses with another bottle of wine.

"Isn't that a bit much?"

"There is nothing as too much of anything."

"I must admit, it's my first time eating with the dead."

I look around, and it's not exactly romantic, but it's us.

"It's a first for me too, but I keep taking them."

"Taking what?"

"All of your firsts. They're all mine."

"That's not fair. What do I get?"

My eyes fix on her mouth as she eats a piece of cold meat with cheese. Her tongue swipes across her bottom lip. Her eyes are still watery from crying. "You have what no one else will."

Her other hand begins to pull on the blades of grass, ripping them out next to Alicia's grave. I lean close, sliding a piece of meat inside my mouth. "It's not your time, my love. I have things I want to do for you. Places I want to take you. If it comes to that, I'll bury myself with you and die a happy man." My lips are inches from hers, my cock screaming in agony, wanting to take her somewhere, but I can't shake the feeling I have inside when I look at her. The expression on her face tells me what all the words in the dictionary couldn't. That she loves me, but she's afraid.

"What are you afraid of?" I ask. I break off a rose from its stem and trace it on the smooth lines of her cheekbones. "Tell me so I can take it away."

She smiles in the way she did when we first met. Gone is the Veronica with fire on her tongue. I like both versions of her, but when we have these moments, moments like the first one we had four years ago, I like this version of her. It's private in that way. Lovers have secrets only the two of them share. A look or a smile.

"You think you can just save me, don't you?"

"I do."

It isn't a lie but a promise. No one will touch her ever again.

"I'm afraid they will take away the one moment I had with you. The one where you told me you loved me for the first time."

"You're the only one that could make me feel, and no one can take that from you. You chose Veronica."

Tears slide down her cheeks. "I did."

"Prey choose," I whisper. She nods. "Don't cry." I lean in and lick her tears. She wraps her arms around me, and we stay sitting on my cousin's grave, and the two sentences she wrote me on a simple piece of paper make more sense than anything ever could. Every language is silent. Every prayer is heard. "Every language is silent. Every prayer is heard," I repeat out loud. "I hear you calling for me, my love. I hear it now." Her sobs rip through her, and then I hear it. Her whisper.

"I love you."

"Then, stay with me. It's not your time to go yet. I need you."

I never thought I would fall in love, but I knew I did that night. Veronica is my first love and my last.

I feel it while looking at Alicia's grave as Veronica waits for me at the cemetery gates. I swear I can feel her energy. Her words were written in letters to both of us, full of love for her friend, completing a promise she never uttered. Death is a mystery. But there is a way to communicate between the dead and the living. They say math is the universal language to solve everything. Books are written about religion to maintain morals and instill faith. But love is and always will be the universal language. My cousin found and risked her life for the one she loved because, without it, you're dead anyway. Love is universal. It is said in prayer because love is all we need and want. Love is what we kill for. Every language is silent because love is all that needs to exist.

I kiss the palm of my hand and place it on her grave. "I'll take care of her now. I promise. I love you, Alicia. Thank you for bringing me happiness." I look over at her boyfriend Chase's grave. "You take care of her now." I look up, and a crow lands on his grave. Its shiny feathers and black beak make a cawing sound.

"Are you sure we can't stay?"

"There is no way to take a shit or use the shower. I'm remodeling all the bathrooms."

"You didn't have to."

I place the fourth suitcase inside the Rolls trunk and press the button so the door can close automatically. I reply, "I did."

"The other house is quieter, and you can study for your finals in peace and no bathtubs."

I made sure all my homes were remodeled with showers and threw out every belt buckle I owned.

She smiles, but I don't miss the whimsical eye she gives when she passes the garage that houses the blacked-out Bentley she practiced on that night. She passed the written driver's exam, and she was able to get her learner's permit last week. I slide my cell phone out and dial my driver. She glances at me and sighs, walking toward the Rolls Royce.

"Take the Bentley to my estate, please," I say into the phone, watching her eyes widen as I open the door, so she can slide in the passenger seat.

There is nothing I don't notice when it comes to her. She likes sex before bed and in the morning when she wakes up. Hard and fast at night, full of chains and an occasional anal. Soft and slow in the morning after I eat her pussy.

She's perfect.

Sometimes it's what scares the shit out of me the most. How perfect she is. There are two sides to her, and I can't figure out which side I like better. Like a precious coin, you can flip over and over and can't decide, so you admire both sides as much as possible.

"You didn't have to take the Bentley."

"It's your favorite. Why not. Do you like specific colors?"

"I like that one."

"You don't want a new one?"

She shakes her head. "No, I like that one because it reminds me of you and the first time I drove it."

"Got it."

I slide my hand in hers, letting that tingling feeling over me, touching her hand in mine. "I'll transfer it in your name. It's yours."

"But—"

"Don't. I want to give it to you."

"It's expensive."

"I can afford it."

"Cocky much."

"You should be proud; your man is loaded. I got bank."

She snorts. "Oh, God. I am proud, but not because you have money."

"It's because I have a huge dick. You can't live without it."

She shoves me, and I laugh, but her face suddenly goes white, and I panic.

"Veronica!"

She holds her stomach and grimaces. "I think I'm going to be sick." Her face turns an ashen color, and I stop on the side of the road. She undoes her seat belt and opens the door and starts to vomit.

"Fuck."

I jump out of the car, and she's retching on the side of the road. I hold her hair back. "It's okay, baby," I say softly. "Get it out. Is it something you ate?"

Her eyes are watery from the effort, but she manages not to get any on her clothes. "I don't feel well," she sputters.

"Can you make it if I drive to the gas station? I can get you some crackers and water."

She nods.

After getting Veronica some water and crackers, I call the doctor so he can take a look at her at the house.

"I'm fine, Alaric."

I'm not taking any chances with her. Maybe she caught something at school or at work. She worked the night shift, and the guys told me she threw the trash out back. Those days are over for her. I'm not going to have my girl work in a restaurant when she could be in our bed watching her favorite horror flick after a day at the spa.

I kiss the top of her hand. "I want to make sure you're okay. I love you."

She looked pale when her body was doubled over, half hanging out, gripping the car door, and the sounds of her vomiting. Her face went white like chalk, but it regained some of its natural color after she ate the crackers and drank some water.

"I'm okay. Maybe it was something I ate," she says with a wane smile.

But she hasn't eaten much. I noticed that these past couple of days, she has left food on her plate, and when I ask if she is hungry or wants me to take her to dinner, she refuses or says she already ate.

"The doctor will run some tests just to make sure."

But I have a feeling I know why. It's all coming together.

CHAPTER 30
Veronica

"You're pregnant," she says with a smile, sitting in front of me.

We are at the Galleria with Jess and four bodyguards standing around us like we are celebrities or something.

Portman gives me a side-eye when Gia giggles.

"What is so funny? I'm not pregnant."

"Oh yes, you are. You don't eat. You sleep all the time or,"—she winks—"not sleep. I know this because I'm pregnant."

My eyes widen. "Oh my God, Gia! I'm so happy for you." Then a thought pops into my head.

"I see that look."

"What look?"

"The same one Jess is giving me."

"It doesn't matter who. We talked about it already. It won't matter anyway. Whoever has one first, that child inherits. It's good that it comes from me and no one else."

I can see her point by looking at it that way and falling in love with twins. "How is it?" I ask.

"How is what?" she asks curiously.

Jess snickers and drops a piece of bread on her plate. "She wants to know how it feels to be fucked by twins."

I laugh when Portman and the other two bodyguards stiffen.

"Oh."

"Who takes the front and who takes the back, or do they take turns?" I ask.

"Take turns doing what?" Dravin asks, sliding into the seat next to Gia and kissing her lips.

"Fucking your wife," I answer.

Jess tries to stifle a cough, placing her hand over her mouth.

"Hmm, I see bad Veronica is coming out to play today." His eyes lower to my stomach. "How are you feeling?"

My eyes narrow. "Why do I feel you know something I don't."

"I don't know what you are talking about. Alaric said you weren't feeling well these past couple of days, and this is your first time out in like forever." His light eyes tell me they hold a secret. A big one.

"Liar."

"What did the doctor say?" Jess asks.

"The results should be in later today. It's the third day." I turn to Dravin.

"It depends on the mood."

"It's his," I blurt, looking at Gia.

He grins. "She told you, and you don't know that."

"She married him legally. You made sure the first child was yours. Fair is fair."

He shakes his head like what I said is crazy, but I know Draven. He's been fucking Gia and pulling out or giving her anal so his brother can have his heir. Poor Gia will be pregnant again when the kid turns one, or should I say lucky.

"Either way, I'm happy for you three." I turn to Jess. "Why is Reid taking so long?"

She knows I mean for her to get pregnant with a little Riordan.

"He's waiting for you and Alaric."

"I'm not married and—" I trail off, rubbing the back of my neck where the tattoo was placed. A reminder of what I am in the grand scheme of things.

I still have to marry Dorian at the end of graduation. I'm not free.

Dravin clears his throat. "We'll see."

After class on Friday, I head over to Babylon to meet with Jess and Gia. We began a sort of routine after school since I got the results from the doctor. I'm pregnant. I don't know how if I'm on birth control. I didn't miss a pill and have been keeping up with filling my prescriptions.

When I walk in, it's packed. There needs to be a seat at the bar. Three bartenders are running around serving drinks. The pool tables are all taken. My eyes scan the booths, looking for Jess and Gia in their normal spot.

I know I've found them when Jess smiles and gestures me over. A hand slides around my waist as I enter the crowd. "Where are you going, princess?" My body stiffens, and my chest tightens as fear grips me when I hear Dorian's voice over Seether's "Fake It."

I pull away. His smile is full of capped teeth glowing white under the dim light of the bar. He's wearing a white t-shirt under a leather jacket, trying to fit in.

My eyes sweep over him in disgust, reminding me of something foul. Like the smell of trash when you walk behind a building. "What are you doing here, Dorian? This isn't your crowd. Aren't you too old to hang out with college kids?"

"Alaric does."

I bare my teeth. "That's because he fucks me better than they do."

"I can do better."

I snort. "I think I'll just ask your secretary. She obviously got bored of you."

It bothered me that Alaric slept with her, but I'm a big girl, and

I've done bad things. It's all in the past, and right now, I carry something more important than regrets and hate inside me.

Dorian gives me a wintry smile that suddenly turns into a frown. "You're a long way from the city, Dorian. I didn't think you hung out here chasing college pussy," Valen says behind me.

Dorian glances at me and then at Valen, then back at me. "I don't. I prefer real women. The kind that don't fuck little boys. I'll just have to show you, Veronica."

My lips turn into a salacious smile. "Oh, Dorian. You couldn't make me come the way they can, but I prefer chains to warm baths. Just ask your perverted dad. He can tell you all about it. How much I hate baths."

Dorian's nostrils flare when Alaric shows up with the twins, and Adam overhears the last part. "Damn, Black. You keep it in the family. It's kind of sick." Alaric leans closer. "I know all about it. It's pathetic that your daddy had to pick your wife for you, too, getting off with his three-inch dick, but don't worry, I have something special lined up for you both." Alaric slides his hands protectively over my waist, erasing Dorian's touch and kissing my neck hotly. "And for the record, I'm not a little boy."

"Have fun with your daddy," I chirp.

Dorian's jaw hardens. His eyes seem desperate, but he gives a sharp laugh. A laugh when someone doesn't get their way but knows he's outnumbered and can't do shit about it. I would be afraid of him if I wasn't in a bar full of people and if the sons of Kenyan weren't all around me. Protecting me.

When I slide into the booth next to Jess, she asks, "What did that pathetic piece of shit want?"

"To get under her skin by showing up in random places everywhere, like the creep he is," Gia says, popping a French fry in her mouth.

"The guys should get rid of him," Jess chimes in.

"I'm working on it. It's going to be a real party," Alaric says, sliding into the wooden booth beside me. "How are you feeling?" I turn to Gia, but he's looking right at me.

"He's asking you, not me," Gia says with a smile. "You think he wouldn't find out?" She snorts. "They know everything."

"We do," the twins both say in tandem.

"You knew."

"I did."

"I'm scared. When he touched me—"

"I was there. I saw it," Valen says. "We won't let him hurt you, Veronica."

My heart begins to beat faster, and my stomach has those little butterflies that swarm. I read that some women can experience those kinds of things in early pregnancy. When I found out, I immediately began Googling pregnancy and what to expect. I was happy, nervous, and afraid.

"Fuck," I blurt.

"That's how it starts," Adam teases.

I laugh. "What now?"

Alaric curls my dark hair around his fingers and says softly, "I take you home, and we celebrate."

"How can you be so calm?"

But the intense look in his eyes tells me he has a plan.

He always has one.

Walking out of the restroom, I bump into a hard chest. The spicy scent of Alaric's cologne causes me to smile, knowing it's him. When I glance up, his mouth lifts into a grin.

"Ready to be my bad girl?"

"Always." He pulls me toward the back exit and pushes me gently against the brick wall of the building. He lifts me, my legs wrap around his waist, and my arms around his neck. My pleated skirt is rudely shoved around my waist. My ass is in his hands, his eyes focused on my mouth as he takes my lips. His cock crowns my opening, the crotchless panties he prefers for me to wear, allowing him access whenever he wants. His slides inside me. "Mm."

I'm so sensitive and horny. I'm already wet and ready for him when he plunges deep with a growl. "Fuck."

"Mm, right there," I say breathlessly when I move faster, hitting me in the spot that drives me over the edge. I want to come. Every time we have sex, I come more than once. Sometimes two and three times.

My fingers grip his hair when he goes harder. Pumping inside me with everything he's got. I realize that any moment someone could walk up and see us, or they could exit the same way we did, getting a front-row show of us fucking like rabbits against the building.

"Someone might come and see us," I whisper against his cheek, loving the feel of the stubble from his facial hair.

"Let them see what a bad girl you are," he says between breaths.

My head dips, and I lick his lips like an animal. I grind my hips and hold myself up against the brick wall, glad I'm wearing a jacket and don't feel the rough texture every time he thrusts into me. My hands slide up the wall, and our eyes lock; I bite my bottom lip when the first orgasm rips through me, knowing he won't stop. The door screams open, and Gia and Jess are the first to step out, followed by Reid and the twins.

"Damn. They couldn't wait to get home and celebrate." I think that was Draven.

"She looks gorgeous," Gia says softly. "Take me home."

"I want to watch," I hear Jess tell Reid.

I pull Alaric's cock out and unwrap my legs from his waist and slowly kneel on the ground and take him in my mouth. I give a loud moan tasting myself and his salty precum from the tip. I run my teeth over his piercing. "Fuck, you're such a bad girl," he says with a groan, placing his hand against the brick wall and holding himself steady. I take him deep, relaxing my throat. I glance up, tears sliding down my cheeks. "You're so beautiful. Marry me."

"Let's go. He's proposing," Jess says.

"I want to see if she says yes," Reid teases.

I almost choke when I hear the twins. "Me too."

I pull him out, licking my lips, and he turns, putting himself away. "I love you."

"I think that was a yes," Jess says.

"How did you join the Consortium?" I ask Adam, placing the clean plates on the serving counter.

It's my last day at the restaurant. I wanted to help Dorothy and Adam out until Melody can start part-time tomorrow. She needs to get into college and wants to save money and her brother wants to help her out.

Adam clears his throat, closing the door to the dishwasher after loading the cups. "Valen came and offered me a sweet deal."

I draw my eyebrows together because the sons of Kenyan don't ordinarily allow anyone into the Consortium that isn't from the Order.

"How's that? You attending high school then OSU."

He smiles. "I'm not the only one, Veronica. They have people everywhere and only the loyal ones are allowed in." He lowers his voice. "If you fuck up, you're dead. How did you think I got the QB1 spot?" He leans close. "Perks of taking care of their girl."

I shake my head in confusion. He rolls his eyes. "The night of the frat party. I was already one of them, Veronica. Alaric showed up and the rest...I can't go into detail. That is all I'm allowed to say."

Adam was one of them the whole time?

"Did you know I went to Kenyan before?"

"What do you think?" he asks, moving to the napkins and rolling them over the silverware.

He did.

"I think you are more involved than what you're telling me, but I get it. You're sworn to secrecy or they will cut your head off."

He nods. "I'm glad you understand." He looks toward the window. "Do you need a ride?"

"Nope. I'll wait for Alaric's driver." I bend and grab my bag. "I'll be off."

"Are you sure?" I reach on my tippy toes and give him a peck on the cheek. "Yep."

I walk over and give Dorothy a tight hug.

"You be good now," she says in a raspy voice.

I look up and scrunch my nose. "I will if you promise to stop smoking."

"Stop stealing my Virginia Slims and I won't buy more cigarettes."

I raise my hand in the air before pushing the exit door open. "Excuses excuses. Bye. Love you guys!"

I walk down the three steps, looking left and right for the familiar black SUV, but I don't see Portman. I pull out my phone, sliding the text app open so I can text him, and walk deeper into the parking lot. I hear footsteps. When I look up, a large hand clamps over my mouth. I try to take gulps of air and thrash my arms dropping my phone. I kick my legs, trying to get free, but I can't. I can hear breathing from behind me and then something black covers my nose that smells funny. Adrenaline floods my veins in panic when my vision goes dark.

I bolt upward needing oxygen and feel the clinking sounds of chains. My arms feel heavy. I blink rapidly, my eyes trying to focus. The smell of dirt filters my nose. It's dark. I blink a couple of times, trying to get used to the light.

"It's about time." I hear Dorian's voice.

I close my eyes, trying to calm the racing of my heartbeat. I glance down and I'm lying in a dirty bathtub. A shudder runs through me. I begin to gag.

"It's normal. Halothane can cause nausea after it's inhaled."

I look up and see the pathetic piece of shit sitting in a chair. Another chill washes over me, and when I look down, I notice that I'm naked. My wrists are bound and the clinking was from the chains rubbing on the edge of the tub.

"Where am I?" I croak.

"Wouldn't you like to know."

"Let me go." I look at him defiantly. "He's going to kill you."

He leans forward in the chair, causing it to groan. "Oh, you mean your little boyfriend." He chuckles. "I was wondering when he would fuck you out of his system and let you go, but I think he's getting attached. Again." He slides his finger over my arm and I pull my arm away, causing the metal to bang. He chuckles harder. "You'll get used to my touch. I wonder if he'll still want you after I fuck you?"

I take three calming breaths. *He'll come for me. Alaric will come.*

I smile and allow a little laugh to escape, wiping the one off his face. "Is that what you think? Honestly?" I get up on my knees. "Do you know how many men I've had to fuck? Pussy I have licked?" I use the pad of my forefinger to make little circles over the white porcelain tub. "And you're worried about little insignificant you." I laugh. The sound echoing.

"You bitch. You're nothing but a whore."

"But you want to marry me. The woman your own father jerks his wrinkled cock to while I bathe myself."

He walks up and yanks the chains so that I'm facing him on my knees. He undoes his belt and I inwardly cringe, hearing the sound of the belt buckle. He pulls himself out and rubs the tip of his penis near my mouth. "Suck it," he demands in a lethal tone.

My eyes flick up. My lips break into a smile. A flicker of confusion crosses his expression. I'll take my chances. Fuck him. His grips my hair, wrapping it around his fist and pushing his hard cock into my mouth, making me want to gag, but I don't. He pinches my nipple, but I block out the pain of the sting.

"I've always wanted you like this. I've been waiting a long time to have you, Veronica. Do you know how it feels to watch someone get everything, including the woman he wants."

I open my mouth and he slides his pathetic excuse of a cock in my mouth and I bite down. I bite down hard with my molars.

"Aahhhhhh! Ahhhhh! You bitch!" he screams.

The taste of copper fills my mouth. He releases my nipple and tries to push me off his cock, but I lock my jaw. He manages to push me off him in one hard push, but I feel my teeth scrape his shaft. His eyes widen when he looks down at his mangled cock. Blood is dripping everywhere. Down my chin. All over his thighs.

"Oh fuck!" His voice croaks on the last part. "You bit my dick"— he grabs it, doubling over— "You crazy bitch."

I spit the blood from my mouth at his cock in that way I 've seen football players do on the football field. "That's just a preview. The next time I'll bite it off." I smile. "Don't worry. You'll get used to my touch."

The sound of a boom from a door opening comes from behind him. My heart is beating like a wild racehorse. A chill racks my body, hoping there isn't someone else with him. I hear footsteps behind him coming from the shadows. Dorian slides his pants on and runs into the darkness in the opposite direction. There is only a small construction light shining down on me like a spotlight, but it's keeping me from seeing. My eyes try to focus.

I hear Valen's voice. "Veronica?"

I sag in relief, crying and laughing like a mad woman. When I see Alaric rush up behind him, looking at the chains binding my wrist, he lifts my chin to see if I'm bleeding. His brows are furrowed and his jaw is clenched.

"Are you hurt?" he asks. "Tell me where?" he says while his eyes inspect my face and body.

"No." I sigh with relief but feel a wave of dizziness when I take a deep breath.

"I can get the chain off from the back," Valen announces behind me, hearing the sound of the chains rattle against the tub.

"You're bleeding," he says while removing his t-shirt. "What did he give you?"

I shake my head softly. "The blood...It's not mine. He drugged me...made me smell...something."

"Motherfucker."

"I got it," Valen says out of breath. My arms sag when the chains are released and Alaric loosens the metal rubbing on my irritated wrists. "Get her in the car and I'll go see if I can find this asshole."

"Alright but be careful."

"Where am I?" I ask.

"Abandoned house four miles from Kenyan," he replies, placing his black shirt over my head, beyond glad that is falls right above my knees.

He picks me up and I wince at how dizzy I feel once the adrenaline wore off.

"How did you get blood all over your mouth and chin?"

"I...bit his...dick."

"Good," he says in a hard tone and I'm glad I don't have to explain further.

The scene he and Valen walked into doesn't have to be explained.

"Did he..." He trails off, carrying me into a dark hallway that feels like a maze, reminding of a dark haunted house.

"No...you came in time but he ran."

"Don't worry, baby. I'll get him. You're more important than revenge right now. The doctor is on the way."

I close my eyes and lay my head on his shoulder, relieved that he came for me. *He came.*

CHAPTER 32

Alaric

I lean back in the driver's seat of my car and let out a deep breath. The doctor said she was fine. The baby has a strong heartbeat and whatever Dorian gave her was not enough to cause any issues with the pregnancy.

I hear the passenger door open and look to see Draven slip into the passenger seat. "She's good man. Don't worry. Gia and Jess are with her."

I look at my hands, feeling the leather under the palms of my skin from gripping the steering wheel. The feeling of needing to kill someone for hurting her growing with every second that goes by.

"He's at the church with his father and some other members of the Order. Most likely in on all the shit that her piece of shit stepfather has her involved in." I nod.

That's why he came here...to tell me. "What do you want to do?"

I turn my head. He throws a t-shirt and I catch it, not realizing I was still shirtless. All I could think about is the woman I plan to make my wife. The one carrying my baby. The one they almost took from me. Sliding the shirt over my head, I reply, "What would you do, Draven?"

He scoffs. "The same thing that must be going through your mind right now. Put the car in drive. The guys will meet us at the church. I'll send a clean-up crew when we're done. After all this shit, you're going to marry that girl and we'll fuck up whoever has a problem with it."

"D-do you think she really wants to marry me?"

I'm nervous. I put her through so much shit, I wonder how she could ever forgive me for being the biggest asshole who never fought for her.

"I'm not going to lie and say I don't feel a sense of guilt for what she's been through. I didn't know, but I think she's been in love with you since she was in high school. I also think she's been waiting for you to save her. So...fucking save her, Alaric."

"You're right."

After the ten-minute drive, I park my Ferrari in the visitors' parking lot by the right side of the cemetery. We walk by the side entrance and already see Dorian's father in deep discussion with the fake priest the Order assigned to make sure no one enters the church after hours, except the members of the Order to conduct their meetings.

"We had him make something up so they wouldn't get inside. The rest of the Consortium are waiting for us. Come on," Draven whispers, pulling to the front of the side entrance.

Once the door slides shut behind us with a soft click, Valen walks up and hands us our robes and masks. "Come on, he can't hold him off any longer."

"You all planned this."

"If you didn't come, I would've killed them myself," Valen says, handing me my knives and a rosary.

I hold up the knife, making sure it's sharp enough. "One way to kill a snake is to start at the head and work your way down, splitting it open and making sure it's dead." My eyes flick to Valen. "You know how I feel about snakes and you damn well know what I'll do for her."

"Took you long enough," Valen says with a smile. "Let's get these sick fucks."

I walk down the aisle and look up at the black cover covering the cross, taking a seat in the middle. The ten members, including Adam, sit in the scattered in the pews facing forward still as a statue. Five members on each side with plague masks on their faces.

Waiting.

I grip the knife in my hand under my cloak. My head is pounding. I can hear roaring in my ears, but when I blink behind the mask, all I hear is the sound of footsteps as the main door of church opens and closes. I can sense them. Six men to us ten.

"What the fuck?" I hear one of them say.

None of us move.

Not yet.

I feel a buzzing sensation in my hands in anticipation. Every time I kill, I feel it. The numbing. The roaring in my ears right before it happens. The manic episode is what they call it. The doctors call it an episode derived from explosive anger derived from a motive. My motive is fear of losing the one thing I value most in this world.

Her.

"One is moving! Ahhhhh!" Mr. Black is the first to scream, drowning out the first rumble of thunder as the main door of the church is shut.

CHAPTER 33
Alaric

I t's ten o'clock on a Sunday night, and I'm pacing back and forth. "Relax, sir," Sergio says, before stepping out to see if Veronica needs anything. I can't. I want it to be perfect. Tonight, has to be perfect. I close my eyes and let out a deep breath.

"Cold feet?" Draven asks behind me when he walks in, closing the door.

"It's not mine I'm worried about."

"She's here, and she isn't going anywhere," he assures me.

"I know that, but what if she remembers all the fucked-up shit I've done to her and changes her mind."

"I have already told you, she's loved you since she was in high school. She's done things she's had to do. I see the look in her eyes when she looks at Gia and Jess. She's ashamed. It doesn't matter how often we tell her it wasn't her fault, but one thing she isn't and was never ashamed of was being in love with you. Everyone knows that. There's one man in this world Veronica loves, and that man is you. It was always you, Alaric. Since the first time she laid eyes on your sorry ass, she knew."

"I know, but I didn't fight for her when she needed me."

He steps closer, fixing the red rose on my tux. "You are now. Right now, this moment." He looks up, a fierce look in his eyes. "This is how you show her you're fighting—for both of them. It's not just her you're fighting for. You're fighting for your future with...her and your child."

I nod, my heart filling with an emotion I can't describe. Tonight, I'm marrying the woman I love, and I don't give a shit about rules or what the Order thinks.

After a few seconds, he slaps me on the shoulder, trying to comfort me. "Come on, man. We're starting."

The church is decorated with black and red roses. I asked the priest to marry us, and he approved when I mentioned who I planned on marrying. He got permission from the church without the Order finding out on such short notice. Graduation is looming in one week. The cathedral was cleaned, and it smells of hundreds of candles and roses and a perfumed scent. Nothing at all like death; it's filled with the promise of life.

The pews shine with all the members of the Consortium in attendance. Sixty-Seven, including Adam. His sisters, Dorothy, and the wives of the sons of Kenyan are all seated. Reid is standing to the side, waiting with Jess as the best man. Jess is in Alicia's place. My chest is tight with emotion, and needles prick my throat. Not of sadness but a distinct happiness I have never felt. If I think about the best night of my life, this sums it up. I'm marrying the woman I love, making it my mission to steal all her firsts. Her vows in return for making all of her dreams come true.

I swallow, hearing a click in my throat. "If anything happens to me, she gets everything, Draven. If I live or die, she will be Mrs. Riodrick-Riordan."

He nods. "I know. It's done."

I stand to the left side in front of the priest waiting...waiting for my wife to walk down the aisle.

Evanescence's synthesis version of "My Immortal" begins to play; everyone stands, and she takes her first steps in black and red silk with a dark laced romance dress. Her dark hair is in waves down to her waist. Her eyes are like clear blue diamonds, almost aquamarine, under the candlelight. She looks breathtakingly beautiful. Her waist is still small despite being pregnant with our child. I could not hold back the tears watching my wife come to me. My chest is thick with emotion.

We can't stop staring at each other, lost in our world the whole ceremony. We almost don't hear the priest when he says it's time to say our vows.

"Please," the priest says softly.

I hold her hand and look into her eyes, sliding the halo cut, ten-carat solid diamond with hidden black diamonds around her finger. "With this hand, I shall bear the weight of your sorrows, lifting them as if they are feathers carried by the wind. Your cup shall remain forever full, for I am to be the crimson essence that fills it - a dark and intoxicating wine of companionship. I will light a candle, and its gentle flame shall illuminate your path through the labyrinthine corridors of darkness"— I slide the ring on slowly— "This ring, a circle unbroken, symbolizes my desire for you to stand by my side, an unbreakable union. As twilight embraces the day, your life with mine, forging a bond as timeless and impassioned as love itself."

Tears shine in her eyes when I glance up, and it's her turn. She takes my hand in her delicate one, doing the same with the platinum band on my finger. She begins, "With the grace of my hand, I shall lift the burdens that weigh upon your heart, holding them delicately like fragile petals in the breeze. Your cup shall know no emptiness, for I shall pour into it the essence of my devotion, a love that overflows endlessly. I accept your ring, a symbol of eternity." She slides on the ring. "I present this ring as a token of my deepest longing, heart, and soul. With the twilight stars in the night sky as our witness and in the eyes of God, I ask for your hand in a journey where our souls intertwine in love as profound as the eternal night. Life is where we love amongst the living and in death where we sleep amongst the rested."

"You may now kiss your bride," the priest announces.

I take her lips, placing my one hand softly on her womb, one hand cupping her cheek and kissing her passionately. The church erupts in applause and sniffles.

I pull back, whispering across her lips, "I love you, Mrs. Riordan."

CHAPTER 34
Alaric

I watch the bastard sitting in his office with his horned-rimmed glasses. Lighting up a cigar, reading something on a piece of paper. I wait a few seconds and then walk inside.

"Who let you in?"

I sit unbuttoning my suit jacket. "I think you have an idea."

"You think because you have my daughter, you can waltz in here like you own the place."

"In a fashion. Yes, and we both know she is not your daughter."

"My name is on her birth certificate."

"I could put Al Pacino's name on her birth certificate. It doesn't mean she is his daughter."

"You're a cocky little shit."

"I am, and I'm not little. Ask your stepdaughter."

He chuckles, puffing on his cigar. You can tell he's a prick, even in the way he holds it in his fingers.

"You've been having fun with her. I can tell."

A message comes through on his phone. He picks it up, and a wicked gleam crosses his eyes when he opens the message. He holds it up, and it's a picture of a young woman with her legs open, showing her unshaven pussy. "Now she has an amazing pussy."

"Let me guess, she's French. And you fucked her without a condom," I answer dryly.

He guffaws, throwing his head back. When he calms down, he opens a little drawer in his desk, takes out a little bag of coke, snorts a line with a hundred-dollar bill rolled up like a straw, and holds it out to me.

"I'm good."

He shrugs. "It's all just a little fun, and you're right. She is French. I met her in France while the wife was sleeping in the hotel room. I went to have a drink after a meeting, and she offered."

"How much did you pay her?"

He doesn't answer and smiles, but it doesn't reach his eyes. No man likes another one to point out that he has to pay for pussy.

"Why are you here, Alaric?"

To kill you.

I lean forward. "I need the names of the men who attend your little rituals," I say confidently.

I have them, but I want him to know that I know. I'd like Charles Devlin to know why he has to die. The smile slides off his face, his expression cold with hatred. I'm sure no one has ever asked who the bastards are that jerk off and hit my wife with their belts while they watch her bathe. Telling her she needs to be cleansed of her sins.

"I'm afraid that is above your head, even for you."

"I'm afraid," I mock, "I have been above your head since the day I was conceived. I don't think you understand. I want all the names. I know Dorian Black's father is one of them. Just like I know you jerk off to your stepdaughter, watching her bathe herself and then beat her with a belt, careful not to leave marks on her skin."

I watch his face turn ashen when I pull out a serrated knife and slide it into his throat, blood spraying all over his desk. His eyes bulge, quickly filling with blood. The copper smell mixes with the cigar now dropped to the floor. Gurgling sounds can be heard as he chokes on his own blood. His arms twitch like a mechanical robot. "We all have to pay for our sins, Mr. Devlin. Your first one was the day you touched my wife." His eyes roll to the left full of blood. "Don't worry; this is just the beginning. Oh, did anyone mention that I have a thing for knives?"

Walking inside the church, I had the younger members cover Jesus nailed to the cross and the altar. The higher leaders of the Order take their seats. There are eight chairs with an oversized black cloth covering each seat.

"Where are the rest?" old man Caruthers asks out loud.

Mr. Bedford, my father, grandfather, and uncle remain quiet. Gia, Jess, and Veronica are all home with armed security. The sixty-seven members of the Consortium file in each of the pews, wearing plague masks just like mine. I'm one of the few that announce that I'm part of it.

"Why are we here, Alaric."

"In front of you..." I pause when I hear grunts and rustling of paper. "I apologize, it is not Page Six with some juicy gossip but something that pertains to someone very important to me."

I hear chuckles. "We see," Caruthers says.

They don't, but they will.

"What are you doing?" Dorian asks in a hard tone, sitting sideways in the pew.

I inwardly smile. "Canceling your contract," I reply. "Didn't you hear, I kill people?"

I copied pages from the book in the library with the rules on Prey and the rituals, passing them to the higher members of the Order. I can tell which ones are aware, which means they have seen them. You can tell from their expressions when they look at something familiar. Something they have seen. But like my grandfather warned, I can't kill everyone. Not yet, anyway, just the important ones.

Strategy is key.

"Veronica is Prey and wasn't born into the Order as some may think."

"He's lying!" Dorian bellows.

"Son." Caruthers points at Dorian sitting in the front pew. His face is so red; he looks constipated, trying to take a shit, but I don't miss the way he tries not to grimace from the pain. "One more outburst, and I'll throw you out." Caruthers turns to me. "Continue."

"Even if she is recognized by a member of the Order, she is still Prey, and Prey chooses."

"That's true."

"Well, it is well-documented the night she lost her virginity that she chose as Prey without the mark. It means she's mine. Some of you have stood by and conducted rituals for sins committed by coercion and manipulation of Prey, which is forbidden in the Order."

"I'm afraid it's too late, son. She has the mark and has been initiated for years."

I nod, so the twins remove the coverings and hear gasps and coughing. "Son, are you insane?" Caruthers snaps. He's the oldest member on the voting board of the Order.

"I'm afraid Dorian's father, Mr. Devlin, and his cohorts have been busy with their pricks in their hands." I point at Caruthers's wrinkled face with his eyes full of anger. "To answer your question, I'm afraid I am," I smile, "but you already know that."

"Riodrick," Caruthers calls on my grandfather.

"It's justified. He already married her, and she's pregnant with his child."

"I see," he says solemnly.

I smile like watching all of the old farts trying to avoid looking at the eight men with their cocks stuffed inside their mouths and their eyes missing from inside their skulls.

Dorian is kneeling on the floor, watching his father's head with his cock stuffed in his mouth with tears running down his face. He looks up at me. "You motherfucker."

"I've been called worse, but I'd be careful if I were you." I look up at the higher members, addressing them with the facts. "Dorian Black knew she was Prey that night when she chose and interfered with a higher member's decision and then had you all vote under false pretenses. She has been enslaved as Prey under manipulation. Our law states either way that her true master is the one she bears a child to or is impregnated, so I married her. She's mine and a Riodrick-Riordan by law. Married in this very church. The death of the eight was voted in favor by the founding fathers. I just sped things along."

"Is this true?" Caruthers asks, turning to our fathers.

They all nod in agreement, and the gauntlet is thrown.

The Consortium members walk outside the church silently, and I follow, watching Dorian hastily head toward the parking lot with a limp in his step.

"What do you want to do to him?" Valen asks.

"Let's cut off his hands and make sure he chokes on tampons when he dies."

"Tampons?" Valen says, with a muffled laugh under his mask.

"Yeah." I turn to him. "Hang him from the cross outside Kenyan Preparatory High School."

"Alright. Who's driving?"

"I am," Adam says, walking up to us.

CHAPTER 35
Veronica

"Police are investigating the crime scene at Kenyan Preparatory High School where a man was hung from a cross, both hands severed and his mouth full of feminine hygiene products." I shut off the local news, tossing the remote on the bed and biting my bottom lip.

Alaric walks in fresh from a shower, his body dripping wet with a towel around his neck. "Was that you?" I ask.

"It was."

"Are you going to stop or should we move on to the secretaries too," I say sarcastically.

He's killed almost everyone like a serial killer on the loose out for blood. I can't sit here and say they didn't deserve it because they did.

He looks up and grins, stopping at the foot of the bed, "If you want. I'll hold, you kill. I suggest we make it quick before our child arrives," he says like we are deciding what color we should paint the nursery, but I know he is dead serious.

"It was a joke."

He grins showing white teeth. "Lie down on the bed, gorgeous."

I lie down on the bed and he kneels between my thighs. "What are you doing?" I ask.

He glances up from between my legs, holding them wide open. "Worshipping you."

Want a sneak peek at
Forbidden Flesh

PREORDER ON MY WEBSITE FOR THE
EBOOK OR PRINT BEFORE IT HITS
RETAILERS.

https://carmenrosales.com/shop/

I walk into Dr. Wicks's office, close the door behind me, and sit, late for my first therapy session of the year since the semester started. Everything is riding on this year. I'm captain of the swim team. I have to get married once I graduate to a bitch I hate.

"So, you've started school, and it's your senior year here at Kenyan."

"It is."

"How are you doing?"

I grin. "You mean, how many random women have I fucked?"

"If that is how you like to refer to it, then, yeah. How are you coping with your impulsivity?"

"By coming, Dr. Wick. I cope by coming on a woman's face, stomach, or throat." I chuckle. "Kind of like you and Dillion." She squirms in her chair, but I don't miss how she squeezes her thighs. I notice she wears pantyhose that hide the little varicose veins on her legs to appear younger and the short skirts she wears just for me.

"I'm not here to discuss me, Mr. Vikiar."

"Oh, Dr. Wick. We're past last names. Except I like yours. It rhymes with dick."

"How clever. Did you think that up all by yourself?"

"I did. Did you know that a male sex addict is a master in making himself come to reach euphoria? Like your pussy, it gets wet every time I'm in here, and you begin one of our sessions, so you go back and take it out on poor Dillon, thinking of all the ways I could fuck you. I bet you think it's me sometimes fucking you with your legs over the handles of this chair spread open while I go to town on that middle-aged cunt of yours, making it come so many times you pass out."

"I think this session is over."

"I think not...I need something from you."

"What can I do for you?"

I lean my head back on the wall looking at the ceiling. "So, there's this girl...."

Acknowledgments

I would like to thank all my readers and new readers for purchasing my book. I hope you liked the fourth book in the Prey series and will love to see your edits and reviews. Head over to my readers group on Facebook Alpha Addicts. I would love to hear who was your favorite character, what was your favorite scene, or what do you think is going to happen. It means a lot to me. I want to thank you for supporting me on this journey.

I would also like to thank my editors, beta readers, bloggers, ARC readers, and everyone that helped make this series happen.

Thank you for everything.

About the Author

Carmen Rosales is an emerging Latinx author of Steamy, and Dark Romance. She loves spending time with her family. When she is not writing, she is reading. She is an Army veteran and is currently completing her Doctorate Degree in Business and has the love and support of her husband and five children. She also writes under Delilah Croww for her DARK romance horror stories with really dark themes that is coming out soon.

Join her VIP list- www.carmenrosales.com

She loves to see a review and interact with her readers.

Scan the QR code to follow her on Social Media and sign up for her Newsletter:

Printed in the USA
CPSIA information can be obtained
at www.ICGtesting.com
LVHW091300131223
766027LV00068B/1894